THE HOUSE ON DEVIL'S LANE

S. L. IRELAND

RED FERN PRESS

Copyright © 2024 Sandra Low Ireland

All rights reserved

The characters and events portrayed in this book are fictitious. Any similarity to real persons, living or dead, is coincidental and not intended by the author.

No part of this book may be reproduced, or stored in a retrieval system, or transmitted in any form or by any means, electronic, mechanical, photocopying, recording, or otherwise, without express written permission of the publisher.

ISBN-13: 9798333998415
ISBN-10: 1477123456

Cover design by: Canva
Library of Congress Control Number: 2018675309
Printed in the United States of America

*To Grandad Ron.
Enjoy your 90th year!*

CONTENTS

Title Page
Copyright
Dedication
CHAPTER ONE   1
CHAPTER TWO   6
CHAPTER THREE   12
CHAPTER FOUR   17
CHAPTER FIVE   22
CHAPTER SIX   26
CHAPTER SEVEN   33
CHAPTER EIGHT   38
CHAPTER NINE   42
CHAPTER TEN   47
CHAPTER ELEVEN   55
CHAPTER TWELVE   62
CHAPTER THIRTEEN   68
CHAPTER FOURTEEN   74
CHAPTER FIFTEEN   79
CHAPTER SIXTEEN   84
CHAPTER SEVENTEEN   90
CHAPTER EIGHTEEN   95

CHAPTER NINETEEN	99
CHAPTER TWENTY	104
CHAPTER TWENTY-ONE	111
CHAPTER TWENTY-TWO	117
CHAPTER TWENTY-THREE	124
CHAPTER TWENTY-FOUR	132
CHAPTER TWENTY-FIVE	138
CHAPTER TWENTY-SIX	144
CHAPTER TWENTY-SEVEN	150
CHAPTER TWENTY-EIGHT	157
CHAPTER TWENTY-NINE	164
CHAPTER THIRTY	170
CHAPTER THIRTY-ONE	175
CHAPTER THIRTY-TWO	181
CHAPTER THIRTY-THREE	185
CHAPTER THIRTY-FOUR	193
CHAPTER THIRTY-FIVE	200
CHAPTER THIRTY-SIX	205
CHAPTER THIRTY-SEVEN	212
CHAPTER THIRTY-EIGHT	217
CHAPTER THIRTY-NINE	223
CHAPTER FORTY	230
CHAPTER FORTY-ONE	237
CHAPTER FORTY-TWO	243
CHAPTER FORTY-THREE	249
CHAPTER FORTY-FOUR	256
CHAPTER FORTY-FIVE	262
CHAPTER FORTY-SIX	269

SIX MONTHS LATER	274
Acknowledgement	277
Praise For Author	279
Books By This Author	281

CHAPTER ONE

My mother, peering into the open fridge, lifts her narrowed eyes to mine. I've been caught red-handed. Silently I hand over an opened plastic bag of shredded cabbage.

"Where's the rest of it?"

"Down my bra. They say it's good for cracked nipples. I read it in my baby magazine."

From her seat at the kitchen table, Leanne sniggers. "You know what's also good? A bottle. There's no way I'd be feeding him if my boobs were on fire."

"She's right, Kat." Mum slams the fridge door and shakes what's left of the cabbage into a pot. No doubt she will boil the life out of it and serve it with chicken Kyiv and oven chips. It's her signature dish. From the bedroom, Matthew's wails reach a crescendo, competing with *Friends* on the kitchen TV. "Have ye just shoved it doon there? You're supposed to mak' a poultice."

She nods to my breasts, which have turned into two sea boulders. The baby is hungry, but every mouthful feels like he's sticking hot needles in me. I nod and pluck miserably at my tee-shirt.

My mother shakes back her crazy mane of hair and flushes water into the pot.

"Tak' it oot, for heaven's sake. I'll groupchat the girls. Marianne's lass has just had a bairn too and she was bletherin' about some miracle cream. You can put it on your stitches and all."

"Mother!" Leanne slaps her magazine down on the table. "Can we not talk endlessly about babies and all that shite? It's bad enough having to share a bedroom with him. I can hear every snuffle. I'm exhausted."

Leanne's love affair with being an aunt had lasted all of five minutes. By the time Matthew and I were passed fit to leave hospital, it had dawned on my sister that nothing had changed. We are still two girls who don't particularly get on, sharing the same poky bedroom we had as children. But now, there's a new little person in the mix.

I'm sure Leanne thought it would be like adopting a kitten. Maybe we all thought that. Matthew would sleep and feed and be picked up and played with and then remain quiet until one of us felt like repeating the cycle, but it hasn't been like that. Matthew has a loud voice and a big personality which fills the whole flat, not just the bedroom. He is quick to let me know if things aren't right, and nothing ever seems right for him. He goes from whimpering to full-on, face-reddening, fist-thumping fury in sixty seconds. My siblings are no help -Ryan turns up the volume on the TV, Leanne reaches for her noise-cancelling headphones.

The baby things I'd stashed so carefully prior to his arrival have now migrated to the four corners of the place, only to be tidied away or mysteriously dumped. When I should be resting. I'm either feeding the baby or searching for his soother or his vest or the nappy cream. My mother tries to help, but she's already working full time on a supermarket check-out and stretching her meagre income to accommodate another soul has been a challenge. I'm grateful, of course, that she's prepared to look after us, but ultimately, Matthew is my responsibility. For life. Even when I'm dropping with fatigue, I lie awake worrying about that life sentence.

Mum turns on the oven.

"I remember when I had Dan. Didn't have a clue. But you learn, lass. We've all been through it. Leanne, set the table. Billy will be in soon."

A chill blows through me, imaginary tumbleweed spinning around my stomach. I've been feeling like that a lot lately, lost, aimless, as if something has been taken from me. With the baby on the inside, I'd been solid, secure, like we were a unit, a platoon of two, able to take on the world, but now with Matthew on the outside, he's become one of *them*. Demanding, abusive and working against me. His roar fills me with dread, but my body operates to its own schedule, swelling with milk, waiting to deliver.

Hastily, I pull up my top, fish the soggy bits of cabbage from my bra and consign them to the bin.

"I'm not really hungry. I'll get something later."

"Can we not sit down for a family meal, just for once?" Mum calls after me. I can't say it out loud, but I know why such a thing is impossible.

Because we're not a family.

Mum's boyfriend, Billy, is five years younger than she is. Maybe that's why she tries too hard, cultivating long, tousled curls and dressing like Leanne, very biker chic. She loves to boast that she swaps clothes with her daughters and on the rare occasion she's mistaken for our sister- usually by some rat-arsed guy in a bar- she goes around singing for a week. We are sort of alike, I suppose. Our hair is the same shade of dark blonde. Mum's is a bit tarnished, Leanne's has some help from L'Oreal and mine is as nature intended. Who has time to overthink things? Leanne has a make-up kit that would put a film production unit to shame. When we were teenagers, she'd harboured grand plans to work on lavish period dramas, but like the rest of us, she missed her calling. She now works on reception at a local beauty spa.

We are all very skinny. Mum and Leanne because they don't eat enough, and me because I've been through the sort of stuff that makes you lose your appetite. I remember a lovely Irish midwife giving me a stern talking to at one of my ante- natal checks.

"I'm not saying you should eat for two," she'd said. "but I'm curious to know if you're eating for one?"

I tried to do better after that. I hate letting people down. I can't shake off the feeling that my father would have come into his own when I discovered I was pregnant. I think he would have had my back, sorted things out. It's pure fantasy, of course, because I haven't seen him for years. My mother swears we were well-rid, that he was a complete waste of space, but I'm not convinced. I have one photograph rescued from the hearth. I must be about two, and he's holding me up high and smiling the sort of besotted smile only your kids get to see. He doesn't look like a waste of space. He has a kind face.

I sit down on the bed and attempt to feed Matthew again, breathing through the initial burning agony of his latching on, in the same way I'd tried to breathe my way through his birth. Once he starts suckling greedily, the rawness subsides a bit and I'm able to relax and tune into the cluttered quiet of the bedroom, the baby's snuffly little grunts, the traffic outside, the dull roar of the TV through the wall. I stroke his soft fat little leg, which is kicking idly, as if it will somehow speed up the milk flow. His optimism makes me smile. How cool it must be to have nothing more to worry about. Today, he is wearing stripy navy socks and a matching sleeper suit, which is starting to look a bit snug. I wonder idly how long it will take him to grow out of his gifts, and how soon I will need to start looking for a job and who will I get to mind him. Everything feels overwhelming.

There's a heavy knock at the front door. My stomach convulses automatically before reason kicks in. Family members don't knock, they just waltz in as if they own the place. I hear a yell from the kitchen.

"Somebody get that!"

Nobody comes. I sit there helplessly. Our flat is on the ground floor, so from my bed, I have a view of the hall and the front door, with its rippled side panes, currently filled with waves of dark colour. Black trousers, I muse. Could be the postie or a delivery driver. I don't know if there's a protocol for breastfeeding. Can you just scoop up the suckling baby and tote him around with you? I've seen women breastfeeding with a towel draped elegantly over their shoulder, but I've never felt comfortable doing it in public. I lack elegance. Ryan would be mortified, Leanne disgusted and Billy way too interested.

So I sit, frozen, until the knock sounds again.

In the kitchen, something is dropped furiously onto the counter.

"For fucksake. Leanne, check on those oven chips."

Mum marches into view, wiping her hands on a tea towel. She yanks open the door so aggressively the glass rattles. I can't see her expression, but I wouldn't like to be on the receiving end.

"Yes? Oh." She appears to be checking someone out. I can hear a male voice. My name is mentioned, and I tighten up. Matthew stops sucking and whimpers. Nothing gets past him. My mother glances at me. "She's busy right now."

"Who is it?" I call out, raising the baby to my shoulder. I hope he's still hungry because my right breast is hard and tender. This is a delicate operation and cannot really be disturbed.

My mother is listening to the reply. She turns to me again. "It's Steve. He has flowers for you. Do you know a Steve?"

My face floods with colour. "Um- yes. I do know Steve. I'll be out soon. Ask him if he'll wait."

CHAPTER TWO

Earlier...

Steve rings the door buzzer, and again, and a third time. A voice crackles over the intercom.

"Assessment and Delivery Suite reception. How can I help?"

"I have a- there's a woman, about to give birth."

"Name please?"

"Kat Riley."

"Did she call ahead?"

"Yes. Hurry- please. I think she's about to have the baby right now."

"I don't have a Kat..."

"Katherine, then. Katherine..." He sweeps a hand through his thick black hair.

"Ah yes. Katherine Riley. Just come in."

The door clicks open.

I hear my name, but it doesn't seem to belong to me. I am in the car, but strangely absent, as if bent on some secret mission known only to me. My fingers, locked beneath the front passenger seat, are like anchors. I concentrate my mind on the intersection of flesh and fabric, riding a wave of agonising tightness. Every muscle in my body clamps around that poor little baby. How will he ever get out?

"What goes in must come out," my mother would say, darkly, whenever I mentioned how scared I was. She has a munitions dump of one-liners for every eventuality. "You've made your bed…" is another favourite. I've heard that one quite often these last nine months.

I bite my lower lip until I taste blood. The taste makes me want to vomit. I've been off coffee and sausages for ages. Blood too, apparently. When Steve returns and hauls open the passenger door, I almost lose my grip.

"Come on, love. Can you stand up?"

"No! I just want to stay here. *Agh!*" Fresh pain cracks through me. I've been trying to time the contractions, just as they'd told me over the phone, but I've lost count. They are coming with dizzying regularity. I grip the seat tighter.

"I- can't-move." I force the words through my tight jaw. When I try to relax, my teeth start to chatter through cold and fear.

Steve attacks his hair again. "You can't have it in the car. I'll get you a wheelchair."

Again, the buzzer. It spikes through the jagged red behind my eyelids. A disembodied voice.

"…be there now…"

And then, miraculously, a hand is holding mine. It is assured and cool and moist with sanitiser that smells of authority.

"I'm Claire. I'll be looking after you today. Let's just get you into this chair and we'll wheel you in. We've had a few babies born in the car park, but it's something we try to avoid!"

The transfer is made, slowly, painfully. My belly is rock hard, resting on my thighs like a package ready for the mail. I wish I could post the baby to myself. Special delivery. I imagine an Amazon carton on my doorstep and laugh, a bit hysterically. Steve is checking out his upholstery, but I feel reasonably intact. No bleeding, no gushing waters. With a sinking feeling I realise that all that is in front of me. Raw, visceral hours of being dismantled, and maybe put back together differently. I hug my bump. I will never be the same again. The nurse takes charge.

"Can you grab her bag, Dad? In you come. Chop, chop."

All three of us are buzzed in. My mother is right. There is no avoiding some things.

I am gripping Steve's hand so tightly, he yelps.

"I cannot do this!" I growl at the midwife, twisting in the bed like the girl from The Exorcist. "It's been hours! I'm never fucking doing this again."

"We all say that, love." Claire is watching the monitor. "I've had three! But I *will* call my colleague…have a little look…"

She exits, and I listen to her rubbery footsteps melting down the corridor. I glare at Steve. His stressed hair is standing up on end like a toilet brush.

"Oh my God! Something's wrong! I know it is."

"There's nothing wrong, love." He adjusts my death grip. I've left deep red welts in his skin and I don't even care. He deserves it. All men deserve a dose of this pain. Steve folds his big warm hands around mine. It comforts me a bit. That is one of the few things I remember about my dad, his shovel-like hands, made for fixing bikes and lifting me on his shoulders and safe-breaking. I'm sure Steve puts his to better use.

"They have to be cautious," he says reasonably.

"I don't want to be cautious. I want this baby OUT!"

"It'll come out in its own time."

He doesn't sound very certain. Indeed, I can see beads of sweat standing out on his nose. I'm sweating too, but I have good reason. But, none of this is his fault, so I moderate my tone.

"Can you get me some ice?"

"Sure. Would you like me to call someone? Your Mum? She might be the best person to deal with- all this." He nods towards my splayed knees and the tight, exposed mound of my belly. It feels odd to have no shame. "Dignity goes oot the windae!" That's another Mum-ism. She's right about that too. Once they've checked to see how far you're dilated for the tenth time, it's open house.

"You're not even at the business end," I remind him. "You get the pretty bit."

My attempted smile goes badly wrong as another pain twists me. Steve leaps up in alarm and tries to rearrange my pillow. I slap him away.

When the contraction recedes, I try to make amends.

"I'm sorry. I really want you to stay. My mum will make such a fuss and try and tell me what to do and…" I bite my lip. "Please don't call her."

"Okay. If that's what you want."

I nod solemnly. "You can go get the ice though."

The midwife, Claire, returns with another woman in blue scrubs who introduced herself as Chima. She's kind but brisk. They poke and prod me and check my stats.

"We have a protocol, Katherine," Chima says. "If labour is not advancing…"

They are speaking words at me. I no longer understand what's going on. This exhaustion is all-consuming and I just want to sleep. Theatre is mentioned. And forceps. Steve still hasn't returned with the ice. I start to panic- what if he doesn't come back? Even now, he could be speeding away from here like Lewis Hamilton. I will have to do this alone. Totally alone.

"No. No! I don't want to be moved. I just want to stay here and have my baby. I want Steeeeeve!" The last came out in a wail.

Steve, shellshocked, appears in the doorway, clutching a paper cup of ice.

Claire smiles briskly. "We'll get you fixed up with some scrubs, Daddy. Don't worry, it won't be long now."

"We can see the head. He has lovely black hair, just like his Dad!" Claire's face is so close, I can see her freckles above her mask. Her hair is covered in what looks like a J-cloth, and the rest of them, illuminated in the stark overhead light, look like strange, probing aliens. Even Steve is wearing a J-cloth. I think I am too, but I'm scared to move. I have wires and tubes coming out of me. Steve looks like he's on the verge of passing out, and I feel horribly guilty. I try to smile at him but my face isn't working.

A lifetime ago, or so it seems, they'd given me an epidural, so all I can feel is the tugging. I've grown accustomed to the fact that my body is no longer solely mine. It belongs to the baby and the strange aliens who are trying to get the baby out. I am just a carcass to be hauled about and dissected and stitched up again. As the epic battle of life and death plays out, I am just an onlooker who can't see a thing.

There is a point when I feel like I want to float up to the ceiling and crouch on top of the lights. I will have a grandstand view, looking down at it all, see my baby's head pulled clear of the wreckage. I want to be the first to say hello to him. But something happens. I'm not sure if I actually did float upwards, but suddenly I am slammed back in my body and the tone has changed.

The team throw glances at each other. Above the masks, their eyes are sharp and watchful.

"Get a paed." Claire mouths to one of the junior staff. Chima, who seems to be doing the grunt work, wipes sweat from her eyes with a forearm. Words like 'lateral' and 'anterior' are bandied about.

"What's happening?" I manage to gasp. "Is the baby okay?"

"Baby's got a fine pair of shoulders on him, that's all." Claire's eyes try to smile. "He's a wee bit stuck."

CHAPTER THREE

Afterwards, all I can recall of the birth is my anguished wail, accompanying the relieved slither of my son. Other people arrive. The baby is whisked away and Steve holds my hand and wipes my tears and tells me it will all be fine. I so want to believe him, but there is only silence from the baby, wherever he is. The urge to jump from the bed and go to him, breathe life into him, is so overwhelming I break into despairing sobs. I stop listening to them all; Steve, the midwives. It feels like a conspiracy, because *I know*, with my brand new intuition, that something is wrong.

Eventually, after what seems like a lifetime, a thin, mewling cry breaks the anxious, professional hush.

"That's him!" Steve pats my shoulder. "His first cry! It's a miracle!"

All the pain, all the fear, of the previous 24 hours seeps away with the blood and birth fluids. One of the nurses starts to clean me up, and just as I am starting to fret about what shape my body will be in, Claire draws close with my swaddled newborn and all thoughts of *me* disappear. After such a forced entry into our world, he looks bloody grumpy, with a pet lip and a Churchillian scowl.

I laugh in delight, but my instinct to reach out for him is impeded by medical paraphernalia.

"I'll give him to Dad!" Claire hands the package over. Special delivery. Steve stares from the bundle to the nurse and back again.

"Actually, I'm not the dad," he says carefully. "I didn't like to say, but- um- I'm just the taxi driver who brought her to hospital."

And now Steve is *here*, waiting on the low wall of our messy front garden. I lay Matthew against my shoulder until he produces a satisfied belch.

"Here-" Mum holds out her hands and I pass the baby over. "I'll change him. You make yourself presentable. This Steve looks like a nice chap- I want the full story!"

I flatten my eyebrows. "Mum! He's just a taxi driver."

"A taxi driver with flowers. Go on."

She shoos me out of the bedroom.

Wrapping my cardigan across my chest, I scurry down the path. Everything about me feels tight, buttoned up and I'm suddenly conscious of the overflowing bins and the balding lawn and what Steve might think of us. My mother has tried to brighten the place up with bulbs in blue glazed pots, but my brothers have turned them into ashtrays and there's a suspicious aroma of pee nearby, as if they've been marking their territory.

Steve doesn't look particularly judgy. He looks relaxed, neutral, sitting on the wall, kicking a leg and nursing a supermarket bouquet.

My face softens a fraction. "Hello."

"Hi. You look a bit better than when I saw you last!"

Unlike mine, his smile is free and easy. I'm shocked at how unfamiliar he seems; a bit like my baby when he first came out. Despite what we've been through together, this man could be any old taxi driver. He seems older than I remember, perhaps late thirties, early forties. When he'd called to collect me the night

I went into labour, I'd been too out of it to study his face. All the other things- the vicious contractions, the empty house, the shock of feeling alone and scared- are riveted on my memory, but not him. I remember every word of my panicked call to the cab company, but only bits of Steve. His arm supporting me as I limped to the gate, his strong, dependable hand, the black hair with a mind of its own.

Despite the awkwardness, I find myself studying his features. His hair has been slicked back with water or gel, revealing threads of silver. There's a whiff of cologne in the air. Ironed jeans and a clean white shirt, sleeves rolled up, uncovering a faded tattoo of some mythical beast on his forearm. He's rugby-player tough, gone a bit soft around the middle. I have no room to talk. Self-consciously, I pull my cardigan tighter.

"I'm really sorry, about keeping you at the hospital." My gaze drops to my trainers, avoiding his eye.

"At least we got you there in time. Oh, here..." He lifts the flowers. "Sorry, it's been weeks, but I just wondered how you were. How's the baby?"

They are a yellow mix of carnations and other bits and bobs I can't identify. The cellophane crackles as he hands them over and I press my nose to them. I want to say how kind he is, how thoughtful, but I just pretend to sniff them, and hope he takes it as a compliment. "He's fine. Cries a lot."

"They do at that age."

I look up. "Do you have kids?"

I shouldn't have asked. It's none of my business and I can't work out why I'm so interested. Maybe I just need some fatherly advice.

"I have two, but they're grown up now. Don't see a lot of them. They live in County Durham."

"Is that where you're from?"

His smile seems to falter a little and his frank blue eyes dim. "Many moons ago."

I'm no good at small talk and I tell myself I'm not interested, but for some reason I keep picking.

"So what are you doing in Dundee?"

"A woman. It's always a woman!" He laughs some more. For an older guy he's quite attractive, and the thought that he's unavailable gives me a surprise jolt of loss. What the hell am I thinking? From somewhere in the depths of the house Matthew starts to cry, and the milk percolates in my breasts. I have a sense of strangeness, talking to this man, with all this new stuff going on in my body, in my life. This is not what I need right now.

I half-turn towards the door. "I have to go..."

"Oh yes. That's a hungry bairn!"

I feel myself going red. Even though he's seen me at my very worst, and probably caught sight of bits of me he'll never unsee, this feels too intimate.

I wave the flowers. "Well, thanks for these."

He doesn't look like he wants me to go, but then he gets up from the wall with a speed that makes me take a step back. He's very tall, maybe over six foot. He clears his throat.

"I've never really introduced myself. Steve Burns." He dusts off his hands and holds one out to me. I take it, and it feels like a whole new experience, despite my hours of squeezing the life out of those very fingers.

"I'm Kat Riley," I say, unnecessarily.

"I know. I had to tell the receptionist about ten times!"

"You were so scared I'd give birth on your upholstery!"

We both laugh, and it's easy and a bit weird. My mother appears pointedly at the door with a furious, flailing bundle. I make a face, and Steve laughs as if he's seen it all before. He reaches down to open the gate and we part like co-conspirators. Long after I've returned to motherhood, I'm still thinking about him.

CHAPTER FOUR

After the birth, they put me in a side room and when I open my eyes, they are all piling through the doorway- my mother, Leanne and Ryan, who is hanging back in the hope they might forget about him and he can make his escape.

My mother, Gemma, is at the head of the posse. She pauses for effect.

"I cannot believe you had that bairn and didn't even call me." Mum always looks fierce. Her hair is so big and elaborately tousled, it makes her look tiny. She wears the blackest eyeliner, and the most jewellery she can fit on her body. Right now, she is properly bristling. The hair has been attacked with volumizer and her hoop earrings are wobbling. "Why didn't you ring while you were waiting for the taxi? I was only down The Anchor! You have me down as your birth partner."

"And me." Leanne saunters in. "It was on your plan. Typical. Bet they never even asked you."

Leanne is carrying a blue helium balloon, with 'IT'S A BOY!" scrawled across it in silver lettering. They are all laden with foil gift bags and cards and chocolates, as if they have just emptied one of the aisles at Card Factory.

My mother approaches in a cloud of Marc Jacobs. Shrugging off her biker jacket, she glances around.

"Where is he? Where's the baby?"

"Have they taken him away?" Leanne snags the clipboard from the end of the bed. "Do you want me to say something?"

"I got you those Belgian chocolates you like." Ryan lays his gift carefully beside my bent knees. He is my youngest and most favourite brother. Of them all, I knew he would be the one to visit. The rest are probably wetting the baby's head in the pub or doing a deal down some back alley.

I struggle to sit upright, colliding with the grim reality of new motherhood: tender breasts, tugging stitches. My redundant belly feels like a deflated, knocked-about punchbag.

"He's in the baby unit."

Her mother scowls. "What's he doing in there? Is he okay?"

"I'll tell them to fetch him, shall I?" Leanne makes for the door.

"No!" I say quickly. This is exactly why I never alerted them to the birth. All the interfering and the questions and the *embarrassment*. There is another reason, but I cannot think about that right now. "It was a difficult birth. He broke his collar bone coming out."

"Oh my God!" My mother sinks heavily into a chair. "You had to give birth all on your own."

"You could get them for negligence." Leanne is already stripping the cellophane from the chocolates. "He didn't break his own arm, did he?"

"He'll be fine, but they're keeping an eye on him and I wasn't alone. The taxi driver stayed with me."

"The taxi driver?" Two voices in unison. Like all the Riley men, Ryan makes himself as scarce as he can, walking over to the window to stare out at the car park. He brushes something off the sleeve of his tracksuit. His white trainers look suspiciously new.

"Is that the father? The taxi driver?" Leanne plumps herself down on the end of the bed and selects a hazelnut whirl.

"No!"

"Have you picked a name?" Her mother, belatedly, pats my hand. "You don't look so good. A bit peely-wally."

"Matthew." I really want to be left alone. I cannot be bothered with my family right now. Even the taxi driver was preferable. They are so loud, so in-your-face.

"Matthew. Is that the father's name?" Leanne demands.

"No! I just like the name, that's all."

Mum raises her barely-there eyebrows. Her lashes are spiked with sooty gloop. "Matthew. It's quite biblical."

"Matthew McConaughy. Matthew Goode." Leanne takes another chocolate. "You could call him Matt."

"I haven't got to know him yet," I say sadly. "Maybe he won't look like a Matt."

"Maybe he won't seem like a Matthew. How about Tyler? Or Zak?"

"Or Ryan?" says Ryan.

Maybe we could call him after the father, if we knew who the father was." Mum gathers up her handbag and jacket. "Are we getting to see him?"

Leanne licks her fingers and gets up too.

"Of course we can," she says. "Ring for a nurse, Kat. Where's the baby unit?"

I feel my cheeks flush with anger. "*I* haven't even seen him yet! Not to hold, anyway. I can't move. I don't even know if I can walk anymore." A note of panic enters my voice.

There's a pause. Leanne extends the box of chocolates.

"Here. Keep your energy up. I'll get them to bring a wheelchair."

A nurse is assigned to whizz me to what they call the NICU. I am the front runner. My family traipse behind, no doubt thoroughly sick at being the also-rans. This is my second trip in a wheelchair and I have to say I'm not a fan, this loss of independence. I feel for those who have no choice, compelled to fight for every little bit of freedom. As soon as I'm out of here- the wheelchair, the hospital, my situation- I will never take my strength for granted again. I will take my son and run.

As we glide down busy corridors, I visualise myself as the black horse in that TV commercial, galloping through streets and woods and sand, even taking on a steam train in some glorious feat of staying power. That will be me. But not right now. Right now I am a broken doll, lost and powerless and afraid.

I have a fleeting sense of triumph when my relatives are denied entry to neo-natal. My nurse stops them with a raised hand and all the authority of a traffic cop.

"Wait here for a while. Mum first!"

I realise that I am the mum she is talking about. I hadn't actually thought of myself in those terms. Butterflies swarm in my empty belly as if I have never met my baby before. We are re-introduced through the wall of his Perspex box. I think I recognise his little scrunched-up face, although he is a healthy, newly-bathed baby colour now, and rocking a smart white hat. His balled fists look determined, reminding me of our last bruising encounter. How can I be sure this is Matthew? They could show me any random baby. I'm not sure what I'm expected to feel. He is alien, a little stranger.

Another nurse approaches. She's wearing a J-cloth hat with teddies on it but it does nothing to reassure me.

"Would you like to hold him, love?"

I stumble. "I- um- my mum wants to see him."

The nurses trade glances, and I realise I need to up my game here, give them what they're expecting.

"But yes- I'd love to hold him."

They relax and smile. I feel hot and sweaty and really, really nervous. I know he is my baby, but why would they trust him to me? He is so much safer in his Perspex box.

CHAPTER FIVE

Later...

If I had to draw a cottage it would be this one. A window either side of the door, a porch with an elegant finial on the steep A of the roof and bedroom windows snuggled under the eaves. The porch is half-glass, half-timber, once painted a soft sage green, but now faded, and the rest is built from rugged local stone. There's a plank bench under one window and a bird table off to the right. Yellow roses and some kind of riotous pink weed fight for space in the borders, but the lawn appears freshly cut, the hedge trimmed, as if someone has been keeping an eye on it.

"I can't believe I'm here."

I open the car door slowly, half afraid to get out, as if the cottage might blow away, or disappear into the mist like in that old film.

I hadn't expected Steve's home to be so rural, so remote. When we'd turned off a narrow B-road and onto Derville's lane, I'd literally sucked in my breath. What would we do if we met another car? The verges were steep, waving with umbrellas of white weed and topped by thorn bushes. I couldn't even see the fields beyond.

We'd slowed to a crawl past a terrace of low-roofed stone cottages before coming to a stop at the far end. My first sight of number 11, and it seemed a glorious situation, perched at the end of the line, bordered by only one neighbour and backing onto secluded woodland. I love woods, although the ones in the city tend to be a dumping ground for old fridges and the occasional dead body. All the cottages are identical to this one, each garden partially concealed by a low hedge. It all very private, contained, as if the place wants the world to stay out. There are no people or dogs or cars. I thought I could hear the monotonous growl of a tractor far off, but I'm no expert on farm machinery.

"It's all happened so quickly." Steve gives my hand a quick squeeze and removes his keys from the ignition. "You go on, I'll get the little 'un."

I step out of the warm car. There's a chill breeze, and the air is thick with farm smells and the bleating of sheep, but otherwise the place is quiet, cushioned. The gate is cold and pitted beneath my hands, and it grinds squeakily as it opens, like an obsolete playground ride. Flakes of green paint stick to my skin. Still, as I wander up the path, I can feel myself falling a little in love with it. The place is dilapidated, wistful, romantic.

Steve is right behind me, Matthew bright as a button in his arms.

"I like it!" I press my hands together under my chin and do a little bounce.

Steve laughs. "Just as well. It's a long way back to Dundee!"

I swoop in for a group hug, Steve and Matthew. My family now. I want to stay like this forever, on the threshold of a new life, with that magical Christmas Eve excitement swirling inside.

"I *never* want to go back home," I tell him, and I mean it.

"What are you thinking? Moving in with a guy you hardly know. And County Durham? You know nobody down there."

"It's not the ends of the earth, Mum."

We're in a Costa in the middle of town, and the place is packed, but, as ever, my mother makes no effort to moderate her volume. Matthew watches us from his highchair like a tennis umpire. He's becoming used to this life, the loud, sudden noises and constant chatter. I wonder how he'll take to the country. I imagine plonking him down on a smooth lawn, letting him run his hand over the tips of the grass as if he's stroking a cat; me kneeling beside him in the sort of floaty print dress I've never owned. My mother breaks into the dream.

"So, you're going to share a house with this Steve and his father, who's an invalid? You've already got one wee man to look after without taking on two more!"

She sweeps back her hair, smoothing it artfully over one shoulder as she's seen Leanne do. Her skin is dehydrated, lips flaky beneath strawberry lip balm. I'd heard her come in late last night, with Billy. I'd lain rigid in my single bed. The streetlight was streaming in through the crack in the curtains, tracking across the wall. I'd traced the line of it, wishing it were the mother ship come to take me home. No such luck. I was forced to listen to their carry on. My mother, shrill and giggly; Billy gruff and demanding. Always pestering her for something. More beer, chips, fags - that other thing that I can't think about. I'd rolled into a foetal position and hugged my knees. Across a narrow strip of carpet, Leanne snored softly, and at the foot of my bed, Matthew smacked his lips, dreaming, no doubt, of me.

"Is it because of our house?" Mum is saying. "It's a bit overcrowded, but Dan and Mark are away now and Ryan will be next. When Ryan goes, you can have his room. We can redecorate."

"It's not about decorating, or space. It's about..." I shake my head. There are things she should know but they are stuck fast in my chest. "Steve's dad is very poorly. He's in a care home, but Steve wants to go back down there so he can be nearby. I might as well go with him. New place, fresh start."

"I told you to get in touch with the council again. Tell them to bump you up the list. It's ridiculous, all of us piled in a three bedroomed flat with a new baby."

"I don't have enough points. There are people worse off than me."

"What's worse than being a single mother?"

"A mother in an abusive relationship? I don't know."

"Well, can't you make something up?"

There are things I don't have to make up, but I say nothing. I'm getting far away from here. Leave it at that.

CHAPTER SIX

Steve hands over the baby and waggles his keys.

"Shall I carry you over the threshold?"

My insides hitch at that. It's always been a bit of a girly dream of mine; the marshmallow dress, the tossed bouquet, all the little customs. What is that old saying? Life happens while you're making other plans. Life has happened to me in a way I never anticipated - a fatherless baby and someone else's home. Steve is waiting for a reaction, so I play along.

"Me AND Matthew? You don't want to do your back in on moving day."

A quick, relieved grin, and he goes to insert an old iron key into the porch door. I wonder if he'll give me a key. He's never mentioned it and it seems rude to ask before I've even seen the place.

"You're right," he agrees. "I'll save my strength for lugging boxes…"

His words stop short as the door jams against a wall of junk mail.

"Man, how is he still getting post?"

"Didn't you clear it up last time?" I ease past the junk mail mountain, and wait for Steve to catch up. He opens the inner door, which appears to be unlocked and I get my first sight of my new home, a box-like hallway, the wall facing me painted bland magnolia and in a white plastic frame, a print of a little boy, his face crumpled with tears. I recoil. *That* will have to go. One crying child in my life is enough. Mercifully, Matthew appears fascinated by his surroundings, head tipped back as he surveys the walls. He's getting strong, and very heavy. I adjust him on my hip.

There is nothing to see other than a hall table with an old-fashioned landline phone and two doors, one to the left, and one to the right. There's an overpowering stink of what is probably supposed to be 'clean linen' from a plug-in air freshener under the telephone table. I wrinkle my nose, wondering what kind of smells it might be masking.

Steve lays a hand on my shoulder, and smiles. He smiles around me a lot, which is kind of refreshing. My mother rarely smiles. She says she hates her teeth.

"Ready for the guided tour? To your right, we have the kitchen-"

He opens the door and lets me look inside. Nothing much to see. It's quite dark, with one window overlooking the front garden, and another above the sink with a view of a boundary hedge. There's a glass-panelled door next to the sink. presumably leading outside. The room is depressingly messy, with a microwave buried under Tupperware boxes and the cooker hob all but invisible beneath an assortment of cookware: frying pan, milk pans, a huge soup pot, a greasy pressure cooker. The entire worktop is cluttered with stuff, save for a narrow margin around the edge. There's a small pine table with four chairs, and that too is stacked like a stall at a rummage sale. At the back of the kitchen is another door, which looks homemade. It's too low and too narrow to be a standard off-the-peg door. Normally, I'd be curious about what lay behind it, but now disappointment is vying with my earlier anticipation. Disappointment wins, and when I turn to Steve he reddens uncomfortably. It must be written all over my face.

"I'm sorry, Kat. The last time I was down- well, I was taken up with settling Dad in the home, and I didn't get any time to clean up, but don't you worry!" He ushers me out and closes the kitchen door. "There's a van coming tomorrow. House clearances. We can just dump what we don't want. Now over here is the sitting room, lounge, whatever you want to call it."

We tread back through the hall and Steve opens the other door with a flourish. He needn't have bothered. What lies beyond would be best left hidden. The place is so full of junk I can barely see the carpet.

Steve stands back and ruffles his hair. "So, quite a bit of clearing out still to do here, but I thought we could get a new…"

He keeps talking, but I'm not listening. My bubble of excitement has shrunk to the size of a pea. The room smells of old age, and I am catapulted back to a time when I was a little girl, being taken to visit my grandma in a care home. I don't remember what she looked like, but I do recall the overheated smell of unwashed clothes and liniment.

I look around me. There's a tiled fireplace with a mirror above it, and the sort of wallpaper you'd see in a Seventies sitcom; fawn, with brown geometric shapes. Beside the fire there is an easy chair with the imprint of a man. I swear the cushions are holding his shape, as if he has simply got up to go to the bathroom and they are awaiting his return. The rest of the room is dark and stuffy and piled with bags and boxes, but my eyes are fixed on that one spot, the deep troughs and dents in the just-vacated cushions. Even the fabric on the arms has been thinned by his rubbing fingers.

I feel a bit breathless. "Your dad- he's definitely moved out?"

"What? Yes, of course he is."

"For good?"

"Yeah, he can't look after himself." Steve glances around. "Hasn't been able to for a while, as you can see. I blame myself. If I hadn't gone away- I was trying to outrun my problems, but it never works, does it?"

I glance at him oddly. Doesn't it? Disquiet, like a lead weight settles on my shoulders.

Steve hurries to shake the offending dents from the cushions and dust off the upholstery.

"Don't worry about all this. It will all be gone tomorrow, and we can start afresh and look-" Triumphantly he steers me towards a sideboard piled with old vinyl records. A dismantled cot is leaning against it; white spars with a blue bunny design on one of the ends.

"Our next-door-neighbour, Len, is very good- he's been cutting the grass and keeping an eye on things. I told him about our situation and he called me the other day and said he'd seen a cot at the auction house and wondered if he should get it. Well, I said yes. Brilliant!"

He pats the top rail of the cot. There's a stripey mattress too, and I can tell straight away it's not one of the special breathable, anti-allergenic ones they sell now. I resist the urge to go over and sniff it. None of this is suitable for a little baby. Homesickness steals over me like the reek from the Glade plug-in.

"Right, if you can find the staircase, you win a prize!" Steve, determined to jolly me along, leads me back out into the hall.

I don't feel jolly. I just want to go home.

Halfway through my first date with Steve, I realised I just wanted to go home.The build-up had been exciting, with Mum agreeing to mind the baby, and Leanne loaning me her red top. I'd even applied lipstick for the first time in ages.

I'm ready way too early, sitting on my bed and staring at the net curtains, with the intensity of someone watching a cop show. From this angle, I cannot see the front gate but I'll know when he gets here. I'll recognise the purr of his cab wheels. After our hospital dash, how could I forget?

He is bang on time. I guess you have to be punctual to hack it as a taxi driver. I let him knock on the front door, in case I seem too keen. He's all newly-washed and minty-fresh and bearing gifts, expensive chocolates, which I leave on the hall table, knowing full well that Leanne will have them eaten by the time I get back. There's nothing sacred in this house.

The drive into Dundee only takes ten minutes, but it's exciting to be out of the house. The smell of male cologne is a bit-overpowering, as if Steve is trying too hard, and the fact that he is makes me nervous. I don't want to be the object of anyone's affections, although I like the way he smiles at me, looking right into my eyes, and the gentle way he says my name, lingering over it as if each letter is special.

We sit in a gloomy old man's pub with a dartboard and scuffed floorboards and he wants to know what Kat is short for.

I sip gin through a straw. "Kat."

His eyes, a lovely deep brown, warm up and crinkle, as if someone has set a match to them. I like having the power to produce that effect. "You were christened Kat?"

"I wasn't ever christened. My mother's not what she calls a God-botherer." I take pity of him and supply an answer. "It's Katherine."

"I'm Steven."

I giggle, glancing up coyly, with the straw still tucked between my teeth. I thought I'd forgotten how to flirt. "Worked that out."

"I can't work *you* out." His eyebrows knit together, giving him a stern look. "You seem very independent but under-the-thumb all at the same time."

"Really?" I put the straw aside. This is the first alcohol I've tasted since I realised I was pregnant and it's made its way straight to my head. There appears to be only melted ice left in the bottom of my humungous glass. Thankfully, Steve is on cola, so he can ferry me home. "Why do you say that?"

"Your mother seems to call the shots. Don't you fancy leaving home?"

"She doesn't really." She does, but I'm not about to admit it. "I can't leave home. I have no job."

"What did you do before?"

"This and that. Admin, mainly, Data entry. Boring stuff."

"Transferable skills. You could work from home. Everyone's at it these days."

"Having a bawling baby in the background isn't a good look. What about you?" Time to deflect away from me. "Have you always driven a taxi?"

"No, actually. I worked in the family business in County Durham, but my dad sold his share to an uncle and I just fancied a change."

"You fancied a woman. What became of her?"

"Happily shacked up with a new man, as far as I know." He gives me a tired smile and I can see pain still lurking in the back of his eyes, like it's still quite fresh. Men generally move on pretty quickly. Perhaps he's planning to move on to me? The gin has dulled my nerves, but now they skitter out from under a stone. I'm already planning on how to rebuff Steve, how to untangle myself. I realise he's just asked me a question.

"What?"

"I said, do you want to have another one here, or go back to mine for a nightcap?"

Oh God. Say something. Say the baby needs you and you have to go home. Say no. Say something. *Say anything.* The sticky tabletop pools before my eyes. A confetti of white snow lies everywhere. I realise I've been shredding a paper napkin and now tears are dripping down my cheeks.

"Hey." Steve reaches for me.

"I don't get out much." That is so lame I want to disappear

inside myself. I don't know what's wrong with me, but he's not asking for an explanation. He just squeezes my fingers, like he did when I was in labour. Quietly, safely.

"Shh. It's okay. Why don't you put your coat on? I'll take you home."

CHAPTER SEVEN

You've made your bed. I can hear my mother's voice in my head as Steve hastily flips the quilt over the bumps and hollows in his father's bed and hurries to open a window, but the bedroom is musky with night sweats and illness, and there's no disguising it. The bedside table is littered with pill bottles, half-empty tumblers of water and tissues. I see a pair of reading glasses and a blue plastic denture container. A discarded hot water bottle lies on the carpet.

"I can't sleep here." The words are out before I can stop them.

"I know it's not perfect," Steve jumps in, "but the ambulance came so quickly, there was no time to tidy up."

So you left it all here, all the private little bits of your dad, strewn about. I feel like I'm about to step into the man's too-big slippers and stagger around in them like a little girl.

I tear my gaze away from the bed. "This doesn't feel right."

"I'm sorry, Kat. I should have come down by myself and cleared it all out. It will be done by tomorrow."

"By tomorrow I'll have slept in *that* bed, and it's not going to happen." I cup Matthew's fragile little head, as if I can prevent him hearing our exchange.

Steve lets out a sigh. It sounds exasperated to me. I don't think I've ever seen him display any bad temper, but I'm convinced I'm in the right. How on earth did he think this would be okay?

"What do you want me to do?"

"Get me alternate accommodation until this place is fit to bring a baby."

"But- but- this is rural Durham. There are no hotels around here."

"Right." I turn to leave. "You can take me to the station then. It does have trains?"

I'm no longer quite sure who I am. An alien has possessed me, an assertive woman who had expected better and been disappointed. Maybe motherhood has released something in me, a crouching tiger or one of those mythical black cats, only ever glimpsed from a distance, but distinctly threatening.

"There's a woman in the next village does B&B."

I turn to face him. Outlined against the window, he looks smaller, slumped. We eye each other across the rumpled bed and I feel my chin lift. I won't look away.

"That sounds acceptable. Book me in for a couple of nights. I'll come back when this-" My gaze lights on the water, the dentures, the glasses. "-is gone. I don't mind visiting your dad in the home, but I don't want to live with his ghost."

The woman who opens the door to me is closed and unsmiling, as if she expects me to be asking for money or pressure-selling PVC windows. The first thing I notice is her shock of long white hair. The ends are tinted a steely blue, and her blue-framed glasses match perfectly.

There's an awkward pause before she recalls who I am and relaxes her defences. Her prickliness reminds me a bit of my mother, which gives me an unexpected pang, but I tell myself it's because they are around the same vintage. Whereas my mother wears inappropriate lashings of mascara, this woman is make-up free, and her unexpectedly dark brows owe nothing to a pencil. She's wearing a black vest top. I note her gym arms and a tiny silver crescent moon pendant nestling at her throat. My imagination immediately casts her as some kind of shaman.

"You must be...Kat?" Her gaze travels to the baby in my arms. I cannot tell if she's for or against, but she doesn't coo at him like most older women do.

"Yes."

"Your husband called. Just one night, is it?"

I don't bother to correct her, either about the time scale or my marital status. We are in Deep Rural here. For all I know, she's ultra conservative and firmly against cohabiting couples. And what will happen if I say I want to stay for a week? I'm certainly in no hurry to return to that stale, smelly house. This lady's B&B, Whitecross Villa, is clean and citrusy- I can smell it from here. I just smile politely, and she smiles in return and swings the door wider in invitation.

"Come in, then. I'll show you around."

The hall is narrow with a staircase to one side, a white glossy banister leading up into the shadows. It's so dark I wonder if the bulb has gone. All the doors off the hall are firmly closed, as if on some level this woman does not want any intrusion. The kitchen is at the end. We go through and, by contrast, the light is so bright, it dazzles me. The sun is streaming through French windows, and I squint at the white cabinets, shelves of delicate china and a vintage Singer sewing machine set up on the pine table. There's a bundle of silky material beside it; sequins glinting in the glare. Maybe she makes her own Druid robes.

My sweeping gaze registers an array of cat bowls on the floor, pretty earthenware ones with CAT in black letters. I wonder if she lives alone with about six felines which she loves more than people, and immediately scold myself for thinking that way. Maybe she has a rich husband and a talent for poker. Never judge a book by its cover.

Somewhere, a hidden draft catches a wind chime. I don't see any windows open, but the sound is melodic and sweet.

"You can have your breakfast in here. You do want breakfast?"

"Um- I haven't really thought about it."

The woman looks at Matthew again. This time, her guard drops and it's like the unveiling of a fresh, clean statue. She leans in.

"I have a travel cot! Yes, I do. Just for you!"

Matthew reacts to her exaggerated nods, reaching out his pudgy fingers.

"Feel free to sit in the garden, too. Your husband wasn't very clear on the phone. Is he not accompanying you?"

"No. We're just moving in, and it's a bit difficult, with the baby."

"Of course. Gosh," she clutches her pendant again. "I never even introduced myself. Rowena Patterson."

We shake. Her hand is cool, as I knew it would be.

"Thanks for having us at short notice."

She brushes that away. "You were lucky. I'm fully booked next month- a bunch of ramblers from Kent – but it's quiet at the moment. At least you'll have the place to yourself, apart from me, of course! Come on up, and I'll show you your room- Here…" She takes my overnight bag. "The house is a bit rambling. Belonged to my husband's family and it's too much for me really…but that's another story. You're on the first floor. Come on."

The room is old-fashioned, with a high double bed and the sort of dark walnut furniture my grandma used to have. There is a wardrobe, a dressing table with an oval mirror and a side table with a kettle and bowl of tea bags and coffee sachets. There's a large expanse of carpet which makes me want to dance. This is all mine! I won't have to share. Gratefully, I inhale layers of product: fabric conditioner, air freshener, carpet shampoo and when Rowena opens a door to reveal the bathroom, Knight's

Castile soap. I am in heaven.

"I'll leave you to it. Feel free to use the kitchen if you need to heat up bottles or whatever, and you're welcome to join me for a glass of wine, when the little one is asleep."

I can't decide if she's lonely or just accommodating. Maybe she makes the same offer to all her guests. The idea is tempting, so I thank her and hope that Matthew will approve of the travel cot and go to sleep without fuss.

"One more thing," she says as she turns to leave. "Do you mind if I ask which house you're moving into? I wasn't aware there was anything for sale."

"Oh, it wasn't. It's been in the family for a while, as far as I know. It's on Derville's Lane, right at the end. Mr Burns' house? Maybe you know it?"

She looks at me with such an expression my blood stops pumping. What was *that*? A mixture of...fear? Hate?

"No, I don't," she says.

CHAPTER EIGHT

Matthew is sleepy, which always fills me with a familiar mixture of anxiety and joy. Is he sleepy because he's healthily tired, and he's about to gift me the luxury of some unbroken rest, or is he coming down with something? The questions never stop, and I suddenly feel a long way from all that is familiar. My mother might give glib answers to most of my questions, but at least she is a sounding board. Steve doesn't know the first thing about babies. I wonder if Rowena Patterson has children. I sit on the edge of the bed and rock Matthew gently, watching his baby eyelids flutter over his bottle. At eight months, he's becoming a real little person. I switched him to the bottle as soon as he started getting teeth and it feels good to be reclaiming my body.

When I first started dating Steve, I was determined to keep him at arm's length. I was suspicious. What did he see in a first-time mum? How on earth could I get into bed with him, to reveal all the damaged bits of myself? Incredibly, after seeing each other for around six months, we still haven't been intimate. He says he loves me, which is probably just frustration talking, and I get the feeling I'm on a bit of a countdown. When I agreed to move in with him, there was an unspoken agreement between us, a sort of silent contract, that we would shift seamlessly into a sexual relationship. Steve doesn't realise it but booking into Whitecross Villa is yet another way of me avoiding my contractual obligations.

"The average couple have sex on the fifth date." Leanne quotes a paragraph from her latest magazine. "Having sex creates powerful bonds, which may complicate a relationship with premature emotional baggage before both partners are ready. Having sex too soon can compel us to stay in a relationship which may not be designed to last."

I fold one of the baby's sleep suits before answering. "And your point is?"

She shrugs and turns a page. "Just wondering what the state of play is between you and the taxi driver."

"He's called Steve, and it's none of your business." I snag another item from the laundry basket'

"But you've seen him what- six or seven times now? Surely you must be doing it?"

"Leanne!" I can feel the blood rush to my face. "I've just had a baby!"

"Three months ago. You must be over it by now."

I fling whatever is in my hand back onto the ironing pile. "Over it? You think I'm over it?"

"Matthew is three months and we still don't know who the father is. Are you sure it isn't Steve?"

"No! Can we drop the subject. I don't want to talk about my private life."

"Ooh! Get you!" Leanne wiggles her fingers at me. "*Private life*. Jesus, we'd all like one of those. Did you phone the council?"

"I'm still fairly well down the list."

"Bleedin' hell. We'll all be living in that room when Matthew is a teenager at this rate."

"Leanne, you could move out. There's nothing stopping you."

She looks at me aghast, glossy nude lips parted. "Me? I don't even have a boyfriend to move in with."

"That's because you sleep with them all too soon and create premature emotional baggage. They run for the hills."

"Bugger off, you." She lobs a tube of Body Shop hand cream in my direction. I dodge neatly, as I've done all my life, and continue folding, smoothing, piling. Pain is building behind my eyes. Leanne has the ability to get right under my skin like a glob of her favourite serum. I haven't slept with Steve and I think it's going to become an issue. He hasn't actually broached the subject yet, but last night we'd come a step closer.

It was our sixth date, as it happened. We'd gone to the pub which serves the ginormous gins, the place we'd visited on our first encounter. I always shy away from the word *date*. I am not *dating* Steve. We are just friends. I like his company.

"I like your company," I'd said to him in the pub, and we'd grinned at each other in a lopsided, tipsy kind of way.

He'd sat for a while, gazing at me with his head tilted, as if he could see something unfolding, and I couldn't resist making eye contact, in the hope that I might see it too. I think I did. A liquid warmth in his brown eyes which made me feel hot and fuzzy. I told myself it was just the gin, but I knew it was something that I hadn't felt in a long, long time. Maybe never. When he asked me back to his flat for a nightcap, I found myself agreeing.

His flat was nothing special; third floor, above a chippy. A smell of curry sauce lingered on the stairs. For a guy, he'd been quite inventive with the soft lighting and mood music, and he owned a genuine old-fashioned record player which fascinated me. I'd sat on the rug and flipped through his vinyl collection.

He'd tenderly laid a throw around my shoulders in case I was cold, although actually I was fizzing with warmth and...joy. I felt happy. I chose Pink Floyd and Steve placed it on the turntable with a reverence that made me giggle. I got up and flopped down on the couch, and as the music swelled through the room, Steve sat behind me and pulled me against him. I could feel his breath on my ear, caught the sting of the whisky he'd drunk earlier. Cushioned by the throw, it didn't feel too intimate. It felt snug, and somehow right.

When his arms tightened around me, my first instinct was to pull away.

"Look, it's getting late," I murmured. "I'd better call a cab."

"You could always stay." His eyes had taken on a sharp hungry edge which made my stomach quiver, and not in a good way. I'd seen that look before. I scrambled to the edge of the couch and stared at the rug. He laid an arm around my shoulders. His voice was soft, persuasive.

"Kat."

"Steve, I want to go home. *I've just had a baby*." The ultimate get-out-of-jail card.

"And I'm at least ten years older than you." He sat back a bit and pinched his spare tyre. "We've all got issues."

I cast a grin at him, but still, I got up. "Sorry. I'm calling a cab. It's too soon."

CHAPTER NINE

Sitting on the edge of Rowena Patterson's solid bed, I go over the problem in my head, as Matthew finally nods into oblivion. It's too soon, I'd told him. The truth is I'm scared, so scared of the baggage. Of everything that goes with getting the baggage. Steve is a saint, a saviour, and in a weird way, so is Leanne. It was Leanne who'd first given me the idea. *I don't have a boyfriend to move in with.* She didn't. But I did. Steve was my escape.

I decide to take Rowena up on her offer of wine. Partly, just for the rare chance to escape from my baby tyrant, and partly because I'd latched onto the idea that she had some kind of beef with the Burns family. **Had I imagined the change of tone? Maybe she was just pissed off that she'd missed out on the local goss.** Country folk are like that, I guess. Perhaps she's peeved about not being in the loop.

My phone trills with a message from Steve.

Are you okay?

I sigh, hoping he's not going to expect a running commentary on my stay. I run my thumb over the screen to create the shortest reply possible.

I'm fine.

Maybe I should stay there with you tonight?

Why?

Strange place. Thought you might want company.

I hesitate before replying. I'll have to share an intimate space with him soon enough, but for now give me this one night, this smooth hush of solo living. I compose a suitably kind response.

That's sweet but I'm going to have an early night. Will come over tomorrow to help x

I add an extra xx to make up for my lack of enthusiasm and with a final check on Matthew, spark out in the travel cot, I make my way downstairs.

Rowena is perched at the breakfast bar and already getting stuck into the wine. She pats the white plastic bar stool beside her.

"Grab the wine out of the fridge, love, There's a glass here."

Like the stool, the kitchen is bang on trend, with one of those industrial refrigerators that spills out ice on demand. I like Rowena's style. As I return to her side I notice immediately that she's donned a smart lime green tunic with foxes on it, and spectacles with forest green frames, which she'd whipped off as soon as soon as I came through the door. I suspect, like my mother, she hates things which age her. I heave myself onto the stool by her side and glance at her paperback (You can tell a lot about folk by their reading material). It's a Mills and Boon with an intense-looking couple on the cover.

"Light reading," she apologises. "I can't be doing with all this dark stuff that they publish now."

"Really? I like a good horror."

She shudders delicately as I top up her wine. "All that bumbling about in the dark. Not for me. Baby asleep?"

"Sound." I take a sip of alcohol and allow myself to relax for the first time in days. Uprooting isn't for the faint-hearted. I feel like a field mouse tumbled from its nest.

"So, what are you doing in this neck of the woods? I detect a Scottish accent."

"Yes, I'm from Dundee. It's very different here. Very- *rural*."

"Oh." She rolls her eyes. "We're out in the sticks alright. So how did you meet…Steve, is it?"

Her attention is so unwavering I feel like a schoolgirl up before the head.

I have rehearsed this. "We've been dating for a while and when Steve's dad got poorly, he decided to come back here. And I came too. And Matthew, of course." That last bit came out wrong. Why wouldn't we accompany Steve if he was, as Rowena no doubt thinks, the baby's father? I didn't want to invite questions, so I added. "It was a no brainer. See a bit of England. I might even get a job."

Rowena opens her eyes wide and nods. Her focus is making me nervous. I glug some more wine, hiding behind my glass.

"What do you do?" she asks.

That stumps me. I shrug. "Nothing much, I guess."

"Apart from mothering!"

We both laugh in an obvious way.

"I was a bit rubbish at school. Every report card said, 'Katherine needs to pay more attention.' It was probably true. I did like English though, so I've had a few admin jobs, done a bit of freelance stuff."

She picks up her glass and gestures widely with it. "Anybody can do anything these days. You can work online, be a mumpreneur."

"A mumpreneur." I slide that around my tongue, try it for size. "I guess I could."

"My niece is big on Instagram. You could start a blog, make some money out of it."

"I might look into that. Cheers." I raise my glass and she chinks hers to mine. I think I may have found a friend. Again, I hear the musical trill of a wind chime, although there is no draught. Maybe she leaves a window open for the cats I have yet to meet.

"So, what's happened to him? Mr Burns?"

"Mr- oh, you mean Steve's dad?"

I expect her to nod, but she says nothing. Her eyes are burning into me. Is she always this intense? Maybe it's me. I'm more used to being ignored. Leanne always has her head stuck in Take-a-Break and Mum spends her life running between home and job and bloody Billy.

"He's not very well. I think he's quite old and he's not able to look after himself. The house was filthy and full of *crap*." I feel bad for exposing him in this way, a frail old man I have never met, but Rowena's vigilant listening is encouraging me. "It was horrible, moving in and finding his- his *presence* still there, like he'd just left. I felt like an intruder. I didn't want to stay there with the baby."

"No," she agrees. "It's safer here."

Safer seems an odd word to use, but I expect she's right. Imagine setting Matthew down on that filthy carpet, letting him roll around amid the dust and sharp corners. I must have made a face, because she laughs and the odd mood is broken,

"You can stay as long as you like. Steve can sort it all out. The most you deserve is a clean house to step into. Will the baby have his own room?"

"Well, I had a quick look upstairs. There's a door in the kitchen which opens onto this really steep staircase. There's a bathroom and two bedrooms at the top. I'd like to decorate one as a nursery- yellow paint, maybe, and a frieze with zoo animals on it and a mobile."

"You've been planning for a while!" She smiles at me with her chin on one hand. Again, I get that queasy feeling, like I'm under a microscope, but I ignore it and warm to my theme.

"I've thought about nothing else since I knew I was pregnant. I couldn't do it though, because I was sharing a bedroom with my sister and a house with a whole bunch of other folk. Family and…drifters. So, poor Matthew was stuck in a crib in the corner and all his stuff piled up because there was no space."

"You and Steve haven't been living together then?"

I spot my mistake.

"Um…no. The opportunity didn't arise."

"Baby Matthew was a bit of a surprise, I take it?" Her eyes crinkle with mischief.

"You could say that."

"So the house on Derville's Lane is your first home together, and Matthew will have a room of his own."

Her lightness has, for some reason, evaporated. Her tone is off, like a cold breeze has passed through the kitchen, making her words not celebratory but something else, and I'm not sure what that is. Just as I'm trying to summon up an enthusiastic reply, she speaks again and her voice is faint and choked.

"There's always a safe place for you here. Remember that."

CHAPTER TEN

Some time earlier...

"I've decided to leave Dundee." Steve announces. "I have to go. My Dad needs me."

I want to tell him not to go. We've only just met. This thing between us- it needs time to evolve. But all I can think of is the practical and mundane. "What will you do for work?"

"Have cab, will travel!" Steve jokes. He jokes a lot, but I know him well enough now to see the tension behind his eyes and the little nervy tic in his cheek.

He rubs his nose. "I expect I'll have to apply for a local authority licence or something. I'll figure it out. I can always get work with my uncle...although we kind of parted on bad terms. Something will turn up."

"You're so glass half-full."

"Glass half-drunk, more like!" He laughs heartily, like he believes in his own resilience. I'm not fooled.

"I hope your dad will be okay. My auntie had a stroke." And then died. I let my words tail off.

"He just needs a bit of support. It's hard, seeing him like that. I'm going down this weekend to get him settled into a place my daughter's found for him. A care home, but a good one, by all accounts."

"What's he like, your dad?"

"He's always been a bit of a rogue, if I'm honest." Steve shakes his head. "A cross between Del Boy and that bloke from the DIY programme on the telly."

"Alan Titchmarsh?"

"Oh God no! My dad was never that laid back. Or that saintly. No, he's more - Nick Nowles- that's the guy's name. A bit rough and ready, but good at getting things done. He always had an eye for the main chance, my dad. Not anymore though."

His sadness hangs heavy on the air. I close the gap between us and let my hand close around his. When he lifts his gaze, it's so dark and intense I want to look away, but it ensnares me.

"I don't want to leave you," he murmurs. "What we have- it's important to me."

I shift my shoulders as if they ache. I know I should repeat his words, interact with this new rawness but I don't know how, so I let it wash over me and all of a sudden he is kissing me with such fierceness our teeth clash. It's not the first time we've kissed, but I don't like it like this. It's unrestrained, unformed. I pull away. His eyes are moist and feel bad for his pain,

"Come with me." His words are hoarse, needy.

"I can't. What about my mum?"

"You're 26 and still living at home, Kat. Break free."

I flounder around for an excuse. "But I need help with the baby."

"Nobody better than me! I was there when he was born- I'd do anything for him. I'd do anything for you. Please come with me. Don't let this be the end."

Back in my room at the B&B, as I fold Matthew's clothes into my overnight bag, I reflect that *this* may be the end, this reluctance to go back to the house on Derville's Lane. Have I come all this way just to realise that I came here for the wrong reasons?

My phone chirps a message from Steve.

Van came early! All clear. I'll pick you up at noon.

What does that even mean, all clear? I'll still be stepping into someone else's life. Idly I scroll through my Instagram feed. Leanne's most recent update makes me feel homesick and, if I'm honest, a bit hostile. She is always so together, like she knows her place in her own limited version of the world. There she is- @beautyismylife – pouting in concentration as she dusts her cheekbones with a luminous powder.

"Paisley and Ball's brand new Moonbeam Pearlescent Highlighter is my new number one beauty must-have! #glow #highlighter #nofilter #paisleyandball #beautybrands #beautyicons #beautybloggers #dundeelife

Trying too hard to be an influencer, I think waspishly. My thoughts drift to Rowena's niece. Blogging sounds like something I could do. I've produced content for business blogs in the past - maybe I could start one of my own? If Leanne can get 2000 followers for pouting, I'm sure I have something to offer. I fall idle for a few moments, lost in thought and watching Matthew inch-worm his way on his tummy across the patterned carpet. Perhaps I could do an online journal of Matthew's progress, inch-by-inch, pound by pound. That would appeal to the parenting community, all those people like me who have become lost in a strange new world. A flicker of something warm ignites inside me. It's a feeble flame which needs coaxing, but it's there! I haven't felt excited or motivated for so long it feels like an alien has taken root inside me.

I pick up my phone and compose a response to Steve, already

practising blog titles in my head- Kat's Korner, Coffee time with Kat, Lost in Motherhood. All of them are a bit shit.

Fine, see you then x

This might not be an ending at all, but a beginning. I am overdue a beginning. The little flame begins to grow and as I wait for Steve, I sit on the bed and nurse it.

My new home looks exactly as it was- the neatly-clipped garden, the bench, the bird table. True, there is evidence of recent comings and goings. Broken bits of hedgerow and loose leaves speckle the path, chips of swept-up crockery and a forgotten teaspoon lies abandoned on the grass. I pick it up, staring at it blankly as if it's a clue to some great mystery.

This time, I enter the house first, like some kind of health and safety inspector, as Steve hangs back awaiting judgement. He doesn't crack any jokes about carrying me over the threshold and I feel like I've suddenly morphed into the sort of person who has to be appeased. This is so unlike me.

The porch door is standing open, the inner door unlocked. I cannot resist a wry glance behind me.

"Do you always leave your door unlocked? Bit risky."

"There are still places where you can do that, despite what you read in the papers."

I let this go. When Steve had suggested leaving the sleeping Matthew in the car, while I took a look around, I'd made a point of firmly unbuckling the baby and hugging him to me as if he might be snatched away. Easy to see Steve had not been brought up in the city.

The first thing I notice is that the hall table has disappeared, leaving the cordless handset to take its chances on the floor. Beyond the orbit of the Glade plug-in, a sharp new fragrance is present- disturbed dust, sweat, outside interference. I'm very sensitive to atmosphere. Unfortunately, the Crying Boy remains.

The sitting room door is standing open, revealing a space miraculously denuded of clutter. What remains looks stressed and hastily rearranged: the sideboard, a gateleg table, the couch, Steve's dad's armchair, its cushions determinedly plumped, as if that action alone will set my mind at rest. It doesn't work. I still feel like an interloper.

"Come and see the kitchen!" Steve is jangling his keys and seems a bit agitated. He's trying so hard. He must have pulled out all the stops to clear the house in a single morning, so I paste a smile on my face. I should probably hug him or stroke his arm affectionately like a regular girlfriend, but instead, I ease Matthew a little closer to my chest.

All the Tupperware boxes and pots and pans that had cluttered the kitchen work surfaces are gone, but the countertop is brown-ringed with tea and age. I wonder if there is any bleach. My mother is a demon with the Domestos and always has three bottles on the go. I bite the inside of my cheek to keep my smile in place, but its rapidly turning into a rictus grin.

"The upstairs is a bit- well, we ran out of room in the van." Steve explains. "I'll just order a skip for the rest. I've taken the cot upstairs, so-"

I stop listening. The strange little door to the staircase is ajar. It quivers as I approach, and a musty gush of air rushes past me. It stinks like the inside of a chimney- cold, ashy, forgotten. Steve must have opened the bedroom windows. I climb the stairs cautiously, Matthew nestled on my hip. The master bedroom is still full of boxes and bags-for-life crammed with belongings which now belong to nobody. The sheets have been changed, but even from the doorway I can smell how stale they are. In the other bedroom, the one I have earmarked as a primrose yellow nursery, the dismantled cot languishes against the wall. The boxes are fewer here, but the thought of putting my baby to bed amid someone else's clutter is disturbing. It's not that I'm unused to living in a mess, but the smell of a family home feels familiar, and this does not. It is alien. I don't want to touch anything, or drink out of the cups or even sit down, and now something else is bothering me.

All the upstairs windows are tightly sealed. Wherever that icy draft had originated, it wasn't here.

The mood remains muted for the rest of the afternoon, and I can tell Steve is at a loss by the way he keeps lifting things up and putting them down again.

"Let me make you a cup of tea, and then I'll put up Matthew's cot. Maybe he'll have a nap?"

"Maybe." The baby feels sack-like in my arms but he's already dozed in the car and I know what that means. He's used up his sleep ration. My mother was always banging on about routine before he came along, and I never listened. Routines were for old people with no life, but now I dread any disruption to the day, because I know the baby tyrant will make me pay. I perch on one of the chairs at the kitchen table, scowling at the surface crumbs. They look fresh rather than historic. I think of Steve breakfasting alone, waiting for the house clearance people, wondering what to keep, what to give away. Meanwhile, I have barely spared his poor dad a thought.

The message alert trills. I check my phone, before banishing it to my jeans pocket. It persists. *Ping.* I will not answer it. I will not. I can feel Steve's curiosity, but he is too polite to ask any questions. He fills the kettle and clicks the switch. There are scrapes on his elbows and what looks like paint, or plaster, and bits of cobweb. His baggy jeans are almost white with dust.

"Why don't you have a bath?" I say. "You must be exhausted. Have a soak, and we can order pizza or something. You do get home deliveries?"

He turns to face me, leaning his hips against the kitchen unit, arms folded, laughing at my expression.

"I've never done it. There's probably a £20 delivery charge. We're really in the Durham boondocks!"

I feel my shoulders relax. "Okay, why don't you take Matthew with you. Go get a curry. And wine! The car will lull him to sleep and I'll get peace to …tidy up." My gaze slips to the sticky floor, the stains on the unit doors. I'm already thinking bleachy water and hoover bags. I have to make this place family-friendly before I can relax.

He brightens at my apparent enthusiasm. "That sounds like a plan. It will give you a bit of peace." The kettle boils and he turns it off.

"Leave the tea. Off you go while there's still a window of nap-time."

Matthew is starting to perk up. Leave it any longer and he'll be awake all evening and probably half the night.

"Right. Okay. Come on, little man." He extends his big hands. I realise that this is the first time the two of them will have been alone together and, oddly, I feel fine about it, but maybe I'm just knackered and looking for some respite. It's really hard being on red alert all the time.

Matthew goes uncomplainingly into Steve's arms, taking the opportunity to peer microscopically at this new face, as if he's committing the very pores to memory. It always makes me smile, this cross-eyed, intense scrutiny.

"Steve. Today must have been difficult. You know, getting rid of your dad's stuff."

He brushes this away, kissing the top of the baby's head. "Had to be done. There isn't much room for stuff in the care home. He has a few bits and pieces, his books, a framed picture of ma and me and one of the grandkids. That sort of thing."

This time, I do go in close, place a hand on his bare forearm. I can feel the heat of him through a forest of hair. His skin is hot and gritty.

"I remember when my grandma died. my mum had to clear the house so she could hand back the key- not that your dad is dead." I bite my lip.

"I know what you mean. Life gets smaller as you age. You wouldn't know about that. You're just a spring chicken."

He hugs me and plants a kiss on my head, just like he did with Matthew. It feels …not patronising exactly- but *paternal*. I slink out of his grasp and wait for him to leave.

CHAPTER ELEVEN

My phone continues to grumble, and although I have vowed not to answer it, the caller will not give up. As the handset vibrates in the back pocket of my jeans, I sink into a place of dread. I'm convinced it's *him* again, but what if it isn't? It could be my mother. Something might be wrong at home. I put down my bleachy cloth, rip off my extra-large Marigolds and accept the call.

It's Leanne, on Facetime. My belly does its usual quivery dance; part-anxiety, part-longing to connect. Leanne has always been top dog in our relationship, so our interactions are coloured by her whims and mood. Even though *she* called *me*, she already looks bored.

"Hey. How's it going? Have you had your first fight yet?"

"Steve isn't a fighter."

"Bo-ring."

I sit down heavily on one of the chairs. My neck and shoulders are aching. She picks up on that immediately.

"You look like shit."

"Thanks, Lee."

"You do. Why have you got your hair scrunched back like that?"

"I've been cleaning."

"You?" A blast of laughter. Leanne picks at a thick eyelash with two pearly talons. "Jesus, you never even changed your bed at home. Mum had to bribe you to do it."

My chin sinks to my hand. "Oh Lee- you should see this place. I hate it." Tears unexpectedly threaten, and I lower my voice. "It's an old man's house. It smells of Old Man and it's dark and creepy. The outside looks really neat. like one of those country cottages you see in magazines, but inside it's...*ugh*."

"Why are you whispering?" Leanne whispers back. "Is the old man still there?"

"No." That comes out all defensive. I want to explain about the imprints in the cushions but it would sound ridiculous. I plead with myself not to cry. Amazingly, Leanne picks up on my mood. She doesn't do that very often, but maybe my absence has had an impact.

"Seriously, Kat. If you're not happy, you can come home. Can't she, Mum? Here's Mum. Hold on, I'll put her on. Mum!"

The shout is so loud it nearly bursts my ear drum. Suddenly my mother is in the frame, the two of them squished together, identical wild curls and foxy features.

"You okay, hun?" my mother asks. "Where's the wee lad?"

"He's out with Steve. They've gone to get a curry."

"What you having- a bhuna?" Leanne demands.

"She always has a korma," my mother snaps. "Don't you, Kat? She doesn't do spice."

Tears slide down my cheeks. They feel so far away; my family reduced to a two-inch square of plastic. Maybe that's why they don't notice my distress.

"Oh, here's Billy! Come in, love." My mother swings away from the screen. I can see the flash of her smile and the swish of her hair and then Billy squeezes his long face between the two of them, chin resting on Mum's shoulder. I can image the weight of it, digging in.

"A rose between two thorns!" He sing-songs. "Hey Katherine!"

I hate him calling me Katherine. Nobody ever does. He uses my full name as if it gives him some power, like a gypsy horse-whisperer. I don't answer, but my mother isn't having that.

"Say hello to your future *father*, Kat!"

"What?" My belly does a backflip. I transfer my gaze from one face to the other. Leanne tosses her hair and simpers. My mother, looking all coy, extends her knuckles to the camera. The sparkly, gaudy diamond is unmissable.

"Last night," she gloats. "He *proposed!*"

Leanne claps her fingers, in the manner of a trained sea-lion.

I don't know what to say, what's expected of me. *Fuck that.* I don't say it out loud. I press the red button and disconnect. Later I send a message to the family WhatsApp:

Sorry! My phone ran out of battery xx

Should I add my congratulations? Maybe tomorrow.

Come bedtime, amazingly, Matthew goes down without fuss in his new cot. I'm still not happy about the remaining junk in here, but I persuade myself things will seem better in the morning. I'll organise paint and order a mobile online. But first, I have this night to get through.

I sit for as long as possible on an old toolbox, gazing at Matthew through the bars of the cot, watching his lashes flutter closed and his little chest adopt a steady rhythm. He goes that pale, still way of all sleeping babies, totally absorbed in the process of growing, developing, regenerating. When I'm convinced he's sleeping soundly, I get reluctantly to my feet.

We'd consumed the takeaway earlier, but the wine awaits. Steve bought two bottles of white, and nuts and cheesy biscuits as a 'house-warming.' When I go downstairs, he's watching some over-loud cop show on the TV and the coffee table is set with two wine glasses and little bowls of nibbles. The fire is crackling in the grate, and the big light extinguished. By the glow of a pair of mismatched lamps, the room looks almost homely, and I'm grateful for the effort Steve has gone to for me, to make me feel relaxed, at home, loved. But there's still an inescapable chill lingering in the outer edges, waiting for us to drop our guard. I shiver as I join him on the sofa. The back of it is draped with a mustard-coloured fleece throw which I recognise from Steve's Dundee flat. He places it gently around my shoulders.

"These old places take a while to heat up. Wine, or beer? I've got both. Is the little lad asleep?"

"Yup. No bother. Wine, please." I sit primly with my knees together.

Steve is not subtle. This is a seduction scenario if ever I saw one. Tonight, comes the trade-off, all *this*- I rapidly scan the walls- for *this*. My gaze drops to where Steve's hand is resting on my knee. His thumb moves in an eager arc against my denim-clad skin. My sigh is more audible than intended.

"I bet you're tired, love? You've worked like a Trojan today."

I'm not even sure what a Trojan is, but I agree with him, and sip my wine. "Steve, do you have a computer?"

"Yes. A laptop. Do you want me to get it?" He looks slightly disappointed as if I'm planning to disrupt his amorous plans.

"Not now, but tomorrow I thought I might get some things for Matthew's room." I have no idea how I'm going to pay for the wish list in my head. Money is an issue. I don't want to be dependent on Steve, but by encouraging me to come here, he's made sure of exactly that. It's a pattern for women like me. My mother made the same mistake, relying first on my father, and then on Billy, allowing herself to be shafted by both.

"I'll give you my credit card. Just get what you want." Steve says.

"Within reason." I shoot him a grin.

"Within reason." He smiles back. Something happens when our

eyes meet. It always does. I cannot deny I am attracted to him, to his qualities, as well as his dark eyes and the ready smile and that unruly flick of hair. The age difference is not an issue for me. I feel safe with Steve, and yet…None of that makes this any easier.

By the time we go to bed, I am pleasantly drunk, although fifteen minutes of flannelling and teeth brushing in an unheated bathroom soon takes the edge off. I daren't risk the shower, which sits overhead a chipped avocado bath tub. I wonder if Steve's credit card will stretch to a new bathroom with a power shower. I'd settle for a new shower curtain. I take a last look at Matthew. He's slumbering on his back, arms thrown carelessly above his head. The room is warm, thanks to Steve's earlier bleeding of the radiators. Carefully, I leave the door ajar, so I can hear him if he cries. As I wander back to our bedroom, my tipsy brain is bursting with paint colours and state-of-the art baby monitors. The sight of a naked Steve lying in wait is something of a shock. Reality hits me with a bump.

He's reclining, facing the door, head on hand and the duvet pushed suggestively down to his waist. His chest is bear-like, furry, which appears comforting rather than threatening, but in the lamplight his eyes are dark and predatory. I've never considered Steve to be a predator but there is no mistaking the sexual charge. Even fully dressed, I feel exposed. He pulls back the duvet some more and pats the mattress. I get a sudden waft of stale laundry and muted tones of a manly cologne. Stripping down to my underwear, I scramble under the covers, away from that laser gaze. I wish I was more like my sister, sexually experienced and always up for a bit of fun. This does not feel like fun. It does not feel like it should.

"Are you cold? It will warm up soon."

His voice is a whisper, he takes me in his arms and the movement of the duvet against our skin is a whisper too, joining us together. Suddenly there is no space between us. We are skin to skin. There is a blooming of sorts; my body grows warm where he's touching me, but as if he's reading my mind, he steers clear of those bits under the protective armour of my lingerie. I force myself to relax, let him kiss me, and nuzzle my neck, concentrating on that little flicker of flame, waiting for it to burst forth. I try to match his enthusiasm, but for so long my passion has been bound up in other things: the fierceness of motherhood, and the sheer struggle for survival.

I am failing, falling short. When his hand smooths across my belly and under the lace at my hip, I clamp my legs shut, pull away from him. In one rapid movement I have turned my back, and I'm curled in on myself like a bud. He hovers over me, His warmth against my back is no longer safe, but sticky and repulsive.

"Don't." Is all I can say.

I feel his exhalation on my shoulder.

"I'm sorry. I...Kat. Look at me. What's wrong?"

The concern in his voice gives me an instant guilt trip. I glance back over my shoulder.

"It's me. I'm sorry- I-I'm just tired and...not in the mood." My voice comes out all peevish. I feel him withdraw from me. He rolls onto his back. I daren't look, but I imagine him staring at the ceiling, one arm over his brow, his Adam's apple working as he figures out what to say, how to handle this.

"You don't have to be in the mood. I mean- we don't need to... All you had to do was say. I'm not the sort of bloke to try and talk you into it. It's fine. Absolutely fine.

And I knew that it was, that Steve would never be that guy, trying to get under my defences, wear me down with bullying and threats and false promises. Steve is a salt-of-the-earth type. Slowly, I unfurl and roll towards him. He meets me halfway and we kiss with genuine affection, but I take care not to close the gap between us completely. He strokes my hair. His eyes have calmed to a simmer.

"Let's go to sleep. I've got a builder coming round tomorrow."

This is so random, I raise my eyebrows. "Why?"

"A while ago, my dad got planning permission to extend. He always wanted a conservatory, a sun room. Sadly, he won't get to use it, but we can. It can be a family room, a place to chill out with a patio door into the garden."

"We can have barbecues."

"We can. I cook a mean steak!" He hugs me closer, but the hunger has gone out of him and I can feel every muscle in my body start to melt. That little flicker of desire has fled and I wonder what it will take to retrieve it. I've burned my boats, and I need to make this work. Still, I've managed to stall the inevitable for another night. I take the initiative and kiss his cheek, tasting the alcohol of his cologne on my lips.

"That sounds perfect. We'll be a proper little family." It's like someone else saying those words, not me, but he responds as I knew he would.

"Maybe in time, Matthew might get a little brother or sister…"

I smile against his shoulder. In time. But not right now.

CHAPTER TWELVE

I come awake in the small hours. The bedroom is in darkness. I'm instantly alert, tensed, waiting for the cry which must surely have cut through my dreams. There is only silence, and the silence is heavy, like an old coat. *Something* woke me up. Flinging off the duvet, I pull on a teeshirt over my bra and pants and shove my feet into my trainers. Matthew's door is still ajar. I wait outside, ear cocked towards the gap. I can hear his steady breathing. Perhaps he'd cried out in his sleep, and that's what woke me? Do babies have nightmares?

Sleep has fled. I don't want to go back to the bedroom and risk waking Steve, and a possible action replay of the night before. Instead, I find the light switch to the staircase and begin a hesitant descent. Some of the steps creak alarmingly, and I make a mental note to memorise each one. It feels important to understand the soundscape of this house, if its to be my home. On the fifth step from the bottom, the little door lets out a groan, opening of its own accord to reveal the silent, dark kitchen. I spot the tail-end of a shadow at the far end. I stop dead, heart hammering.

There is zero draft. No windows are open. Why would the door open on its own like that, as if ushering me through? You get that with older houses, I tell myself. Everything is squint or on a slope. That accounts for a lot, and the shadow? Probably just a trick of the light. I scurry down the remaining steps and fumble for the light switch. The dark is banished instantly. Nothing is out of place, and I chide myself for even thinking that way. Here are the mugs and the wine glass in the drying rack just as I'd left them; there are the remains of our set meal for two, bundled into its plastic carrier. Everything is as it should be.

I close the staircase door firmly, and go to switch on the kettle. I'll make myself a cup of tea. I'm just wondering whether a slice of toast might be pushing it at three in the morning, when an evil squeal breaks the silence. My hands grip the edge of the worktop. Everything about me freezes until all that remains is the steady thrum of blood in my ears. What the *hell?* I know instinctively that it is not Matthew. This was no baby noise and I swear it came from outside. There it is again! Mid-way between a snarl and a spitting noise.

Braver now, I turn the key in the back door. I'm praying that a security light might snap on, but of course it doesn't, and I've left my phone upstairs. Then I spot an old-fashioned torch, heavy as a truncheon, hanging on a hook beside the back door. It provides a faint circle of light. I make a mental note to add batteries to my shopping list. There are two steps down to a path which leads to the rear of the house. It's chilly, and a few spots of rain blow through on the breeze, bringing up gooseflesh on my arms. As I venture forth with caution, the noise comes again, close by. This time, it is less of a disembodied screech and more of an enquiring mew. The torch beam alights on a scrap of ginger fur, a thin little cat, mouth open in a soundless scream, showing off a pink tongue and needle-sharp teeth.

My hand flutters to my chest.

"Oh my God! You scared the shit out of me!"

I'm so relieved I actually want to laugh. It's all so ridiculous, me prancing around half-naked, searching for the unexplained in the dead of night, like I'm starring in my own horror movie. I haul my teeshirt over my bum and plop down on the top step. The cat comes forward and slinks around my calves. Its fur feels electric against my skin, reminding me uncomfortably of my own sensuality, and my rejection of it.

I tickle the feline chin. This cat has no inhibitions; it stretches its neck and preens against my hand. The night is brought to life by its engine-like purring.

"Where did you come from, eh?" I scratch the bony skull. "Was that you fighting? Why don't you come back tomorrow and I'll give you some milk?"

The cat shows no sign of retiring for the night. It is decidedly overfriendly, and I end up having to push it away. Probably some old farm cat covered in fleas. I stand up and brush myself off.

"It's bedtime. If you're still around tomorrow I'll see you then."

The cat stretches its jaws in an agreeable mew and I let myself back into the house. I feel strangely peaceful. They say that stroking a pet has a stress-busting effect. I'm looking forward to a quick cuppa now, and maybe a biscuit, before settling back into bed. As soon as I close the back door, that unexplained breeze springs from nowhere, carrying on its breath a foul-smelling, musty odour. The door to the staircase is standing wide open, despite me having firmly closed it, and worst of all, Matthew is crying fit to burst.

I fling myself up the stairs, slipping and banging my knee, righting myself and scrambling upwards. A gale is howling around the landing. Leaves swirl past me. I am aching to get to my baby, but I feel like I'm wading through treacle. The door to his bedroom is wide open and I can see that Matthew has rolled onto his tummy and is kicking his legs in temper. The window, which had been firmly fastened, is open. Bits of leaves and pools of rainwater have collected on the sill, and the glass is rattling. I scoop the baby from the cot and attempt one-handed combat with the window. The latch is loose and rusty and it takes me several minutes to lock it firmly in place. The cold vanishes like magic. I turn to Matthew. His face is red and wet, as if he's been left to cry for hours, when in reality, I'd checked him not twenty minutes before.

"Ssh, baby. It's okay." I cradle him close until the crying subsides into hiccups. Steve appears in the door, rumpled and sleepy, wearing only black boxers. I round on him like a tigress.

"Why the hell did you open the window?"

"I didn't." He looks genuinely bemused.

"Well, I didn't. You must have done!"

"I didn't." More forceful now. "What are you talking about?"

I take a deep breath. Beneath my chin, Matthew's scalp is so sweaty I wonder if he has a fever.

"I woke up and went to check on him. He was asleep, the window was closed. I went downstairs and…when I came back up it was howling a gale up here. The window was wide open!"

"Did you check the window when you looked in on him?" Steve goes over to ply the latch, up and down, rattle, rattle.

"No, I just stood by the door."

"Maybe it was open then?"

"I wouldn't put him to bed and leave the window open!"

"But maybe it was already open a crack and you didn't notice. These are old windows." He rattles the latch again. "Ill-fitting, and the weather can turn in an instant."

I scour my brain, go through the bedtime routine. Surely I would have noticed if the window had been even partially open? Steve comes over and strokes the baby's head.

"He must have got a fright, poor little chap. Does he need a drink or something?"

I shake my head. "I don't want to wake him up any more."

Steve rubs his chin. "I hate to say it. but he looks wide awake."

"Hmm." As I dither about what to do, Steve comes up with a solution.

"Bring him into our bed. He'll drift off no problem with a bit of company."

I'm about to raise the obvious objections; routine, bad habits, physical danger, but an insidious thought, like an overfriendly cat, weaves its way into my head. A third person in the bed, a body between us, the ultimate passion-killer. Matthew might yet prove to be the solution to my problem.

I wake feeling rested, all the anxieties of the night before a muddled blur in the back of my mind. The day is sunny, warm and calm, as if determined to prove a point. When the builder calls, Steve takes Matthew with him, and from the sitting room window, I watch them pacing the back garden, animatedly discussing footings and materials and the direction of the light. I like observing people, guessing at their conversations, gauging reactions. Being one step removed from real life suits me.

Steve's laptop is sitting open on the gateleg table. He's scribbled down his username and password, and left his credit card in a saucer. I realise with a pinch of guilt how fortunate I've been, to have a way out. I love him for that, even if I cannot show it.

I log on to a few home shopping sites. I'm soon immersed in cot bedding, clown friezes and babywear. The minutes tick by as I browse and click. It's almost a surprise when Steve appears at my elbow.

"How are you doing?"

I lift my head, feeling slightly dream-like, as if I have been in a cartoon world of candyfloss and peach.

"Oh- yes, I've managed to get a few things. How was the builder."

"Good. He's going to pull together a quote. He says he can start pretty soon. We'll have a sun room for the summer!"

"Sounds wonderful." I sit back in my chair. All of this- the garden, the sun room, the credit card- it all feels a little too good to be true. An insistent, unwelcome voice in my head taunts me that it probably is.

CHAPTER THIRTEEN

Steve decides to go into town for Polyfilla, silicon and other DIY supplies. He says he'll take Matthew with him, which provides me with a sunlit window of possibility. Perhaps I'm taking advantage, but Steve and Matthew seem perfectly content in each other's company, so I agree happily. I ask him to bring enough paint to cover the walls of Matthew's bedroom.

"What colour?"

"Yellow. A bright, sunny colour like primroses."

"Okay. Anything else?"

I shake my head and he ruffles my hair.

When they're gone, the silence folds itself around me. A farm vehicle and trailer pass with a prolonged metallic rattle, but other than that there is no traffic noise. Perhaps local drivers try to avoid Derville's Lane. Time is such a luxury I become overwhelmed with the prospect of how to fill it, so I take a five-minute break to make some coffee. Above the roar of the kettle I hear a familiar mewling sound. When I open the back door, the ginger stray from last night saunters in as if she owns the place, rubbing her chin on the rung of a chair.

"Did you used to live here, puss?"

I find a saucer and fill it with milk. Maybe she's Steve's dad's cat? Steve might not even know about her and here she is on the doorstep, literally starving. On a whim, I text Steve.

Please bring cat food

He replies almost immediately with:

???

That makes me smile. He definitely isn't aware of the cat. I place the saucer on the floor. The cat is skulking under the kitchen table, and when I stoop down to get a better look at her, I realise she has something in her mouth. She drops it with a retching motion and walks away. I steel myself to run for the dustpan and brush. If *that*, whatever it is, moves, I'll be out of that door faster than Usain Bolt. I cannot stand mice, and I've already found evidence of them in the cupboard under the sink. I send another text.

And mouse traps.

The cat wraps itself around my legs as I decide what to do. The *thing* is very dead. I sweep it out from under the table with a long-handled brush, and the cat turns her nose up at it as if to say, 'I'm done with that."

It is the skeleton of a rodent, just the bones, not a scrap of skin or hair to be seen, although there must be gristle or sinew of some kind holding it together. It strikes me as a bit odd that a cat would be interested in a skeleton, but the lack of any visible organic matter makes me feel better able to deal with this. I sweep the remains into a dustpan and head towards the outside bin. The cat is a nuisance, winding around my legs and almost tripping me. It's only when I'm scraping the corpse into the bin that I realise the skeleton has a red thread tied around the top of its spine.

Steve is away so long I begin to worry. I've made the best use of my time, setting aside the internet shopping to focus on my career path. I spent an hour researching blog sites and blogging, choosing a template with care. I even set up an Instagram account, although I've never had one before. In seconds I get my first follower. Leanne.

She sends me a WhatsApp:

WTF?? @buildingsitebaby?

I smile with satisfaction and type:

Good, eh? Visit my new blog https://buildingsitebaby.com

There's a pause, and then she comes back with:

You haven't done any posts!

All in good time! I've loads of ideas. This is going to be BIG!

When my phone starts to ring, I answer it, assuming it's my sister. Only when I hear his voice do I realise my mistake. *Fuck.* Jaw clenched, I growl into the handset.

"What do you want?"

"Don't be like that!" The voice is light, up for a bit of banter.

"I'm not like anything. Just- just leave me alone."

"I *have* left you alone. That doesn't mean I've forgotten. About us."

"There was never an *us*." I've gone all clammy; brow, hands, the back of my neck. Nausea swirls in the pit of my stomach, and I fight the urge to hurl the phone across the room.

A soft laugh. "Stop kidding yourself. I'm travelling down for the footie in a couple o' weeks. Thought I might drop by."

"No!" Calm down. *Breathe.* In, out, in out. "There's nothing for you here."

"We both know that's not true, sweetheart."

"No." The word is a whisper now, I can feel the fight leaving me, fear welling up in its place. I try a different tack. "You don't know where I'm living."

There's a faint rustle. "Number 11, Devil's Lane, according to the note you gave your mother."

I do not correct him. Instead, I disconnect the call with damp, shaky fingers. Cold dread descends on me like the sort of sea mist you see in old horror movies. I'm rocking back and forth on the chair, as if I'm trying to lull Matthew to sleep, but Matthew is not here. I am on my own with this burden. Completely and utterly alone.

When Steve is not back by 4pm, I call his phone. It goes straight to voicemail. My heart gives an involuntary flutter. If it was just Steve, I wouldn't care, but what if something is wrong with the baby? Last night I thought he was coming down with a fever. I should have given him baby paracetamol. I should not have let him go with Steve, and after receiving that phone call…well, my mind goes through all the sorts of dread possibilities, as I sit at the kitchen table stewing in a cold sweat, hand clamped around my phone. When it eventually rings, I jump up and press it to my ear.

"Steve! Where the hell are you?"

"Just….errand….soon."

"You're breaking up, Steve!"

"In the car…losing signal…"

"Bloody hell!" My fingers tear through my hair in frustration. "Just get back here ASAP."

I disconnect and continue to stew until I hear a car pull up outside. I run down the front path, leaving the door to swing open. I've gone from cold sweat to boiling rage.

"What the fuck are you doing? Going off with Matthew like that?"

Steve stares at me, half-in, half-out of the driver's seat.

"You told me to."

I haul open the back door and unclip Matthew from the car seat. He's perfectly fine, although his nappy feels wet and bulky.

"I didn't think you'd be gone for hours on end. I'm not used to leaving him with anyone, Steve. It's always been him and me."

I'm on the verge of hysteria and Steve realises it too. He must think I'm a complete flake. He comes around to steady me by the elbows.

"I was in the DIY shop and I got a call from the care home. My dad needed me to run a few errands so we did that and then when I popped in the staff insisted I have tea with him at 3pm and they were making a fuss of the little lad here, and…"

"Wait. You took Matthew into a care home? You took him to see your father, who I've NEVER MET and then passed him around like a parcel?"

"It wasn't like that." Steve worries his hair. I turn on my heel, hitch up Matthew and storm back up the path. I'm probably being totally irrational, but I cannot bear to imagine my son being cooed at by a bunch of people I don't know. What about Steve's dad? He could be a Creepy MacCreeperson for all I know, and there's my innocent baby being toted around like a sponge cake and what if…

Oh, I know it's all in my head. There was never a possibility of any real danger, but I'm on a roll and cannot stop. I stomp up the stairs with Matthew and set about changing him. Steve follows, apologising, but oblivious to what he's done wrong. He tries to make out I'm being unreasonable, which makes me madder than ever and the whole thing escalates. I pop the final stud on the baby's onesie and stand up, chin jutting.

"I'm going back to Rowena's."

"Who?"

"Whitecross Villa. I'm going to stay a few days while you decorate the nursery. You did remember to get paint?"

"Yes, I got paint. And mousetraps, and cat food, even though I don't know what the hell that's all about. But unlike you, I don't *question* everything."

His voice harbours a certain iciness, which makes me recall last night when I'd accused him of opening the window. I wonder if I'm pushing him too far, but now I've embarked on this course, the cleanliness and order of my own room at Rowena's is too tempting.

"Just for a night, or two."

"Or two," he echoes bleakly. "I'll go and call her."

CHAPTER FOURTEEN

Rowena opens the door with a smile.

"In you come."

"Sorry about the short notice."

I negotiate the doorway with Matthew and the changing bag and an enormous teddy Steve bought him in town. The baby is trying to suck the fur off its paw. As Rowena closes the elegantly panelled door, I hear Steve rev up and pull away. Even the car sounds injured. I actually hate myself right now.

"No problem. I told you there'd always be a bed for you. Place still in a mess?"

I follow her through to the kitchen.

"It's better," I say slowly, "but Steve's painting the nursery, so we're staying away from the fumes."

"Primrose yellow?"

"Of course!"

"Have you eaten? I'm just having salad and quiche, but you're welcome to join me."

I'd packed loads of formula and puree without even thinking about myself. The quiche must be in the oven; the fragrance of baked cheese wafts up my nose and my stomach growls.

"I wouldn't say no!" I place Matthew on the white tiles and he starfishes across them. Rowena smiles and goes back to fixing the salad. She'd been chopping tomatoes on a wooden board. I slouch against the breakfast bar and we lapse into a companionable silence. Her phone is next to me, tuned into to some kind of radio broadcast which I cannot help but hear. A man's voice with a Yorkshire accent is chatting matter-of-factly about hauntings. My skin starts to prickle.

"As we heard in episode one, poltergeist activity is not confined to the Sixties and Seventies. Even these days, hauntings are a frequent occurrence, especially in our smart digital age, but people rarely want to talk about them. Ironically, there is arguably more stigma attached to paranormal experiences now than say, forty years ago. Why? Well, people are afraid of negative push back on social media platforms. But believe me, poltergeists are still -dare I say it- alive and kicking! Hello! If you've just joined me, I am Harry Bryce and this is Paranormal Cold Case, the podcast for the believers, the unbelievers and all those inbetween."

Rowena turns around and walks towards me. She has the sharp knife in her hand, dripping tomato juice, and a very odd expression on her face. My stomach plummets for an instant, but she merely leans in to turn off the podcast. Her eyes meet mine.

"Do you like beetroot? I pickle my own." And then she walks back to the chopping board.

Did I imagine that strange, pinched expression? Why did she turn off the programme so deliberately? I search my memory bank for what had been said. Harry Bryce. Paranormal Cold Case. Hauntings. Coincidence? Rowena is making conversation about her vegetable garden, so I shelve the strange feeling for now and focus on her words. Yes, I agree, teaching young children to plant seeds is a lovely thing to do and no, I've never had a garden back home. The whole thing has left me a bit perturbed, and when the quiche is finally served up, I discover I'm not as hungry as I thought I was.

Steve must have worked like this Trojan dude to finish the

nursery for when we returned home at lunchtime the next day. The room has been cleared, leaving the cot standing on bare boards, with just a minimum of furniture dotted about: an old oak dining chair, a modest table and a chest of drawers. The windows are thrown open to let in air and light, and a new rail has been affixed for my circus-themed curtains which should be arriving shortly. The walls are a lurid shade of mustard.

Disappointment hits me in the solar plexus.

"What do you think?" Steve is still wearing paint-flecked coveralls. His hair and forearms are liberally sprinkled with mustard dots. "Just the curtains and the frieze to go. What do you think, little man?"

He chucks Matthew under the chin. The baby kicks against me and babbles happily.

I force out some kind words. "You've worked really hard. It's-bright, and- um-uncompromising."

To avoid Steve's quizzical look, I wander to the nearest wall and pat it with my fingertips. It's still a little tacky. My vision of the perfect nursery slowly starts to crumble.

"Once the curtains are up, it will be awesome. Your own special room!" He eases the baby from me and takes him to the window. "Look, you can see the garden and the birdies!"

Matthew pulls a face and tries to grasp the breeze in his pudgy fingers. Liberated, I take stock of the furniture. A desk, a chair, a drawer for storing stationery... Pressing my hands together, I whirl around to Steve with a genuine smile.

"I can use this as my home office!"

He looks surprised. "You could, I guess..."

"Just during the day. Obviously not when Matthew's asleep. I could put the laptop here on this desk and this chair will do for now, although a proper office chair would be great. Once I start earning some money."

I'm imagining it all as I had once imagined a primrose yellow nursery. I could put up a pin board, buy one of those fancy ring lights for my insta posts. Ideas come thick and fast, impeded only my Steve's doubting tone.

"Why do you need an office, Kat? And what's this about earning money?"

I realise that, once again, I have neglected to share my thoughts with him. I sit down on the chair. It's a bit wobbly, but with a couple of cushions it will do for now. I tell him about Building Site Baby, how I can post regular updates on Matthew's progress and the house renovations, endorse products, amass followers and basically conquer the world.

Steve still looks doubtful. "Well, I've got to hand it to you- you're a tryer. You say you get free stuff?"

"Yup. I can do product reviews and if I have affiliate links on my website I can make actual money."

"All from this professionally-painted bedroom?"

I get up and go over to him, loop my arms around both of them. "It is very professional. Thank you for doing this for us. Becoming a blogger is my way of giving something back. You've taken on me and somebody else's baby. That's huge."

He hugs me back, touches his brow to my hair. "I want to do it. I love you, and I think you'll be a fantastic blogger."

I pause for a heartbeat. "So…can I borrow your laptop then?"

Everything is ready, the ring light over to the side, my I-phone on the special stand (which arrived this morning, courtesy of a publicity-hungry start-up tech company). Behind me, the circus curtains flutter in the breeze and Matthew is standing up in his cot, gripping the bars like a bored prisoner. He's sucking on his dummy like the baby in the Simpsons. I've had to employ new tactics in order to keep him sweet for filming.

Roll camera.

"Hi everyone! My name is Kat, and welcome to this first video from Building Site Baby! This will be a record of my journey with my baby as my partner and I renovate a cute little cottage on the edge of the Durham dales. Come join me as I wrangle nappy cream and teething, rewiring and bricklaying. What can possibly go wrong?! But first, meet the star of the show, Master Matthew Riley!"

Grab camera and pan to the baby, who obliges with a wobbly cot dance. Suck, suck, bob, bob. Back to me.

"And the other star, is of course- the cottage. Ta da!"

Pan around the walls.

"This is a work in progress. A yellow blind and lovely fluttery circus curtains from All About Babies and this rich ochre paint- such a change from pastels- which is called Corn Moon. Oh, and here is my desk. A bit rickety, but bear with me, guys. This is a *journey* and we're all on it together!

Okay, so I'll see you next time when I'll be introducing Matthew to a spot of gardening!"

And sign off.

I switch off the camera and the light. I'm sweating. I can feel the thick cosmetics Leanne has recommended melting on my skin. My eyes are so heavy with unaccustomed gloop, I no longer feel like me. Behind me, Matthew spits out the dummy and begins to cry. My stomach clenches. I need to work out my new software, edit and upload the video to Instagram and Youtube.

"Ssh, Matthew! Let me think."

Releasing the video to the world might just be the easy bit.

CHAPTER FIFTEEN

The first comments begin to trickle in. Leanne is first, on Insta.

This is ma wee nephew! #BabyMatt #BuildingSiteBaby #babiesofInstagram #AllAboutBabies #CornMoon #nurserystyle

Numerous 'follows' follow, a steady steam of @beautyismylife fans, treading the party line. After twenty minutes, Leanne WhatsApps me:

You're welcome, Sis! Best of luck with your venture!

A warm glow of satisfaction settles in my tummy. Not only have I gained approval ratings with my sister, I feel part of something, perhaps for the first time in my life. I flip back to Instagram and read the comments.

"So he'll be around in about an hour."

Steve's voice breaks into my virtual trance. I pull my eyes from my phone screen, noticing that my triangle of toast has gone cold in my hand.

"Who?"

"Gary the Builder. Kat, have you been listening?"

I shake my head, unabashed. Steve sighs, not in his usual indulgent way but with a release of impatience.

"I said, I've accepted his quote and he's coming round to stake out the foundations."

"Okay." I perk up. "That's brilliant."

Across the breakfast table, Steve narrows his eyes at my

enthusiasm.

"Are you excited, about the sun room?"

"What? Oh yes. And maybe Gary will agree to a wee interview!"

"Interview?"

I dive back into my comments.

@paintedlady: Love that colour! What make of paint is that?

@buildingsitebaby: Isn't it bright?! New range from @harrowandburgess #cornmoon

Two minutes after that, somebody for the ACTUAL paint company likes my post and comments:

Thank you so much for the mention! Hope #BabyMatt enjoys his new @harrowandburgess #nursery #nurserypaint #babydesign #interiors #cornmoon

"So I have to pop over to my uncle's, but you'll look after Gary?"

I lift my eyes momentarily. "Gary who?"

"This is Adam, my apprentice," The builder says, by way of introduction. "We're just going to peg out the site today. Steve not here?"

Gary is good-looking in a rough and ready way- he has a very direct gaze. I'm quite glad of Matthew's presence in my arms. He's like a shield. Guys don't hit on new mothers as a rule, and it's a relief. However, I have an agenda. Gary is a proper hunky builder. He is going to have great Insta appeal, if I can persuade him to pose for a photo. I wonder if he has a hard hat. I'm just pondering how to phrase such a request, when he notices the baby.

"Didn't know Steve was a dad! Kept that quiet."

"He's not," I say quickly. I don't elaborate, but rush on, "Look, Gary. I've just started a blog for parents and I'm going to be writing about my experiences of bringing up a baby while renovating a house…"

"Are you planning on doing more?" Gary surveys the eaves with interest. "Plenty potential. Downstairs bathroom, underfloor heating…You could convert the attic, like they've done next door. Adds value."

I try and get him back on track. "For the blog- would you mind if I took your picture?"

Gary shrugs. "Yeah, no problem. Do you want to be in it? Adam can take it."

"One more thing." I give him an awkward smile. "Do you have- I dunno- a hard hat and maybe a hammer?"

Later, I upload the image to the laptop. It's perfect, and I spend far too long appraising it with satisfaction. It says everything I want to say about Building Site Baby. My earlier experience in the field of content writing has suddenly come to the fore- have I discovered a latent talent for self-promotion? As unlikely as it seems, the final draft of my first blog post is self-deprecating, easy and readable. It hits the right note, if I say so myself, and I feel punch drunk with possibility. If I can increase my traffic, I could easily reach out to all the firms whose products I aspire to. I need a new car seat, and a changing table, a baby monitor and maybe, eventually, one of those cross-country strollers. I picture myself hiking with Matthew, taking videos in wild places and beside waterfalls. Stick to brand, I warn myself as I get carried away. Stay with the house renovations for now. I embed the new photograph at the top of my blog post.

Adam had fished two yellow helmets from the white van, along with a heavy masonry hammer. Gary and I had put them on, posing rather stiffly as the apprentice aimed my camera phone.

At the last minute, Matthew made a grab for the hammer and the resulting image is offbeat and fun; a tug-of-war between a rugged workman and a rascally tot, me giggling, my hair cascading from the over-large hard hat. I look relaxed and game for whatever life might offer. This version of me is so far from the truth I want to frame it, remind myself every day that this is what is inside me, waiting to be brought out. Conversely, the more I look at it, the more it makes me sad. Wiping a tear from my eye, I press 'publish.'

"He's your child, but I certainly wouldn't be putting him all over social media like this."

Steve is fuming. He's been away all day- something to do with a family summit involving his uncle- and I'm making an omelette and chips for tea. I need to see about getting a grocery delivery. I can't keep depending on Steve to bring things home. The weeks are passing quickly and I've been busy with my fledgling business, but I'm starting to feel like a prisoner.

"He's gone viral! Hashtag Baby Matt." I turn down the heat beneath the frying pan.

"Kat, be serious. If you want to do the blog, fine. But it's like you're…selling Matthew."

"No, I'm not."

"And God knows what Gary thinks of all this." He sits at the table, hunches over his phone. "As you know I don't do all this shite, but my *cousin* sent me this!"

I can see the image on the phone, one of the many now, with me laughing up at the builder, and Matthew framed between us, as if *we* are the family unit. A shiver of disquiet runs through me.

"I told my daughter Laura about your blog this morning, and by lunchtime, she's shared it all round the office. Kat, it's like throwing a lit match into a forest."

I divide the omelette in two and flip it onto our plates.

"It's what I want." My voice sounds petulant. Is this what I want? To lose control of things? Again. Why does being around Steve make me want to dig my heels in?

Steve makes the photo disappear and sets down his phone. His face is dark, burdened.

"No more photos of Matthew. You don't know where they'll end up."

I sit down opposite him. "You just said, he's my child."

Steve just grunts. We eat in silence.

CHAPTER SIXTEEN

Steve has managed to get a new job, or perhaps a new version of his old one, with the family firm, now run by his uncle, which is apparently the 'biggest importer of garden furniture in the north-east'. I'm not sure how true that statement is. Nor am I convinced this the life path Steve imagined for himself. If I'm honest, I have never asked him about his hopes and dreams for the future. Some of them are self-evident. He wants me to open up to him, love him, without reservation. He wants a sun room. He wants to earn some cash. All pretty basic stuff, but I have been so wrapped up in my needs, I have neglected to dig deeper. I'm not sure I can, without committing to a deeper level of intimacy. I'm not sure how deep I want to go.

Anyway, Steve now spends his days driving a delivery van with a youth named Tyler. They offload cedarwood tables to spa resorts and picnic benches to council facilities. I wonder if we'll get a staff discount when it comes to furnishing the new room.

The back of the house is not sunny, and I'm surprised nobody has clocked that but me. Gary the Builder is just keen to have a job, and Steve wants to provide- sun, space, happiness. He's a good man, and now an absent man. Part of me is relieved.

Today the sun is determined to lure me out of the house, reminding me that it's not a day for being slumped in front of a screen. It's a toss-up between a third coffee and making the most of the sunshine with Matthew. The baby wins.

It takes me ages to strap him into his sling, and by the time I accomplish that, he's getting wriggly and fractious. We both have red faces and I'm desperate for another caffeine hit, but undaunted, I march into the back garden, past the new foundations, which are conspicuously quiet. I suspect Gary is multi-jobbing- he hasn't put in an appearance for days.

The lawn is short, but the margins of the garden are overgrown in a romantic, abandoned way. I love the idea of a secret garden. Beside a dilapidated shed lies the remains of a vegetable plot. It's stony and fallow, but I can see the ghost of rows which once held fresh vegetables and there are a few straggly raspberry canes bearing early fruit. I pick a few. They yield to my fingers with a satisfying pop, and I put one in my mouth, the sweetness making up for this morning's coffee deficit. I pick a small one for the baby. Can babies have fresh raspberries? He can manage rusks and pulped up grown-up food. I press the fruit to his lips; they are the same new shade, fresh and new. Matthew gapes like a baby bird, and I squeeze a drop or two of juice onto his tongue. His contorted face makes me laugh and when he recovers, he claps his hands in delight.

"We'll grow our own, Mattie. Fresh carrots for your puree. How about that?"

He says nothing, just sucks reflectively on the ear of Bobo his favourite teddy, and we walk on. There is a wood beyond the boundary, and a ramshackle gate, reinforced with baler twine. The untreated timber is the same hue as the tree bark. I've never considered myself to be an adventurer, but all this newness is intoxicating. It has a flip side, unfortunately. I realise how passive I've been, waiting for life to happen; how tolerant I've been of things I should have forcefully rejected. Why haven't I ever stood up for myself, and fought for *me*, with all my might? A lump comes to my throat. Where did all this spring from? I blame it on the trees, as if somehow their complex root structures are undermining me, creeping under my shell.

We pass through the gate with some difficulty. It seems resistant to its own function. The trees are very old- I have no idea what species they are, I'm just conscious of the delicious space between them, and the waving of branches overhead. They are whispering to each other. Hot on the heels of my emotional blip, a feeling of peace steels over me. I am at home here. I breathe in the musky scent of the wood. It smells of animals, as if wild creatures have slipped past, very early in the morning, while we were sleeping. All those generations of wild things; foxes and badgers and deer, have made a track for me, as if they knew one day I'd come.

I tickle Matthew under the chin and laugh for the sheer lunacy of my thoughts. It's so unlike me to be this fanciful. But I like it. Matthew tips his head back, fixes his gaze on the jigsaw of sky between the leaves. I like it here. I love it. I am so lucky. This becomes my inner refrain for the next leg of my journey. The wood wends its way uphill, and the trunks become sparser as a summit comes into view. There is something so satisfying about reaching a summit, even if it is comparatively tame. It's hardly Ben Nevis, and there is no panorama once I've reached the top. Just more trees.

We sit for a few moments on a flat slab of stone. I take Matthew from the sling and sit him on my knee, but he is desperate to get down. He leans so much to one side, I relent and let him sit on the ground, where his tiny fingers explore the dirt and his padded bottom gets covered in twigs. Eventually it's time for home.

As we troop back down the hill and in through the secret gate, the sun goes behind a cloud. It's like someone dimming a light. For some reason my mood dims too, as if I don't really want to go back inside. That's not the case. I have plans. I've managed to obtain a Baby-Go-Sleep musical mobile from a company who wants a review on my blog. My first free stuff! It was so exciting when I emailed them and they actually replied. My site traffic has been rocketing and the most recent image of Gary the Builder now has over 200 likes.

Despite all the positive progress, a grim feeling winds itself around me and I cannot seem to shake it off. It's almost as if I've caught something in the wood and brought it back with me. As we pass by the forsaken vegetable plot. I can see the back elevation of the shed, and all the abandoned accoutrements of a keen gardener: a grass rake, a dented iron watering can, a collapsed tower of plant pots and some black nylon netting folded around some stakes.

That's when I become conscious of the smell. Motherhood has definitely sharpened my nose. I'm always on the hunt for stale laundry or dirty nappies, but this smell is rank, like rotten meat or manure. It's heavy, weighing my spirits down even more. I want to get away from it, but I also want to find its source. It doesn't take much. Not a metre from my feet, a blackbird must have got its feet caught in the netting and died a horrible death.

I slap a hand over my nose.

"Oh no, the poor thing."

It's dead. I can't do anything about that, but I vow when Matthew has his nap, I'll get some scissors and free the poor thing, give it a decent burial.

It's only when I'm trying to settle Matthew for his nap, that I become aware of a second disaster. Somehow, we've lost Bobo the teddy, Matthew's favourite toy. A bear has been left behind in the woods. It feels like the beginning of a very dark fairy story. It also means I have to negotiate with a selection of substitutes before the baby will eventually consent to lie down.

When all is quiet, I collect a pair of scissors and the over-large Marigolds, which I'd bundled behind the bin after the unsavoury incident with the cat, and venture out into the garden. I'm reminded that I'm not good with small bony things and my stomach starts to tie itself in a knots. A few years ago, we had mice in the kitchen at home. Nobody knew, until my mother had reached under the sink and pulled out a live mouse inside a bundle of cleaning cloths. Shrieking is not a word that can do justice to the ear-splitting, primal sounds that came out of our souls. Leanne and I had been sitting at the table. I'm not sure what registered first: mum's demented scream or the demented mouse, fleeing for its life. I've no idea where it went. By that stage, all three of us had stampeded up the hall and out of the front door. Mum texted Ryan from the garden- he was still in bed- and we refused to enter the kitchen again until he'd appeared in his pyjamas, yawning, to set a trap with a lump of Leanne's Dairy Milk.

We'd laughed about it afterwards. I still remember shaking with adrenaline, and, a few hours later, hearing the snap of the mousetrap, and Ryan bearing the mutilated corpse away on its tiny stretcher. How could we have been scared of *that*, we'd scoffed. But fear is fear, and you make light of it at your peril. I know this to my cost. You should always pay attention to your gut. Perhaps that's why Mum's doom-laden pronouncement after the mouse incident stayed with me. "There's never just one," she'd warned ominously. Maybe that's why I've got into the habit of waiting for the next threat.

I may not like tiny dead things, but a sense of decency compels me to do the right thing by the beautiful former blackbird. Maybe country life is going to be more stressful than I'd anticipated, and I'm so taken up with that thought, a sudden movement in the garden next door startles me much more than it should. In fact, I nearly drop the scissors and my heart starts banging along to some weird new rhythm.

I see a moss green cap first of all, an old man's cap, and indeed, there's an old man wearing it. He has the sort of craggy, granite face you'd see in a reality show about rural vets. His tweed jacket, patched at the elbows, looks like it might have fishing flies in the pocket, a handful of boiled sweets and maybe one of those white cotton hankies with a manly blue border. Beneath the cap, his white hair is a bit out-of-hand, but he's quite dapper, with a neat shirt and tie, which doesn't quite fit my first impression of him as a hill farmer. I'm not sure I've ever met a farmer, but I'm pretty sure they dress down.

"Good morning." He touches his cap.

"Oh, hello." I feel a bit tongue-tied. I've never been good at small talk, but he's staring at the scissors in a way which makes me feel I have to explain myself.

"It's for the bird. At the back of the shed. It's dead."

He waits a beat. "Oh."

"It got stuck. In some netting."

"Feet, was it?"

I shrug. "I think so."

This conversation could drag on, so I make a move to go about my business, but my neighbour seems in no hurry to go about his.

"You'd be Steve's missus, then?"

"Yes, I'm Kat."

"Aye. Steve said. Len Langton. Look, do you want a hand?"

I realise I'm biting my lip. When he says that, I can feel the tension ebb away.

"I would. I hate the thought of…" I wave the scissors towards the shed with a grimace.

Len nods soberly. "I'll come round."

He disappears. When I see him again, he's letting himself in our side gate. I expect he knows the place like the back of his hand.

"Gi' me them." He holds out a flat, scuffed palm and I gratefully relinquish my weapon.

CHAPTER SEVENTEEN

After the burial, I offer to make Mr Langton a cup of tea. It seems the proper thing to do, but I'm secretly pleased when he refuses.

"You're alright, love. I'm just off, as it happens."

"Somewhere interesting?" I shouldn't have asked. Maybe he's visiting his wife's grave or something.

"Auction rooms. Go there every week- always get a bargain. Do you need anything for the babby?"

He jerks his neck inside his collar, as if the mere mention of babies is women's talk. I recall the cot, which I'd scrubbed thoroughly before committing Matthew to it. I've just emailed a UK manufacturer of car seats and have my fingers crossed for a good result. Len is waiting for an answer. E-commerce and online influencing are so far from his world, I won't even attempt to explain.

"Not really. I've got it covered. But thank you for finding the cot. That was really kind."

He brushes this away.

"Well, some other time- for a cuppa?" I say.

"Aye, love. Next time. If you have any more trouble wi' livestock, you just give me a shout."

"I don't suppose you know who owns the cat, the wee ginger one? I wondered if it had belonged to Steve's dad. It seemed very familiar with the house."

He makes a face. "Never been a cat here, as far as I know."

"I heard it yowling and hissing one night." I pause, not sure how much I should confide in him. Maybe I just need to get it off my chest. "I spoke to the cat, and then I went back upstairs, the baby's window was open, and neither Steve nor I had opened it. These are old houses- do they have problems with the windows?"

I hadn't meant that to sound accusatory in any way, but there's a definite shift in Len's expression, as if I've touched a nerve. Maybe living in an adjoining house makes you sensitive to criticism- all those boundary problems that can cause tension; overgrown branches and snaking tree roots, leaky chimneys and dilapidated fencing.

"My house is properly maintained." Len slips off his cap, smooths down his wild hair before replacing it at a neater angle. His gaze flickers towards the eaves. "*This* house has always had a mind of its own."

When Len departs, I let myself in through the side door, mulling over his parting shot. *A house with a mind of its own.* Alarmingly, the description fits. Predictably, the door to the staircase, which seems to have developed a problem with remaining shut, is now firmly closed, even though I'm pretty sure I would have left it open.

There is no sound from the nursery. Quickly, I stow the rubber gloves and the scissors under the sink and creep up the stairs, carefully avoiding the creaky risers, buying myself a little extra time.

Matthew is still out for the count. I envy the way little kids can sleep so soundly in the middle of the day. They say you should sleep when your baby sleeps, especially in the early days, but I could never do that. I was always watching, waiting, perpetually on duty.

Now, though, I have a distraction. A delicious little sidebar to my life as a mother. I can do it right here, from this very bedroom. I've painted the old table pale blue, and padded the chair with cushions and Steve's fleecy blanket. His laptop is set up, with an anglepoise lamp and a range of notebooks. I have plans to get my own laptop, although to be fair, Steve doesn't seem to mind me commandeering his. It's not as if he uses it for anything important, just checking the weather and his lottery numbers, or the odd game of online poker. I've discovered that, if I'm suitably mouse-like, I can write blog posts and update my status without disturbing the baby's beauty sleep, which also gives me an excuse not to indulge in any cosy Netflix chilling with Steve. I know where that can lead.

A few days ago, I did a live stream outside, when the sun was threatening to shine and Gary the builder was threatening to do some actual work.

"Smile, guys!" Juggling Matthew and my phone, I walked cautiously backwards towards the foundations. Gary and Adam mugged to camera, giving jaunty thumbs-up.

"Remember folks, Gary Fogarty, for all your building needs. Unless you're watching from HMRC!" Gary mouths.

"And Adam!" chipped in Adam. "Apprentice of the Year!"

Ignoring them, I continued. "So, moving away from the building works, here is the back of the house. As you can see, it's very old and it needs a bit of TLC. A work in progress, if you will. I'm thinking of having it painted in a nice pastel colour, maybe reach for that Mediterranean vibe…"

And on I went, showing off to my anonymous audience the old shed and the ruined vegetable garden which, I promised them, would soon be burgeoning with our healthy five-a-day. By the time I'd signed off, my mouth was dry and my palms wet. I felt like a performer in a one-woman show. That's what it was, a performance and who is in the audience, I cannot tell; the lights have been killed.

Despite any misgivings I might have, I'd posted the video online and the comments are still creeping in. I settle onto my cushioned throne and begin to scroll through them. A few of the newer ones catch my eye.

SassyJuno: I love pastel colours! It will be ace, @buildingsitebaby. What about that lovely blue colour you see in Greece?

DearHound: Better check your building regs. Some councils don't allow a change of paintwork, but I'm sure it will be fine.

CamSam: Hunky builders!

MelodyHughes: So excited to hear about your garden. I'd plant herbs, if it was mine.

MountainAsh: Congratulations on your blog.

Elan Del Silver: I wouldn't let my baby anywhere near that builder.

That last one makes me jump to my feet. I stare at the screen as if I expect some monster to crawl out of it, my heart banging in my chest. Even though Matthew is sleeping soundly behind me, I cannot stop myself from going over to check on him. I stroke his soft, hot forehead with a fingertip, as I agonise over what to do.

Leanne gets trolled. all the time. People comment on her pout, her eyes, her hair. They speculate on her earnings and her morals, and that's just the women. The men are worse, and I've seen some of the things they tap out behind their anonymous keyboards, full of vitriol and aggression. Leanne has a thick skin, but on several occasions, Mum has threatened to rip our broadband out by the roots.

"There's always the off switch," is her mantra, but we all know that social media is Leanne's oxygen. She would rather lose a limb than her internet connection, and before I'd entered this world, I was firmly on Mum's side, but something insidious is happening. I'm not thinking, "What is this doing to me?" I'm thinking, "How is this going to affect my stats?" So, I rationalise it. Just some random creep with an axe to grind. Maybe I've even misread the comment?

I turn back to the laptop and approach it with the same resigned panic as we'd experienced on re-entering the mouse-invested kitchen all those years ago. Words are too small to hurt you. But still, I cannot look away.

@ElanDelSilver: I wouldn't let my baby anywhere near that builder.

CHAPTER EIGHTEEN

The comment has not gone away. I can hear Leanne's voice in my head. *Do not engage.*

@ElanDelSilver: I wouldn't let my baby anywhere near that builder.

I want to reply. "What exactly do you mean?" but instead I ignore it and react to the other commentators instead.

"I'll run my paint charts by you, @SassyJuno. I agree @CamSam, Great tip, @MelodyHughes. Thank you, @Mountain Ash- follow me on Instagram!"

Instinctively, I bodyswerve @DearHound- I could do without a lecture- and take one last look at the offending remark. Did the poster know something unsavoury about builder Gary Fogarty? Maybe they'd had a bad experience with a loft conversion or something. Gary does seem to be a bit unreliable. Yes, that was probably it. Nothing more sinister than a bad review.

I close down the screen, and take a last look at Matthew before going downstairs. Fingers crossed for an undisturbed coffee before he wakes. As the kettle boils, I check my Instagram. More comments about the video - all complimentary. My shoulders sag with relief. The urge to scroll is like a nervous tic. I swear phones are addictive and I will never let my son have one until he's at least sixteen.

The podcast Rowena had been listening to pops into my mind. What was it again? *I am Harry Bryce and this is Paranormal Cold Case, the podcast for the believers, the unbelievers and all those inbetween.* I think I might classify myself as an 'inbetween'. I've never actually encountered anything spooky, so I'm unsure how I'd react. I like a good horror story, but I'd never read or watch anything supernatural late at night. That's asking for trouble, isn't it? As I mull this over, my questing thumb has found Harry Bryce. There are a number of episodes, ranging from black dog spirits to haunted pubs and the current offering, which is entitled *The Poltergeist House.* Was that the one Rowena had been listening to? I press play, and a rich male voice bursts into life.

"...so you were about sixteen at the time?"

"Yes, that's right." The interviewee is female. "It was happening all through my early teenage years."

"It must have blighted your life?"

"I suppose, in a weird way, I learned to live with it. It was my parents who were scared. You would be, wouldn't you? All these random things happening around your child?"

"Yes, indeed. Very traumatising." Harry softens his voice like a concerned uncle. "So, it began with the knocking?"

"Mainly scratching, at first. In the walls. We thought it was rodents, or even birds nesting, but it got so loud it used to wake me up. Then I'd sleep in and be late for school. It's not something you can explain to your teacher!" The woman's voice relaxes into a soft laugh, but there is a hollowness behind it. In the background comes the distinct ethereal trill of a windchime.

"No," Harry agrees. "And can you tell us about the objects that went missing?"

"It was random items at first- forks, spoons. They'd turn up in unexpected places, like the garden. Once I found a mug hanging on the branch of a tree in the woods behind the house. And not just mugs. There were other things."

As the woman is recounting all this, I'm preoccupied with digging a spoon into the coffee jar. I stare at the object as if it's come to life in my hand. Is this the teaspoon I found in the front garden? How did it get there? *Stop it!* I give myself a mental shake. It had slipped out of one of boxes in the middle of the clear-out, *obviously*. I'm about to switch off Harry and his ghostly goings- on, when the interviewee's next words stop me in my tracks.

"...And then it started messing with my things. Books went missing, a sock, a shoe, and then, at the height of it- my hamster, Betsy."

I turn up my nose. Poor Betsy. I'm not sure if I want to hear this. There is a mewling cry from upstairs.

"Okay Matthew, I'm coming!" I chuck the spoon in the sink. Instead of switching off the podcast, I turn up the volume and slip the phone into my back pocket, as if I cannot quite bear to be parted from this conversation, and begin to climb the stairs.

"And what happened then?" Harry Bryce probes. "Did the hamster turn up again?"

Matthew has stopped crying. He must have found something to play with in the cot. His door is open, and I can hear a steady tapping sound inside, which instantly makes my breath freeze. What the hell?

"Oh she turned up," says the female voice in my pocket. "Dead."

I enter the room. It's cold. The blind is half-drawn, just as I had left it, but the window is open and the breeze is making it *tap, tap, tap* against the frame. I haul at the plastic beaded cord and it shoots upwards, flooding the room with light.

"How had she been...dispatched?"

Matthew is still asleep. He hasn't stirred or made any sound. The mewling is coming from another source. I cannot believe what I'm seeing,

"We found her little lifeless body on the doorstep. Thought at first she'd been caught by the cat – we had a little ginger cat at the time- but it was no cat. Betsy had been strangled with a red shoelace."

A cat is sitting in the cot with my sleeping baby. The same scruffy ginger cat who had got into the house before. It starts to purr, a sinister, throaty, mechanical sound. Smug. In control. A scream builds in my throat, but my whole system is so paralysed with fear, I cannot make a sound.

CHAPTER NINETEEN

Telling Steve about the ginger cat should be simple, but when I rehearsed it all in my head, it sounded a bit ridiculous, like the residue of a bad dream. Was I over-reacting? I can get pretty hormonal and I *know* I am a bit overprotective...My confidence in my version of events is wavering, and even before I open my mouth, I'm already conscious of how ridiculous it all sounds.

Steve repeats my words back at me.

"So, the cat was in the cot with the baby?"

"Yes."

"You must have left the back door open and it slipped in while you weren't looking. If you think it's a stray, I could try and catch it and hand it into the animal shelter."

My teeth are clamped together so tightly, I can barely get the words out. "I didn't leave the door open. I *didn't*. And you're not listening. *It left a mouse skeleton under the cot.*"

"They do things like that."

"It was the *same one* I'd put in the bin! It's impossible."

"How do you know it's the same one?"

"Because of the red thing round it's neck." I shudder at the thought. "The skeleton had a red bit of string around its neck. What was left of its neck."

I'm thinking of the podcast. I'm unable to think of anything else, but of course Steve does not know about the podcast, and I'm not sure how to tell him without making myself sound crazy. What *happened* in the nursery had mirrored exactly what I had *heard*. That was the chilling bit. The dots were connecting horribly in my head: the hamster; the red shoelace. The teaspoon in the garden and that floaty jingly windchime. Rowena has a windchime. Was Harry Bryce interviewing Rowena?

It was hard to tell. The sound quality on my phone isn't great and it seems unlikely that Rowena, the rather ordinary proprietor of a B&B, would be an interviewee on such a niche show. But when she mentioned woods behind the house, and the poor hamster with its red garotte, something clicked.

I *had* put the carcass in the bin, hadn't I?

Steve rests his palms on my shoulders, and I submit. The weight of them is comforting, but I'm longing to shrug them away.

"All of this-" his gaze does a sweep of the ceiling, "- is all a bit much. It's been a big upheaval. Maybe we could go away for a few days? Or a day, at least. I could take you to Durham to see the cathedral. It's lovely there beside the river. Very tranquil."

I want to say something really cutting. but he's trying to be nice, so I go along with it.

"I'm fine. I'm sure you're right."

"Tomorrow, why don't you ask around, see if you can find out whether the cat is a stray? It'll give you a chance to meet the neighbours."

Steve gives my shoulders a final pat and moves away, leaving me silently fuming. What just happened? Steve has talked me out of what I know to be the truth and I have kept my mouth shut and let him. I *will* go and speak with the neighbours. But I won't be asking about the cat. I'll be asking some awkward questions about this house.

My first impression of the houses on Derville's Lane is that they look like a random selection of people- some are smart casual, others are a bit rough around the edges. I can talk. I've scraped my hair into a knot, my tee-shirt smells of baby sick and I'm shuffling around in crocs with Matthew clamped to my hip like a permanent fixture. Which he is. Maybe I should have taken a bit more time over my appearance, first impressions and all that.

Too late now. I skip Len Langton's house and try the one next door. This is quite genteel; carefully tended borders and a sleek black cat on the windowsill. He eyes me up. He doesn't look like he would have a scruffy ginger cousin, and anyway, despite applying my thumb to the bell push at least three times, there is no answer. The same happens with the next house, a bit messier this one, with a furiously yapping terrier behind the door. Maybe people have jobs here, regular nine-to-fives.

Feeling a bit discouraged I push open the gate of the next house along. This is a daft idea. The cat is merely a symptom, a sign. The question I really want to ask is, "Excuse me, can you tell me if my house is haunted, please?" I lean on the bell. There's no *bing, bong*, so I tap the letterbox for good measure.

Almost immediately the door flies open and I am confronted with an angry teenage girl. She has golden skin, and a crown of afro curls also tipped with gold. Her gaze is the most direct I have ever seen, and she seems to tower above me, with impossibly long legs in micro-shorts The afterburn of a quarrel fizzes around her. I was a teenage girl once, so I remember the score. She juts out her chin.

"Yes?"

"Um- hey, I'm Kat. I've just moved in with Steve at number 11."

The girl's gaze drops to Matthew. There is a war raging behind her eyes; innate politeness versus whatever was going on in her head when she threw open the door.

"Hey. My mum is in. *Mum!*" She calls casually over her shoulder, before turning back to me with a regretful little smile. "I'm just going out."

I stand aside to let her stalk past me. A woman takes her place. She looks really frazzled, so I guess I must be right about the argument.

"Sorry! Boyfriend stuff."

I arrange my expression politely. "Oh, that's okay. I have all that teenage stuff ahead." I hitch up the baby as if to demonstrate. "It's just that I found this cat in my garden…"

"Did I hear you say you'd moved into number 11?" Without waiting for a reply, she comes out onto the step and peers up the road. The teenager has disappeared, even though there is no place to disappear to. It's a mystery, but the woman just sighs and apologises again in a weary manner. She's a pretty, blonde, white woman, but currently rather pink and very flustered. "I'm Joss Baker, and that *was* my daughter Tamsin. Look, do you want to come in?"

I don't, really. Some of their prickliness has rubbed off on me and I just want to go back home, and yet I step into the hall. It's the same shape as ours, but decorated in trendy geometric stripes and instead of a crying boy, they have a gallery of family photos, dominated by Tamsin. Only child, I guess. The father appears to be a good-looking Black guy in some kind of uniform.

Joss catches me looking, and her face softens with pride. "That's Charlie. He's a pilot. Long-haul. He's away in Canada right now."

She ushers me into her kitchen. Unlike ours, it is ultra-modern with no trace of a steep, strange staircase. They've knocked through, and I can see sunlight bursting through a conservatory to the rear.

"Would you like a drink?"

I would love a gin and tonic sitting on Joss's squishy cane sofa, but that's the stuff of fantasy. I am not here to socialise, so I decline the drink. Joss is making big eyes at Matthew, trying to make him smile.

"I remember that age well. You think it's non-stop worry. And then they turn into teenagers."

Her face falls and she turns away. Feeling a bit uncomfortable, I launch into my rehearsed speech.

"The reason I called is...the thing is, we have this ginger cat hanging around the house and I'm really keen to find its owner."

"A ginger cat? Gosh, no, I haven't seen it, sorry. I haven't a clue who it might belong to."

I let out my breath. "Yesterday, I found it in the baby's cot."

"Oh, how awful." She frowns. "That is rather creepy. Goes with the territory though, doesn't it?"

My heart stutters. "What do you mean?"

She shrugs. "Well, creepy cats in the dead of night. All part of the folklore of that place, isn't it?"

I smile faintly. This is *exactly* what I wanted to hear. Evidence that I am not losing the plot. "So, there *is* a story connected with Number 11?"

Joss quickly backtracks. "What am I saying? Ignore me. It's a lovely spot, and great to have a new neighbour."

I am literally over the threshold before I realise I've been hustled out. Joss is still chatting ferociously about the neighbours and the lovely countryside and the summer barbecues, but there is no mistake. She's wants rid of me.

"It was so lovely to meet you. I'll keep an eye out for the cat. Bye, then!"

The visit is at an end. Matthew squirms as I wave goodbye and walk down the path. By the time I get to the gate, Joss has already closed the door. I pause for a second and look back at the house. In one of the downstairs windows, a curtain twitches. The visit may be over, but I'm still being watched.

CHAPTER TWENTY

I have so much going on in my head I cannot get a grip on my thoughts. What the hell did she mean 'part of the folklore'? If there is any folklore attached to this place, shouldn't I know about it? I spend the next few hours, mooching around, not able to settle. I should get in touch with Rowena, check in with her about the podcast, but I realise that Steve had carried out the necessary arrangements and I don't have her contact details. That's a mistake. Am I going to let Steve arrange my whole life?

Unreasonable feelings of resentment simmer as I make lunch for Matthew and myself. Old wounds pop open, leaving me struggling to function. Automatically, I spoon baby lentil soup into Matthew's waiting mouth, and then sit at the kitchen table, lost in thought, as he smears buttered bread into his hair.

There had been no sign of the cat when we'd returned home. I'd checked, thoroughly, and the mouse skeleton, or whatever it was, had long vanished. I think I'd left it for Steve to deal with, and I have no idea where it has ended up. If I don't know, I cannot torture myself with the details of an unexplainable resurrection. Despite Steve trying to talk me out of it, I *know* I put the bloody thing in the bin. My mind fixes on this detail and chews it over until there is nothing left. I need more information. More evidence.

I need something else to happen.

With a heavy air of inevitability, I reach for my phone and press play on the Harry Bryce podcast.

"So, what was the most frightening thing to happen to you in the house?" says Harry

There is a second or two of dead air, as if the interviewee is picking over the possibilities. Are there too many to choose from? Eventually, she clears her throat and seems to take a deep breath.

"Gosh, I think it may have been when they brought in the Ouija board, Harry. My father didn't approve of that sort of thing, or my mother either, come to that, but we had so many people turn up and offer a solution- all kinds of mediums, and spiritualists - and *cranks*, if I'm honest, although at sixteen, I think I could be forgiven for not recognising the cranks. Anyway, it became like a competition. Yes, there was a definite competitive edge to what was happening. Everyone thought they could solve it, come up with the answer. In modern parlance, I expect you could say that everyone thought they *owned* this situation. They thought they owned *me*. Like I was property, or something. A haunted doll to be exorcised."

Harry makes a noise of empathy. "That sounds very distressing, Rowena."

Rowena sighs. "It was very distressing, Harry. I felt all my power had been taken away, and there was one man in particular- it was his Ouija board, actually...They say that poltergeist activity can be a cry for attention. But what if it's a cry for help?"

Somewhere in the background, a windchime tinkles in an unseen breeze.

Matthew pushes his plastic bowl to the floor, and the crash fills me with seismic waves of panic. Breathlessly, I jab the pause button. I knew it! Harry Bryce's podcast guest is Rowena. Surely, the Poltergeist House cannot be this house? But a shrinking feeling says it is. Everything points to it. The woods at the back, the ginger cat, the hamster who met a sticky end with a red shoelace.

It is insane, but plausible. Even though Rowena had denied any knowledge of this house, I had seen something play across her features. At the time, I didn't understand it but having listened to her talk, that seems to fit too. She is angry, still disturbed by what happened to her three decades ago. Perhaps even still looking for answers.

And I have become unwittingly, treacherously, caught up in all that past history. If Number 11, Derville's Lane is Rowena's former home, the implications are horrendous. It means my new place of residence has been the focal point for a host of dark, unexplained occurrences; strange knockings and Ouija boards and…poltergeists. What if it still is?

When I get up from the table, my limbs feel heavy and uncoordinated. I clean up the mess and scrub food from the baby's hair. I clutch him to me and climb the stairs, trying not to make a noise, not to *disturb* whatever is lying in wait. I tell myself not to be ridiculous, but sometimes your rational brain cannot get the upper hand. I assess the nursery as thoroughly as if I'm sweeping for landmines, but nothing appears out of place. Matthew settles down for his afternoon nap straight away, sucking his thumb until his eyes flutter closed.

I check the window, making sure the latch is secured. I can see Len in his garden, the moss green cap bobbing over some gardening task. I'm still smarting from the fact that Steve has withheld this information from me. He must know! Perhaps he things it's all just hogwash, or maybe he doesn't want to scare me, but either way I am annoyed. I should be the judge of that. I have a right to know the circumstances surrounding the place I live in.

Perhaps if I approach him the right way, Len might be inclined to fill me in on the background. Certainly, Joss Baker looked like she wanted to cut out her tongue after blundering into such territory, but people are weird, and their reactions to ghost stories even weirder. Harry Bryce's tagline springs to mind. Maybe Joss is an unbeliever.

I make my mind up to run down and confront Len. He can only say no, he doesn't want to talk about it, but I will at least know I have the right house. If I'm going to have nightmares, I'd rather not have them for no reason.

And then, I intend to get hold of Rowena's details and grill her about the podcast. There's a chance that she was exaggerating for the benefit of Harry Bryce's ratings, but again, I need to know what I'm up against. That last thought fills me with dread. I feel like a warrior tooling up against an unknown beast.

By the time I reach the garden, Len has disappeared into his house. *Crap.* I hesitate about going to his door. My maternal instinct has long since sketched out a distinct orbit for me, an imaginary border over which I dare not stray. I'm not sure what that might look like in square metres, but there's definitely some unwritten rule that prevents you from straying too far from your sleeping child. While the idea of chatting to Len over the back garden fence is acceptable, a trip to his front door is a step too far. What if Matthew wakes up? Still in two minds, I venture into our front garden and waste a few minutes peering over the hedge, as if expecting Len to magically appear. When his front door does open, I'm caught out, forced to arrange my expression into something less intense. To my surprise, it is not an old man in a cloth cap who exits the property, but baby supermodel Tamsin.

This is decidedly not what I am expecting, and she isn't expecting to see me, either. She dithers for a second on the doorstep, managing to look ruffled and self-possessed all at the same time, before breaking eye contact to close the front door with a soft *clump*. She just shoots me an enigmatic smile and carries on down the path, looking every inch a person who has a right to be there.

"Tamsin?"

"Oh, hey."

She pauses on the other side of the hedge, and I have suddenly no idea what I'm going to say to her. I've been rehearsing questions about the history of this house, but it seems pointless directing them at Tamsin. The Seventies must seem like the Middle Ages to her.

"I was just wondering…is Len there?"

Of course he is. I saw him in the garden not ten minutes ago, but Tamsin looks puzzled.

"Um- yeah, I guess so." Just as I'm trying to interpret that, she rushes on. "Do you ever need a babysitter? It's just that my folks are always at me to get a job but I have to take two buses into town which is such a drag and there is NO WAY I am applying for McDonalds."

I'm somewhat taken aback. "Um- well, I haven't really thought about it." A babysitter on tap would be a luxury, but I haven't quite worked out my feelings about Tamsin. She doesn't seem exactly maternal, and I get the distinct impression that she's labelled me as yet another boring adult. Is that what she's doing at Len's house, earning some pocket money cleaning? If she doesn't rate McDonalds, she'd hardly going to volunteer for some domestic drudgery. I'm not sure how to respond.

"Are you old enough?" I blurt out.

Her sudden, wide smile makes her look younger, more approachable.

"I'm seventeen. How old is your baby?"

We've somehow drifted together, the front hedge forming a barrier between us.

"He's going on nine months, but I haven't really left him with anyone."

"I've seen that Steve putting him in the car."

"I live with Steve."

"But do you trust him?"

"What?" This conversation has taken a strange turn. Tamsin's gaze is frank and intimidating, and I cannot look away. "What sort of a question is that?"

"I just mean, you can trust me. I'm hard-working, reliable. Very punctual."

The oddness dissipates. She's just a kid, applying for a job.

"I'm sure you're ideal babysitter material, but…"

"Let's swap numbers, and then if you need me, you can call me up. You know, like a dope dealer."

The analogy is unsettling, but I guess she means well. I find myself taking out my phone and then suddenly I'm in the middle of a conversation about social media and profiles and followers.

Tamsin's phone case is set with crystals. She goes to work, manicured fingers flashing like fury across the screen, until she has not only secured my phone number but followed me on Facebook and Instagram.

"@buildingsitebaby- that's cute!" She scrolls through my images and posts. It's unsettling. We've hardly exchanged words, yet here she is, soaking up my intimate moments like a sponge. "You should do Tik Tok. Lots of oldies do it."

"Right. I'll think about it. I have enough on my plate at the moment."

"I'll follow your blog. It's super cool."

Placated by her approval, I smile and make a move to leave.

"I have to go check on the baby. He's asleep."

She looks up from her phone, startled, as if the baby is news to her.

"Asleep? In the daytime? Weird. Okay, so remember my name if you want a sitter! Later."

And off she goes, sauntering back to her life, phone in hand. I am still reeling from our interaction. I'd come out here determined to interrogate Len on the history of my new home. Instead, I've just given away my personal details to a perfect stranger.

CHAPTER TWENTY-ONE

It's a bit ironic, given the tiny, crowded home I grew up in, that I've always had an issue with personal space. I don't like getting close to people, or rather, I hate people getting too close to me. *I have the power to back off, keep my distance, but what if some moron invades your space?* There isn't a lot you can do.

I cannot pin this unease down to anything in my childhood, but my mother is a hard woman, both physically and emotionally. Although she loves us fiercely, she would dispense slaps rather than hugs. I suppose it was difficult, being a single parent to six of us. The lack of positive physical contact never bothered me much, although maybe it warped me in some way. I do have a vivid picture of Leanne and myself playing with dolls. We'd made them a field hospital out of Kellogg's boxes and spent ages bandaging them up with toilet roll. No benign illnesses for these creatures. They were all victims of violent crime.

I remember another time- I must have been very young, because my father was still on the scene - we'd been out somewhere, the whole troop of us, maybe visiting relatives or something, but I remember there'd been drink involved. I know that, because the older boys had pinched some half-empty beer bottles and were staggering around, pretending to be rat-arsed.

We'd paraded through the city centre, my neck craning to see the tops of the buildings. How pretty they were against the night sky, all that grand stone carving, and then the mood changed.

We seemed to have taken a shortcut down some dim old close, and Mum and Dad started arguing. Mum was in a right mood, slagging him off, trying to provoke him, and she did. He slapped her. I still remember the crack of his hand against her face. We all fell silent, and a bottle got dropped and rolled into the gutter.

Dad started to say he was sorry, but Mum was notoriously good at holding a grudge. As we watched, she picked up a half breeze block. I can see it now, the grey dusty lump in her hands and the streetlamps shining on her bare, straining biceps. It was cold, and she was wearing a thin strappy top. I could see the hairs rising on her skin like the hackles on a dog. She steadied herself, legs splayed like a weightlifter and shot-putted the block at my father's head. She missed, luckily, but he did not come home with us that night. He never came home, and we eventually gave up asking for him.

My mother's strength haunts me. The steel biceps, the fierceness of her. No, she is not built for warmth and nurture. There are things she should know, but I can never confide in her. My mother is notoriously good at holding a grudge.

I go back into the house, check on Matthew and take out my phone to message Steve.

Hi, do you have Rowena's number?

Adding the afterthought: xx

There is a pause. Steve is usually quick to reply but now, on this one occasion where I'm all fired up to take decisive action, my phone remains stubbornly silent. I cannot settle to anything, and end up walking round the house idly rearranging things. I need to speak to Rowena, confirm her story. I need to know what I'm dealing with here. I stand in the middle of the sitting room, noting the deathly hush, waiting for *something*. A slight sound from behind the skirting makes my heart leap like a frog. Instantly I recall Rowena's interview:

"...Mainly scratching, at first. In the walls. We thought it was rodents, or even birds nesting, but it got so loud it used to wake me up..."

My ears strain for further noises, but the walls remain resolutely silent, as if they are testing me. Has the temperature dropped? I feel suddenly cold, and start rubbing the shivery tops of my arms until they tingle with heat. My phone is as uncooperative as the house. Damn Steve and his inconsistent replies. And then an insidious voice in my head: *You could always Google this address...*

Yes! I could simply type 11 Derville's Lane into a search engine and see what pops up. But what if I don't like what I see? I press my hands to my stomach, trying to quell a sudden feeling of nausea. My phone beeps.

Having a bit of a family situation here. Try laptop. Email contacts. Will phone later.

The nausea persists. That sounds serious. I hope nothing is wrong with Steve's kids. I've never met them- Laura and Sam- but I guess I will do, one day. I realise with a kick of regret, that I've never even asked Steve about them. He's told me all the relevant details, of course- Laura manages the office for the family business, and Sam is engaged to someone who's name I've already forgotten. I should have paid more attention, shown more interest. I'm just so wrapped up with my own offspring... Inadequacy overwhelms me and I flop down into Steve's dad's armchair. Inadequacy and guilt. I send a reply.

I'm so sorry. I hope it's nothing serious xxx

And then because I feel like a monster: *xxx*

When no response pings back, I take myself upstairs. Matthew is still snoring softly, and I cannot resist stealing a photo for Instagram, capturing the cot and the mobile and the curl of his baby fingers. I post it absent-mindedly while booting up the laptop. Once in, I type into the browser bar: 11 Derville's Lane.

And wait.

A list of property sites reveal themselves. *Current house prices*, with the caption at the top. *Did you mean Devil's Lane?* I feel like something is sitting on my chest. No, I did not mean *Devil's Lane*. Scrolling through the possibilities, I spot Derville's Road in a place called New Romney; a Devil's Lane somewhere else and a World War One Battle of Derville but no Number eleven. And then, on the next page:

11 Derville's Lane. The most famous poltergeist case you've never heard of!

I'm just thinking that this may be a ploy by Harry Bryce to promote his podcast, when I find myself staring at the blog post of someone who obviously likes a scary tale or two. The site is called The Haunted Hut (I imagine some dude typing feverishly in a garden shed) and the page is edged with black, like a Victorian death note. There are random images of ectoplasm and seances. And there, in front of me is an old photograph of *this* house. It's dated 1977, and in there's also a body of text:

There are many famous cases of poltergeist activity. Think The Enfield Hauntings, or Borley Rectory. Perhaps you've heard of some notorious addresses- 30 East Drive, perhaps? But what about 11 Derville's Lane? A modest end-terrace in the Durham countryside, it's hard to believe that this cottage was the location for such bone-chilling paranormal activity that a constant stream of mediums, scientists and researchers flooded the home in the mid-1970s. The activity seemed to focus on a teenage girl, Rowena Howden, who reported strange scratchings and knockings in her bedroom. Objects disappeared, only to reappear days later, glass shattered and furniture was ruined. Even the family hamster came to grief. No explanation was ever found, although local psychic Thomas Burns held a spirit board session in which he claimed to have made contact with a dark entity...

Hurriedly, I make the blog disappear. The hairs on my arms are prickling and I want badly to slam the laptop closed, but I cannot seem to tear myself away. Thomas Burns? Could that be a relation of Steve's? It has to be. Same surname, same house.

I type 'Thomas Burns' into the search engine. A list of Facebook and Linked-in profiles pop up, and then a newspaper article dated 2005, which, in attempting to rehash old news, has reprinted an interview with the teenage Rowena - the strange noises, the hamster, furniture moving- and also included scanned images of contemporary newspaper entries. The lurid headlines make me feel sick: Poltergeist Strikes Again! Terror of Young Girl in Haunted House and, more worryingly, Local Psychic Branded Fraud.

I try to maximise the image. The font is tiny, but I can make out the gist of it. Thomas Burns was attacked by Rowena's father and thrown out, Ouija board and all.

This time, I do slam shut the laptop, wincing as the noise rings around the nursery. Matthew begins to stir, and my inner maternal clock judges that I have perhaps three minutes left to myself. I pick up my phone and open Instagram. Matthew's nap time photo has multiple likes and ten comments.

@beautyismylife: Oh my days- my gorgeous baby nephew! Xxxx

@SassyJuno: Loving that clown mobile! Is it washable?

@DearHound: How is it fixed? Read about a baby who pulled down a mobile and swallowed a screw.

@MelodyHughes: Is the mobile plastic? Check out @dreamtimber for sustainable wooden toys.

@MountainAsh: What is that behind the mobile?

@CoffeeBeanz: It's a shadow, right? Looks like a hand!

@AngiBabe: Yeah- a claw!

@ElanDelSilva: Not surprising, in that house.

@AngiBabe:What house?

@ElanDelSilva: It's the Poltergeist House. Strange shit happens.

I grip the desk, clutching my phone, eyes rivetted to the screen. How do they know? Did they guess? Have I made a terrible mistake and given away my address? Rookie mistake 101. And how do they know about the alleged paranormal activity? Perhaps, it's common knowledge and I am the only one being kept in the dark.

Oh my God. Blood pumping, I scroll back to enlarge the photograph. Beneath my pinching fingers, the clown faces loom blurry and grotesque; sinister gargoyles perching above my sleeping child. And there on the wall, a definite area of shade. It's just a shadow, I tell myself, a dark mirror image of the jolly mobile, but a seed of doubt has now been planted. The shadow resembles outstretched fingers, or the rapacious talons of a bird.

I scramble to the window, flip open the blind, and Matthew yelps and squirms against the influx of light. Whatever is lurking in the fringes of the room has been banished. The walls are a smooth, bland buttercup.

I try to steady my erratic breathing, hovering between mortification, that I have compromised my privacy, and irrational fear. *The Poltergeist House.* How do I rescue this? Approaching my Instagram page as if it's a poisonous spider, I summon up a breezy persona and type.

@buildingsitebaby: Just a shadow guys! Nothing to see here. And that is not my address X

I wait, imagining all those anonymous keyboards, lying in wait. Some of them will have already floated off to the next social media hit. Within seconds, a reply pops up.

@ElanDelSilva: Yeah right. We know where you live.

CHAPTER TWENTY-TWO

Who the fuck is Elan Del Silva? I feel like the walls are watching me. Matthew is crying angrily now, and I go to scoop him up, consoling him in a lilting baby voice when I'm really trying to comfort myself. *It's okay. There's nothing to be scared of. It's all okay.*

I have to get out of this bedroom, out of this house.

After a wrestle with the keys in the back door, we are suddenly released out into the fresh, cool air. My face feels feverish. Matthew is still fretting. He needs to be washed and changed and fed, but I am desperate for some breathing space. The panicky feelings start to recede as I walk down the path towards the back garden, but the ginger cat is sitting behind the bins. The sight of it gives me the chills. It backs off when it sees me. I kiss the top of Matthew's hot little head and aim a malevolent stare in its direction. I cannot believe I fed it and made a fuss of it. Mum always said cats were bad news, that they would smother a sleeping baby in a heartbeat.

Making my way as far as the lawn, I take a few deep, cleansing breaths. My head is bursting like an over-stuffed carrier bag. I try to get it all in perspective. The Instagram comments are unfortunate and goodess knows how @ElanDelSilva manged to get a hold of my address. Have I missed something? Have I posted some obvious feature of the house or garden which could be identified by fans of paranormal phenomena? I've watched all the wacky ghost hunt stuff on obscure streaming channels. I know there is an appetite for a spooky mystery, but have I somehow managed to tumble unwittingly into such a world?

I cannot believe Steve hasn't mentioned this story. It's pretty big, after all, your home being at the centre of something unexplained. A portal, that's what they call it on those shows, a place where evil can cross over into the everyday and lie in wait for people like me. Stressed mums with a gutful of fear and already enough on their plates.

I'm now gripping the baby so tightly he begins to protest, and I have to set him down on the grass. He's just about crawling, and manages to scoot in a crab-like fashion towards the foundations of the new sun room. I'm beginning to think foundations are all we'll ever have. Steve has been chasing up Gary the Builder, who has a variety of ready excuses. This week, his cement mixer broke down on another job and he's behind with his schedule.

I snap a photograph of Matthew selecting pebbles from the builder's sandpile. It's really growing quite warm and my thoughts turn to sun hats, Factor 60 and clean nappies. Such practicalities help to settle the churning in my stomach. I'm pissed off with Steve and wary about the house, but I need to get back on track. I promise myself that I'll tune into the podcast again and then contact Rowena. Perhaps it's all a hoax? It all happened so long ago. Maybe people were more gullible in the Seventies.

Slinging Matthew on my hip once more- I swear my spine will be permanently misaligned -I make my way to the back door, vowing to ignore the sinking sensation in my gut. The door is locked.

What? It cannot be. There's no way I could have locked myself out. It's a mortice lock, the kind where you have to physically turn a key, so I'd simply pulled the door after me. Had Steve come back unexpectedly and locked it from the inside? I knock hopefully and press my ear to the glass panel. I can hear something moving around inside. Shifting my head, I stare hard at the frosted glass as if some clear image might miraculously manifest and offer me a clue as to what is happening in the kitchen. I search for a shadow, a tell-tale movement, but there is nothing.

"Steve?"

No reply. I try the door again, rattling the handle, but it won't budge.

"Steve! You've locked me out. Open up!"

There's another indistinct sound, a bump, and then a pause. I get the sickening feeling that, on the other side of the door something is listening as intently as I am. Matthew gurgles, and I place my hand gently over his mouth. His eyes are round as buttons.

Trying to convince myself that this *is* Steve, that he didn't hear me when I called out, or that he's disappeared to the bathroom, I withdraw and walk around to the front of the house. Steve always parks his car on the road, and that's what I expect to see, its charcoal grey roof standing just proud of the hedge. There is only a chilling absence. Even though I run down the path and scan the lane, there is no sign of Steve's car. Whoever or whatever is in the house, it is not Steve.

My stomach contracts. My mouth has gone as dry as toast. Every survival instinct is screaming at me to *go*. Someone has broken into your home! Get out of there, seek help. But I cannot resist trying the front door. The porch, as ever, is open, but the front door has a Yale lock, and even though Steve insists that people can still go out and leave their doors unlocked in 21st century Britain, I am not of the same mind. When I'm home alone, I make sure the snib is on, and, of course, I don't have my keys with me.

My brain goes down an unlit track. What if there is another explanation for the locked door and the noise within? It had started with small noises, Rowena had said. Scratchings and... things that go bump. My brain flies to the staircase door and all its little tricks. Open one minute, closed the next. The dank, evil-smelling odours that spring up from nowhere like sandstorms; the bedroom window, inexplicably opened. An explanation is relentlessly taking shape in my imagination.

Whatever happened here is not over.

It's happening again.

Heart pounding, I sprint around to Len's front door, Matthew bouncing against my chest. My urgency seems to amuse him and he starts to giggle, while all the while I'm thanking whatever force for good is in the world that I hadn't stepped outside and left him in his cot or his high chair. I feel weak at the thought. My shaky fingers find the bell push and pummel it. Len's gruff baritone can be heard, deep inside the house. Is he speaking to someone, or to himself, cursing all cold callers? Presently, the door opens.

"Len, I need help." I blurt out. "I've locked myself out. Actually, I haven't locked myself out because the door shouldn't be locked. I think it's just stuck but I could have sworn I heard someone inside and..."

The old man stalks stiffly past my babbling. For a moment, I'm scared that he's going to totally ignore me, and that he's bent on some other errand, but when he turns left out of his gate and heads up our garden path, I hurry in his wake. He really is a man of few words, but I feel suddenly safer.

Len spends several minutes staring at the back door. Is he listening? I listen too.

"I definitely heard a noise," I whisper.

"*Ssh.*" Len frowns, and carefully depresses the door handle with the rapt attention of a locksmith. To my horror, the door magically swings open an inch.

"I'll stick a bit of WD40 on it for you." He stands back, and I realise I'm going to have to enter first. This is my home, after all, whether I want to set foot in it or not. I am completely bemused.

"I cannot explain that." I step into the kitchen, peering around for anything that might be out of place. An intermittent creaking sets my nerves on edge. I track it to the staircase door, which is standing open. It's rocking ever so slightly on its hinges, *back and forth, back and forth.* In the middle of the floor lies a smashed mug.

I place Matthew in his highchair and stoop to pick up the pieces. It's Steve's favourite mug, a whimsical rural design from a local pottery. The shard in my hand bears a stencilled cockerel in cobalt blue. I turn it over reflectively, staring at the brown tea stains as if they might offer a clue as to what's going on here.

"Cat, shouldn't wonder," says Len from the doorstep. I notice he hasn't attempted to enter.

"The cat was outside." Even as I say it, I'm questioning myself. Had the cat somehow managed to climb in through a window.

"Tricky little buggers." Len rubs his nose. "I'll get off then."

"Len- have you…" I choose my words carefully. "Is this house haunted?"

That is the exact opposite of what I intended to say, but it's obviously the thought uppermost in my mind. Len's gaze shifts from mine.

"Not for me to say." He turns away. "Old Tom Burns would be the man to ask."

Steve returns just as Len is leaving. I hear them exchange words on the path, but I'm still trying to process the Thomas Burns connection, that the dodgy psychic from a Seventies ghost story is undoubtedly Steve's father. I'm not even sure what to do with that information, but I keep getting a mental image of a troubled Rowena knocking back wine in her white kitchen. I need to talk to her. She's obviously okay with telling her story to Harry Pryce's fans, so it's not a secret. Except in this house.

Steve enters and catches sight of the broken mug, surveying it with an expression too weary to care. I feel all defensive and prickly.

"It wasn't me." I go to fetch a dustpan and brush.

He shrugs. "It's only a mug. What was Len doing here?"

"Good question."

Steve pulls out a chair next to Matthew and makes tapping noises on the highchair table. The baby slaps his own hands down in appreciation.

"Has something happened?"

"That back door got stuck. No, it *locked* itself when we were outside." Angrily I sweep up the bits of pottery. "I had to call Len, but I actually heard someone moving round in here. I was terrified, and this…" I proffer the sweepings. "This was on the floor when we managed to get in."

Steve scratches his chin. "How did that happen?"

"You tell me." I empty the dustpan into the pedal bin with as much noise as I can muster. Matthew's face falls at the sudden sound, and he begins to whimper. I watch Steve unclip him and ease him from the highchair. He's buying time. He knows I'm onto him.

He cuddles Matthew to his chest. "I've had a really hard day."

His most recent text comes back to haunt me, and I feel a pinch of guilt. He really does look done in. Maybe this can wait.

"Do you want to talk about it? Is it one of your kids?"

I can see a suspicion of moistness in his eye when he nods. The fight sneaks out of me with a sigh.

"Matthew needs changing. If you do that, I'll see what I can rustle up for tea. I do a mean macaroni cheese."

His face softens. "That sounds like a plan."

I watch him bear Matthew carefully up the stairs. Yes, this discussion can wait, but not for long.

CHAPTER TWENTY-THREE

The evening wears on. Stuffed with macaroni cheese and some Neapolitan ice cream I found in the freezer, we lounge around in the soft lamplight of the sitting room, watching Matthew chewing on his brightly-coloured play bricks and any other soft toy he can gum to death. Even though I have much darker matters on my mind, I let Steve vent about his daughter, Laura, who is going through a messy break-up.

"She hasn't been married long. At least her mother and me had put a good shift in before it all went pear-shaped." He sips a beer reflectively. "Laura's husband is a bit of a dick, if I'm honest. They never had two pennies to rub together. She earned it, he spent it. I'd like to say she's better on her own, but I don't suppose it feels like that to her. I've been a shit dad. Never there when she needed me."

Something creeps over my nerve endings. I fight the sudden urge to pick up Matthew and wrap him in cotton wool, or at least in an unending hug, which would protect him forever from the powers of darkness and doomed love affairs. I would do anything to protect him and I can only imagine how Steve must be feeling right now. He's sitting in his father's armchair, while I am lounging on the couch. Quickly, I cross the space between us and seat myself inelegantly on his knee. He looks surprised and pleased and a whole lot happier.

"Don't beat yourself up." I tell him. "If I've learned anything the last year, it's that parenting is trial and error. I kind of wade from one mistake to the next."

Steve gives me a sad smile, puts down his beer to accommodate me, to wrap me in his arms and we stay like that for a long while, soaking up comfort and warmth. It makes me feel good, and I catch myself leaning into his embrace. When I do voice the million- dollar question, it comes out less accusatory than I'd intended.

"Why didn't you tell me this house is haunted?"

Steve's eyes flicker and he takes another sip from his can.

"That's just old wives' tales. Don't believe what you hear. It's nonsense."

I stiffen immediately. His thighs beneath mine feel like iron, when minutes before we'd been melting over each other like butter.

"So, you admit there *are* stories? 'Folklore' is how one of your neighbours put it."

"Who? Len?"

"It doesn't matter. Steve, you lied to me."

He looks genuinely shocked. "I haven't lied about anything!"

"Okay. Lied by omission, then. That's a thing."

"Kat, I haven't been keeping anything from you. Look, you're upset about locking yourself out, I get that-"

"Oh no. Don't turn that back on me." I square up to him, which is extremely tricky when you're sitting on someone's lap. In fact, he's let his arms drop, which makes my position precarious. Huffily, I get up and stand in front of him. "That door was… stuck…in a way I cannot explain. Nor can I explain the noises or the broken mug or the incident with the cat-"

Steve obviously doesn't like me having the height advantage, so he gets up too. On the floor, the baby sucks a rattle and stares from one to the other of us, wide-eyed.

"There's a logical explanation for all of this," he snaps. "Faulty window catches, old doors, swollen with damp. That mug was on the drying rack along with a stack of other things. It probably just slipped off."

"And the noises I heard?"

"Mice. They're in the walls."

"Mice!" I throw up my hands. "They must be on steroids then. That's how it *starts*."

"How what starts?"

Despite my evidence- the podcast, the online articles- his sarcastic tone irks me so much I suddenly don't want to discuss this with him. He has no understanding of what I'm going through, and no sympathy. And then he comes out with something that completely robs me of speech.

"Maybe you've been on your own too much. It's easy to give things feet and legs when you're in a new place. Old houses are quirky and you're over- reacting, letting your imagination run away with you."

I clamp my jaw shut. I'm furious, and not sure how to play this. There's certainly no point in mentioning the podcast until I hear Rowena's side of the story.

"Let's just leave it at that. I'm going to give Matthew his bath."

Steve smiles, but at some random spot on the carpet, not at me.

"Good idea. Get him settled in bed and we can watch a film. *Lord of the Rings* is on at nine."

Much later, Matthew is fast asleep and Steve is watching some epic battle between hordes of fantasy soldiers. I cannot concentrate and the noise is drilling into my skull. There's a similar epic struggle going on in my brain right now, between the forces of hearsay and conspiracy and the known facts. I mumble some excuse about updating my blog and pick up the silent baby monitor. Actually, I feel robbed of any motivation. I linger in the kitchen for a long time before pouring myself a tumbler of water to gulp down two paracetamol.

Maybe Steve genuinely doesn't think there's any cause for concern about this house. I suppose it all happened a long time ago and if his father was the dodgy psychic involved, he had every reason to keep it from his family. Steve probably grew up not knowing the full story, or trusting some mythical version of it. I bet he's an unbeliever. Only an unbeliever would fail to get freaked out by the sort of things that are alleged to have happened here, that are still happening. Does this make me a believer?

Lost in thought, I sip my water, staring at the night through the kitchen window. Rural nights are so free of light pollution, I can see my own reflection as clearly as if I'm gazing into a mirror. Kat through the Looking Glass. What can I see? I lean my elbows on the edge of the sink and narrow my eyes at the woman in the window.

Without warning, the cat leaps onto the outside ledge. The sudden appearance of its whiskered, malevolent face superimposed on mine freaks me out so much I drop my tumbler into the sink with a crash so loud it reverberates through my core. The cat opens its mouth in a pink, silent miaow. Heart banging, I rescue the glass, which is thankfully still in one piece. I tell myself to calm down. *Deep breaths*. This is exactly the type of reaction that makes people tell you you're *over*-reacting. Steve's words still smart, but there's nothing like a modicum of anger to curb the imagination.

It's nothing more than a stray cat on a window ledge. Fumbling with the cord for the kitchen blind, I let the fabric drop into place, deleting the night and the cat and anything else that might be lurking out there. I rinse and dry the glass, but all the while I'm telling myself that I cannot leave it like that. Some primitive fear is driving me. I need to get rid of that cat and all will be well.

Snatching up the baby monitor, I open the back door, noting its smooth operation. No sign of any stiff hinges. or swollen panels. No rational reason, in fact, for it to become wedged so tight it refused to budge. There is no sign of the cat, either on the path or in the garden beyond. I linger beneath the light of an uncertain moon, the night air cool on my fevered cheeks. Everything looms large and lumpy; next door's hedge, the garden shed, the tall trees beyond our boundary. Rowena's words come back to haunt me:

"Once I found a mug hanging on the branch of a tree in the woods behind the house. And not just mugs. Other things."

My feet propel me onwards, while all the while my brain is roaring at me to stop. I could be cuddling up to Steve right now, watching Legolas ride into battle, or whatever the hell he does in *Lord of the Rings.* But no, something mad and bad in my psyche drives me onward. I don't know what I'm looking for, or what I expect to see, or how far I need to go before I might see it.

The answer is, not very far.

I let myself through the gate into the wood- not the best place to be, in the dark - and proceed with caution, sticking to the path, scanning for tree roots and other trip hazards with the flashlight on my phone. No sign of the cat here either, and no sound. The hush is complete, as if the woods are empty of any living thing. A faint mist plays across the light beam, like something you'd see in a swamp, or a really bad creepy movie. It makes me shiver and I go to turn back.

That's when I see it, out of the corner of my eye. A blurry object, hanging from a low branch. Hanging. I do not want to approach it but my feet have other ideas. I am drawn to it, and I cannot look away. The thing is swaying, very gently, although there isn't a breath of wind. From several feet away, I can see what it is. It's Bobo, Matthew's missing teddy. It's been strung up by the neck with a long red shoelace.

A cold chill envelopes my soul. I don't want to go any closer, but I cannot leave it there, my child's toy. What sick monster would do this? The day my son dropped it in the wood, was someone watching? Or did they find it, much later, and decide to play this hideous prank? Not just any old sicko, either. This was perpetrated by someone, some ghoul, who knows the significance of the red shoelace; someone who knows about Rowena's pet hamster, who is familiar with this house's infamous back story. Somebody who cannot let things lie.

I take down the teddy with some difficulty. The lace is tough nylon, knotted tight around the creature's neck. I have to lay down my phone and the baby monitor to attack the knot with both sets of fingernails. The angle of the flashlight blinds me, and I can almost feel a presence behind me, just beyond the spread of the beam. Why do we always assume we're safe in a lighted area? Things that dwell in the dark don't necessarily stay in the dark. By the time Bobo is freed, I'm so creeped out the back of my neck is prickling. I cannot believe just metres away, Steve is lounging in a warm house, while I am near-paralysed with fear in some eerie limbo-land.

I grab the phone and the monitor and scramble for the gate, almost tripping over my own feet in my haste to get back to the safety of the garden. My heart is racing as wildly as my legs. Whether the hanging of Bobo was the work of a human or the result of supernatural forces is a question for another time. I just want to get back into the house and lock the door before I faint from fear. Anything suddenly seems possible.

As I draw level with the garden shed, I pause to take a couple of deep breaths. I cannot approach Steve like a breathless, gabbling hysteric. I need to present a calm front, so he will take me seriously at last. Even Steve cannot ignore the implications of a teddy bear lynching. Even if it's not the work of a ghost, there could be a psychopath loose in the woods. How did I ever think this was a safe, quiet place? I should have known. What about all those folk horror films set in rural isolation? Strange neighbours with odd ways. How do I know the threat isn't close to home? Len, Gary the Builder, Steve…?

Steve. How well do I know him? I shy away from pinning this on Steve. What about Len? He seems such an upright figure. *Couthie*, my mother would call him. Sweet and old-fashioned. Surely this is the work of a psychopath? What about Gary? I haven't seen much of him lately.

Oh Christ. I'm in the middle of nowhere with a psychopath. My belly cramps with fear. The baby monitor suddenly crackles into life. I'd forgotten about it. All my senses flip to red alert. A snuffle, a little cry. Matthew must be having a bad dream. But then…what was that? Was that a giggle?

Babies do not giggle in their sleep…do they? Matthew is awake, and I'm blundering around outside like a complete fool. I make for the house, the monitor clutched tight in my hand and the unfortunate Bobo clamped beneath my arm. The giggle burbles through the ether again, vibrating against my palm. My son is definitely awake and laughing *at something*.

Stumbling past the shed, I find myself on the lawn, staring up at Matthew's bedroom window as if my maternal radar can troubleshoot from a distance. At his window, the blind is half up, half down, on a drunken slant, as if someone has been messing with it. I know I left it pulled all the way down, because any chink of light in the morning wakes Matthew at dawn. Has Steve been up there? Maybe that's what's happened- Matthew has woken up and Steve has gone up to comfort him and he's making him giggle with some funny faces and…But in my heart I know that is not the case. Steve never stirs from the TV between teatime and bedtime. I always have full control of the baby monitor, just as I do now. Unless I ask, he leaves the childcare for me. He certainly couldn't hear Matthew crying from the sitting room, and he would never think to check on him. Plus, *Lord of the Rings* is about three hours long.

Over the monitor, I hear a gruff male voice. The words are unintelligible, and I don't recognise the tone, but it is definitely NOT Steve. Panic surges like bile. I know I need to run but I'm glued to the spot. As I watch, a black shadow passes across the window. A black shadow IN MY BABY'S ROOM!

CHAPTER TWENTY-FOUR

My limbs have forgotten how to work. Somehow, I manage to get into the house and up the stairs, moving like a puppet, all jerky and uncoordinated. I'm running on adrenaline. There is no time to call for help, or phone Steve. My mind is on that solitary shape in the window, whatever it was, that slick, shifting shadow, that has the power to meddle with blinds, and windows and maybe even doors. What could it do to a defenceless child?

Please don't hurt my baby.

Please don't hurt my baby.

The last few steps feel like a battle. By the time I reach the doorway of Matthew's room I am gasping for air, almost anticipating that dark *something* flying at me, knocking me flat. But there is nothing but a vacancy, an after-kick of a smell I recognise, and Matthew, standing in his cot, clutching the rails. He is unharmed, wide awake, and I waste no time in snatching him from his cot, banging his toes against the rail in my panic.

Clutching him close, I bury my face in his sweaty little neck, inhale the smell of baby and fabric softener and tell him I'm sorry, I'll never leave his side again. When I come up for air, that other, lingering tang is unmistakeable. It's the same ancient ashy smell that had gusted down the stairs; overturned stones, dirt and mould. My heart starts to thump again. Almost afraid to look, I check Matthew for damage. It's then that I notice his fresh pink fingernails are encrusted with dirt.

I rush him to the bathroom, gush water into the sink and tip in all the liquid soap I can find. Hauling off his sleepsuit, I wrap him in a towel and plunge both hands into the water. He objects and wriggles as I check each finger. The nails are black with dust and debris, as if he's been digging in parched soil. What the hell is going on? I want to scream for Steve, but I know he wouldn't hear me, and anyway, I don't trust my voice, or even my eyes. How can this be? The baby starts to whine at this rough treatment, so I have to swallow down my anxiety and make a game with the bubbles. By the time I've managed to clean his hands and face, Matthew is wide awake and restless. How am I ever going to get him back to sleep? I'm certainly not going to put him back in that room.

We return to the nursery to collect a blanket. I'm almost scared to enter, my whole body feels as cold as ice. My gaze scours the room. It doesn't feel right. The clown mobile is deathly still and I imagine I hear a clock ticking, even though there is no clock. It's like a pulse in the walls, or maybe it's me, the aftershock of all that adrenaline thrumming through my system. My workspace looks untouched, but when I trail a hand across the desk, I note that my jotters and my diary have been moved, just a little. It's enough. Swearing, I cross to the cot, and sweep away the duvet. It's still vaguely warm from Matthew's body. There on the mattress lies a foreign object. Something which should not be there.

It's a doll, but it's not one of my son's toys. His toys are as familiar to me as he is. This doll is a little stranger, a cold, dirty thing from another century. It might once have had golden waves and a lacy pinafore, but its clothes are grey and blighted with mould spots, there are bald patches on its scalp and it has only one staring eye. It's staring at me. The stink of decay and mildew is so vile, a grunt of disgust escapes me. Matthew had been playing with this thing. That's why he'd been giggling. That's why he was covered in dirt.

"Steve!" I wail, not caring if he hears me or not. "Steve!"

I exit the nursery, hugging Matthew to my body. We slam into a hard form at the top of the stairs. Steve's strong hands steady my shoulders.

"Whoa. What's wrong?" He soothes.

"For fucksake!" I shrug him off. "What are you doing, creeping around?"

His face stiffens. "I was coming up to the bathroom, if that's allowed."

I take a deep. shuddery breath. "I was out in the garden and I heard Matthew giggling on the monitor and I saw a shape at the window. It was very dark, I'm not sure what it was but the blind had been moved and I couldn't think I just sprinted for the stairs and I..." I run out of words and swallow painfully. "And then, when I got up here Matthew was awake and his hands were all dirty...like there was *dirt* under his *finger nails* as if he'd been outside...and then I..."

"What were you doing out in the garden?"

I stare at Steve. "What was I...? You think *that's* the important bit?"

"Kat, slow down. I'm trying to understand what-"

"Okay. Understand this-" I shove him towards the nursery. "Look at what's in the cot and see if you understand, because I fucking don't."

He winces, as he always does when I swear in front of the baby, but he goes obediently to the cot. Peering gingerly, he does what I haven't been brave enough to do. He picks up the doll. I watch him for what seems to be a long, long time, my insides shrieking.

Eventually he turns to me.

"I haven't seen this before."

My teeth feel like they're stuck together. "Whatever was in here gave it to Matthew."

For a moment, I think I detect a smile, but then he turns away.

"Don't put it back in the cot! Get rid of it!" I sound slightly hysterical. Sensing my fear, Matthew begins to fuss.

"So you don't know where it came from? It looks like its been packed away. It could have been in one of these boxes." He starts rooting through the boxes, which are stacked up against one wall.

"Oh, your dad kept dolls, did he?"

"No, but my mother had some really old ones, Victorian ones, passed down from her granny. This could be one of them." He runs a finger over the dolls scalp. The hair looks like its been gnawed away in patches.

I try to catch him out. "So, you were up here just now and you gave the doll to Matthew?"

He looks genuinely perplexed. "Me? You think it was me you saw from the garden? It wasn't me. I haven't left the sitting room."

"So how did- that thing- jump out of the box and into Matthew's cot?"

He shrugs, glancing from the doll to the boxes and back again as if the clues are all there. "There must be a rational explanation."

"Must there?"

"Of course. Look, I don't know what you've heard, but there is nothing going on here. There are no ghosts. I grew up here. I think I'd remember."

"But what about before? The whole thing- the story- began before you were born. You dad knows about it, doesn't he?"

Matthew is starting to whimper, rubbing his eyes with clumsy fists. He's tired and disorientated, and my anger begins to lose ground. Steve senses my weakness and swoops in. "It's late. We'll talk about this in the morning. Let's put him to bed…" He reaches out as if he expects me to deliver the baby into his arms. I back away.

"You must be joking."

"What?"

"You think I'm going to leave him in here? We'll sleep on the couch."

Steve looks genuinely flummoxed, but he's tired too, and his patience is being tested. I can see a nerve twitching in his jaw.

"At least bring him into the bed, then."

"No. I'm not staying upstairs." I'm already turning away. He catches my elbow.

"Kat, this is ridiculous. You're going to sleep on the couch from now on?"

I shake him off and stare at him, not answering, and he swears under his breath and rubs his neck. His eyes have gone colder than I've ever seen them before.

"You'll use any excuse, won't you?" he says eventually.

"What do you mean?"

"Any excuse to avoid being in bed with me. No, don't deny it." He raises a hand, even though I wasn't planning to deny it. "If I'd know the physical side of things was going to be so…so…"

"So what?" I go on the defensive, because I know he's right. He's sussed me out. The thought of sleeping on the sofa is a relief, safe from ghosts, and the other things that are haunting me. "Have you ever asked me why that is?"

"No. Maybe I don't want to hear the answer." He turns away, but not before I've noticed a suspicious glint in his eye. I know what's going on in his head, all the self-questioning, the insecurity. A middle-aged man with a younger woman. The fight leaves me completely. I suddenly feel older than he is.

"It's not what you think. It's not about you, trust me."

I swallow down my sympathy and head for the stairs.

CHAPTER TWENTY-FIVE

Steve wakes me with a cup of tea. I wasn't even aware I'd dozed off, but his voice comes to me in dream-form and I struggle to rise to the surface. The heavy weight of Matthew is absent from my chest, making me flounder into full consciousness like a drowning swimmer. I try to get up, but Steve eases me back onto the cushions. I remember suddenly that I'm sleeping on the couch, and then I recall why.

"Relax. Everything's fine. Matthew's in his high chair attacking a rusk as we speak. You look awful."

"Thanks." Feeling drained and groggy, I accept the cup and take a scalding sip. For most of the night, I'd lain sleepless, cradling the baby, who'd dropped off instantly, as babies tend to do. My mind was a maelstrom of newspaper cuttings, and lurid claims, possessed dolls and red eyes glowing at an upstairs window. Okay, the demon eyes were a total fabrication, but it goes to show, as Steve insists, how the imagination can exaggerate things. He's right, there must be a rational explanation, but I'm struggling to think of one.

On and on my brain whirled, in some mad eightsome reel, flinging all the facts into sharp focus. The cat is probably just a stray, a mere coincidence, but the rodent bones, with the red thread? The evil-smelling breeze that haunts the staircase? The back door with a mind of its own and the smashed mug? And now the evidence of my own eyes. I know what I saw, and I'm

100% certain I did not find that moth-eaten doll in those boxes and hand it to my son.

And then there's that other world, the shady sub-culture of anonymous commentators who concoct narratives as the world sleeps, regardless of the facts. They have crawled into my reality and found out where I live. I cannot bring myself to call them trolls, because trolls are virtual tormentors. They don't cross over into the real world to brutalise teddy bears. I resign myself to never sleeping again.

Sometime in the small hours, I'd placed Matthew carefully on the cushion beside me and slumped on the edge of the sofa, flexing my aching arms and shoulders. And then I'd reached for my phone, the very thing that all those sleep experts warn you not to do. But I was not listening. Me, who could no longer bear to be in a haunted nursery, was apparently willing to enter a murky digital crypt well past the witching hour.

There'd been an unread message from Leanne, and like an idiot, I'd opened it.

Today. 21.45

Here is something you should see. One of your Insta followers posted a link in the comments and it leads to this...

I couldn't resist a trip down the rabbit hole. It brought me out in an alien landscape, a members-only Facebook group entitled 'Ghost Watch.' With a sinking feeling, I'd pressed 'join,' and within a few minutes been accepted into the ranks without question. 'You are now a member of Ghost Watch.' Obviously, the small hours is when it all happens for paranormal investigators.

It took me a moment to orientate myself. The group's cover photo was a forlorn ghost girl with exaggerated Zombie eyes and sewn-up lips. A pinned post with details of a forthcoming lecture entitled 'Dr Simeon Whittle's Cabaret of Death' did nothing to quell my fears, but there was worse to come. Scrolling down, I discovered the night's hot topic. They were discussing Number 11, Derville's Lane. More horrifyingly, they were talking about me.

Beneath a grainy photograph of this house were a series of comments. The admin, one Bill Bunter (not his real name, obviously), had set the scene, a summary of the story I'd become all too familiar with, but worse than that, they'd included a link to my blog and Instagram accounts, with the caption 'The Evil Continues.' The sinking feeling that had been keeping me company all night turned into a gnawing pain.

I flicked through the comments. Some were from people using their real names. others were hiding under an alias. Most I did not recognise, but some I did. Some were my original followers.

Melody Hughes: I follow this blog! Did you see the shadow on her wall?

Jane Merriman: I saw it! Right above the baby!

Mountain Ash: What about the photo on Insta with the baby playing in the sand?

Jane Merriman: No- what did I miss?

Bill Bunter: Saw the pic. Did you see something?

Mountain Ash: Yup- check it out..

Mountain Ash had reposted my photo, the one of baby Matthew in a sunhat, innocently picking pebbles from the builder's sand. She had encircled something in bright pink digital highlighter. Like all the other ghouls, I'd immediately enlarged the image and scrutinised it. In the garish circle, I could pick out letters, what looked like a capital 'D' and a small 'e', even though I'd never noticed anything in the sand at the time, or even on the image. I clicked back to the comments.

Melody Hughes: WT actual F?

Mountain Ash: We think it was trying to write 'Devil.'

Melody Hughes: The baby?

Mountain Ash: No. IT. Whatever is in the house.

Jane Merriman: Or maybe the baby. Didn't Bill say the last child to live there had been possessed?

Bill Bunter: Devil's Lane. That's what they called it, back in the day. My mother grew up around there. 11 Devil's Lane. The Howdens couldn't sell that place for love nor money.

I couldn't read any more. These people had made up a story I was not part of, and to contradict them, to engage with them, would merely kick the hornet's nest. I felt like a trespasser in my own life. How could they suggest that my baby might be possessed by something paranormal, something *evil*? It was insane. After that, I'd lain awake for ages, an insidious refrain playing on repeat in my head.

Why are you so upset? It was you who invited them in.

In the kitchen, Steve is making moves as if he's going to work. Of course he's going to work. Am I expecting him to stay at home and protect me from something he doesn't believe in? He thinks I'm a hormonal flake. I am so on my own with this. I sit at the table and sip my tea, planning my next move, while Matthew, unchecked, smears soggy rusk on anything he can reach. I watch Steve pack a flask, a tin foil parcel of sandwiches and an apple into his backpack.

"Will you be gone all day?" I already know the answer.

"Yup. We've a container of goods getting delivered. That will take some sorting out and then I'll be out in the van, and then I have to pop in and see Dad. I might be a bit late back. Do you want me to pick up anything from the shops?"

"I want a lift."

"A lift? Where?"

"I want to speak to Rowena. You know she was the girl who lived in this house before you?"

"Rowena Patterson?"

"Rowena Howden she was then. She was the girl who was haunted by a poltergeist." A cold chill descends from the staircase, as if something is stirring, and I suppress a shiver. I cannot decide whether Rowena's history is news to him. His expression is neutral.

"It's only eight am. You can't land on somebody's doorstep at this time."

"You could come back at lunchtime. I can call Rowena and you could drop me off then."

His eyes narrow a fraction.

"I told you, I'm busy."

"You mean you don't want to help me."

"I don't want to help you make a fool of yourself. What will Rowena think if you turn up at her door spouting about ghosts and goblins?"

I bite my lip. I think she will want to hear what I have to say, but I'm not going to get into that argument. It's a waste of time. Let Steve think what he wants. I know there is a problem here. I know my son and I are in danger and Rowena is the only one who can help me. So, I just sip my tea and say nothing.

Presently, Steve picks up his jacket and his keys and leaves. There are more ways than one to escape this house. More ways than one to skin a cat, as my mother would say.

CHAPTER TWENTY-SIX

The bus shelter is on the opposite side of the lane, almost level with the Bakers' house, in fact. It sits in a square reservation carved out of a farmer's field, and is basically a dark timber shed with a pot of withered geraniums at the entrance and a timetable behind plexiglass. Unlike the bus stops in my hometown, it is free of graffiti and smells of creosote, rather than pee. The rural transport links are a hot mess, a confusing formula of numbers and times which I don't have the energy to interpret. I check the time on my phone. It's just after ten thirty. I locate an app which promises to help me plan my journey, but it simply buffers, as if something is conspiring to keep me here. Cold drips down my spine.

Steve had left without confirming whether or not he could come back for me at lunchtime. He might not even have time for a lunch break, he'd grumbled. I knew I had to take matters into my own hands. I'd found a listing for Whitecross Villa on a Visit Durham website and called Rowena on the number provided. She'd answered quickly and didn't seem fazed to hear from me. I fought the impression that she'd been expecting a call.

"Just pop in whenever suits you," she'd said.

I couldn't find the words to explain that I was hoping to *book* in, rather than pop in. It was the obvious solution. There was no way I could face putting my baby to bed in a room that appears to come alive at night. Rooms are supposed to remain static, predictable. They should not have an agenda, and I feel like I've lost control of this one. She might say no, of course. Steve might have a strop and attempt to bring me home. Both of those are possibilities, but I have to take responsibility. I cannot stay at number 11 and put Matthew and myself in danger.

The online stuff is harder to deal with. Can I report the Ghost Watch group to Facebook? I don't have proof that any of them have been snooping around the house- how could I, when they're anonymous? I should ask Leanne for help. She's always been more media savvy than me. I'm beginning to wish I'd never heard of buildingsitebaby.com.

I'm debating all this in my head, while juggling Matthew in his sling, when I get the feeling I'm being watched. Joss's hot husband – was it Charlie? – appears to be home on leave and is in his garden, uncoiling the lead of a lawnmower. He waves across at me, as if he knows who I am, even though we've never met. I guess news travels fast around here. It's not creepy though. He looks pleasant and unthreatening and very much like the kind of guy who could find his way round a bus timetable. Maybe I could ask for help.

I'm just about to call over to him when his attention is distracted by Tamsin. She appears in the doorway looking beautifully sulky. Words are exchanged. I cannot hear them, but I can see her father casting a typically disapproving eye over her bare legs and shoulders. She's wearing the briefest denim shorts and a cropped top in fuchsia pink, with a huge bag looped over her shoulder. She reminds me of me, a long time ago. Pre-baby, pre-everything. Charlie shakes his head with paternal resignation and turns back to the lawnmower. It makes me feel smiley, and a little bit sad. Everyone needs a dad to look out for them. I swallow the lump in my throat and rearrange my expression, as Tamsin crosses the road. She looks surprised to see me.

"You going into Town?"

I'm not sure where Town is, so I shake my head. "Next village."

"Oh." She looks me up and down. "I'm going into Town."

We lapse into silence. I consider complimenting her on the outsize bag, although I'm not sure why I want to get on her good side. Maybe she intimidates me. In the end, we both end up speaking at the same time. Tamsin laughs. It is a pleasing, childlike sound, at odds with her apparent sophistication.

"You go first," she says.

"I was just going to ask you what time the bus is?"

"Could be anytime. It hasn't passed yet, so I figure maybe in the next thirty minutes or so? The oldies call it the shopper hopper. It's always full of pensioners."

In her eyes, I probably qualify as an oldie and my heart quails from the thought of having to make conversation with a mouthy teenager for the next half-an-hour, but she seems to be unbending a little bit.

"Are you taking him with you?" She blinks at Matthew. He reaches out his fingers, intent on catching her swingy, bouncy curls.

I hide my amusement at the odd question. "We're kind of an item."

She grins back. "I suppose. My offer still stands, if ever you want a babysitter. My rates are good."

"I'll bear that in mind."

Her gaze slides from mine. "Oh look. Here's the bus."

Once on the shopper hopper, she sits at the back and I sit at the front and we pretend not to know each other.

When Rowena unlocks her front door, my opening gambit strikes to the heart of the matter.

"The last time, you said there was always a safe place for us here. Do you remember?"

"You'd better come in, love."

As she turns away, I notice the shimmer of silver jewellery in her ear lobes, little crescent moons that match her pendant. Her white hair is piled on top of her head, showing off her ears and slender neck. I wonder if she does a mean side-hustle in spirit totem jewellery. More disturbingly, what is she seeking protection from?

She leads me into the white kitchen. I smell over-ripe fruit and spot a bowl of ruby-red peaches on the counter. They seem at odds with the pristine setting, and I remember the time before, when she was slicing tomatoes with a dangerously large knife. Maybe it's something to do with the contrast, red on white.

I don't waste any words.

"I heard you on the poltergeist podcast. I know it was you." That sounds like an allegation, and Rowena looks quite pained.

"So you're a detective now?"

"Why didn't you tell me, about the house?"

"The way you say it suggests that nobody else told you either."

My turn to look pained. "And now I have a problem. Because of my-um-online presence, I'm being labelled as the girl who lives at 11 *Devil's* Lane."

She laughs without humour and indicates a stool. "Join the club. Please, sit."

I place Matthew on the floor with a teething ring. He seems content here, more settled than he's been of late. The white breakfast bar is so far away from poltergeists and dark entities that I'm suddenly at a loss. Rowena gets straight to the point.

"Have you experienced something in the house?"

Her voice is like that of a therapist. It unlocks something. I nod miserably.

"There's a ginger cat hanging around and I found it in the baby's cot and twice it brought in this *thing*...this skeleton with red string around its neck. There's a wind that gushes down the stairs and the worst thing- the very worst thing....Last night, I went for a walk in the woods and found Matthew's missing teddy, Bobo. It was hanging by the neck from the branch of a tree."

I let that sink in. Rowena's fingers fly to her silver pendant, and her eyes widen a fraction. I certainly have her attention. I continue.

"That's not all. I had the baby monitor with me, and I could hear Matthew giggling, as if he was interacting with someone. I ran up the garden and there was a figure in his room. I could see it. I felt so *helpless*."

"Oh, Kat. I'm so sorry." Rowena looks shaken to the core, as if she is somehow responsible for this, but I don't want to dwell on that.

"By the time I got up there- it was gone. But there was a doll in the cot, a filthy, dusty doll and the baby's fingers were caked in dirt."

"What did the doll look like?" Rowena is staring at me, unblinking, finger and thumb pinching the crescent moon as if it's an anchor. I feel discombobulated. I realise I do not have to persuade Rowena, or try to convince her. Unlike Steve, she is totally on board.

I draw out my phone.

"This morning, I took a picture of it. I- I knew I was coming here. I need your help."

I find the image and extend it to her. She – deliberately, it seems to me- does not touch the phone, but scrutinises the photo in that same unblinking way. Her face is pale and stiff, dark eyes even darker. She averts her gaze and I banish the image to my gallery.

"Well?"

"That doll is…Tommy Burns brought it in as a trigger object. He called it Hetty. The idea was that the…entity…might be drawn to move the doll if it was placed in a suitable location."

I am struggling to speak. "And did it?"

"Let's just say, it did not go as planned."

"What do you mean?"

"Whatever was in the house didn't want to play with the doll. It possessed the doll as a way of getting to me."

CHAPTER TWENTY-SEVEN

One minute I'm perched on a stool and the next I'm standing up, almost hyperventilating, with my hands threaded through my hair. I feel scalded by this revelation. My son has been playing with a possessed doll. The *what if* question invades my mind. I scoop Matthew from the floor and stare into his eyes. He stares back, his gaze still cornflower blue and fresh and curious, Full of love for me. My breathing starts up with a stutter.

"This is *awful*. I don't know what to believe anymore." My voice breaks. "I cannot stay in that house."

Rowena appears at my elbow with something rich and rusty in a thick tumbler. I hadn't realised she'd moved.

"Brandy. Good for shock."

I drain the glass in three gulps and hand it back, gasping. The woman laughs. It's an unlikely sound after all the horror.

"You can stay here. I haven't talked to many people about this. I thought it was all over, and I don't even know why I agreed to do that interview, but if you like, I can show you the newspaper cuttings and the diary I kept. I'm not sure if it will help, but you deserve to have the full story."

"What about Thomas- Tommy Burns? Is that Steve's father?"

She simply nods. I shake my head.

"So why didn't Steve say something? He's acting like this is all in my head." I pace the floor with Matthew in my arms. I don't want to let him out of the safety of my embrace.

"Perhaps he doesn't know," Rowena says softly.

"How could he not know? This is huge. His father was a psychic. How could you not know that?"

"Fake psychic. His father was a lot of things. Do you know everything about your family? And do they know everything about you?"

I swallow. "No."

Rowena nods as if vindicated. "No. People talk when they shouldn't and don't talk when they should. All families have secrets."

She gets up again to collect her scrapbooks and photo albums, leaving me to mull over this. So, if the house was vacant, Tommy would have been able to buy it for a song. That doesn't seem wholesome, after what I'd read online. I was desperate to discover the full story, while all the while dreading what I might hear. But first, Rowena seems determined to fulfil her duties as hostess.

She goes about making an early lunch of oatcakes and hummus, as if there is all the time in the world, and I am not being harassed and driven to distraction by nameless shadows. She sets it all out, very professionally, on the table in the sunny window, along with a pot of peppermint tea.

"Would you prefer regular, love? I have a nice Assam."

"No, this is fine." I don't think I can manage a drop, or a crumb, but Steve's early morning cuppa seems a long way distant and my belly now has that sick, hollow feeling of hunger laced with anxiety. I do my best to nibble away at the food, as Rowena goes in search of some safe kitchen stuff for Matthew to play with; a plastic sieve, some Tupperware bowls and a wooden spoon which he's keen to use as a drumstick. She crouches on the floor in front of him and plays tambourine with a container lid. I let myself smile at the normality of it, even though the darkness is still breathing down my neck. I sip my peppermint tea.

"Do you have children, Rowena?" I ask presently.

A cloud passes over her. She gets to her feet.

"No. It never happened. I was married to a lovely man. James. We had many happy years. He died about five years ago."

"I'm so sorry."

She shakes her head, A few wisps of white hair stray loose, making her look younger and more vulnerable.

"He had heart problems. Ironic, really. It should have been me, after all that I went through, all that I put my family through…" She stops herself. "My dad died of exactly the same thing. He was only in his early fifties. What happened…broke him. He was a very rational man."

I don't know what to say to this. Even though I'm not the most sentimental of people, tears begin to prickle, but when Rowena approaches the table, she is stubbornly dry-eyed. Maybe it's one of those things that are too big to fully get your head around, even when you're a grown-up widowed orphan. I feel a pang of pity.

"Did you have to move out of your house? Is that when Tommy Burns got it?" That seems a bit blunt too. I bite my lip.

Rowena sits on the chair opposite and picks up her own glass mug of peppermint tea. Her expression is set and angry.

"Mum was forced to sell the house after Dad died. He didn't leave her very well provided for. I'd already moved out by that time. I was living in Newcastle- a bit more anonymous- and my mother took work at a tailors in Durham. She was a seamstress."

I remember the sewing machine, which has now vanished, from my first visit.

"But of course- who would want to buy a house with a reputation like 11 Devil's Lane?" Rowena continues. "Mum had to move closer to her work in Durham, and even though she knocked down the asking price, the place sat empty for ages. It got broken into, trashed." She shudders. "Pentagrams and inverted crosses daubed on the walls."

"How awful." I shudder too, imagining the ghost of all that occult graffiti underneath the current layers of paint. "Who would want to live in a house like that?"

"A psychic, that's who. Tommy bought it in- let's see…" Rowena's eyes narrow in concentration. "1985. Yes, he was in his thirties, and married. Think your Steve may even have been on the scene by then. Maybe just a nipper, like the little one over there." She smiles fondly at Matthew, who is chewing on a plastic spoon. "Tommy liked the idea of being a bad lad. Psychic Tommy, the locals called him. He enjoyed having a reputation, even if he was a big fat fake."

She gives her head a shake, an attempt to dislodge all that bad history, before reaching for one of the big blue box files she'd unearthed earlier. I note that it's the exact shade of her current specs, which is probably just a coincidence. When the lid is lifted, I'm faced with a jumble of yellowing newspaper clippings, A4 sheets of web capture and on the top, a dog-eared daisy print notebook marked 1976. Before Rowena can stop me, I lift it free of the box. Instantly my inner voice berates me. What are you thinking? You cannot read someone's diary! Rowena pulls a face at my hesitation.

"Go ahead. It's old history now."

Despite my curiosity, I set the journal aside, and pick up one of the cuttings, which feels like slightly firmer ground.

"It isn't though, is it?" The old newsprint crackles and my nostrils itch with dust. "It's still going on."

We lapse into silence, lost in separate worlds. There are no surprises. The captions scream at me: Haunted House! Horrific Poltergeist Encounters for Rowena, 16. Can He Crack the Case?

My senses prickle at this last one. I read on:

Local medium Thomas Burns has vowed to unlock the paranormal mystery at 11 Derville's Lane. This quiet row of rural cottages has been branded 'Devil's Lane' by fearful residents who say they just want an end to ongoing rumours of poltergeist activity within the walls of the unassuming end-terrace. The case has attracted worldwide media attention, with journalists, psychics and ghost investigators vying to get through the green door of Number 11. The haunting seems to be centred around attractive teenager Rowena Howden, who claims that she is being kept awake by bumps in the night, deathly apparitions and unexplained phenomena. Rowena's parents, Moira and Derek Howden, say they are exhausted with the situation and terrified for their daughter, whose schooling is being disrupted by the ghoulish goings on.

Burns, 25, is one of the youngest psychics in the region, claiming to be the seventh son of a seventh son.

"I discovered I had a gift from an early age, when I saw my deceased grandmother on the landing. I wasn't afraid. She spoke to me, telling me I had a gift and I should use it to help humanity. That's what I intend to do. This family is suffering and I think I can heal it."

Burns refused to reveal which methods he would employ to rid the house of its spectral occupants, but he was quick to suggest that if the entities were evil in origin, he would not hesitate in fighting fire with fire."

I let go of the article and watch it drift and settle on some unseen breath. It includes a grainy school head shot of Rowena, fresh-faced but still recognisable, which somehow makes the description 'attractive teenager' lurid and creepy. The papers loved an attractive teen, back in the day. The interview with Tommy Burns gives me the chills, the thought of this young guy believing he's some kind of spiritual warrior out to save her. It was bound to end in tears.

Rowena is sorting methodically through some photographs. It's hard to tell what she's feeling, or whether seeing all this stuff is triggering anything for her.

"So you reckon Tommy was a fake?" I can't help asking.

Rowena considers her reply. "I think he thought he was the business, but he got in above his head. Like most of the people who turned up, he was driven by things which had no bearing on what was happening."

"What things?"

She counts them off on her fingers, "Money- one of the newspapers paid for his story before he even had a story. Power- he was a kind of hero in the paranormal fraternity."

"Even without the internet?" I cannot imagine a world where people can be influential without social media behind them, but I guess it must have happened.

She nods. Her face is a mask, but I can see pain in her eyes. "And finally, lust. He fancied me. This was a way in. Literally."

I do not like that *literally*. What is she getting at? The whole thing stinks, and more than ever I want to visit Steve's father and see what he remembers.

"So…" I struggle to find words of the appropriate delicacy. "Were you and he…an item?"

"It was a long time ago. He took advantage of the situation. It's all in the diary." She sighs so heavily the newsprint dips and falls like a wounded bird. "Long, long ago. 1976 was the conclusion, in many ways. All the activity had been building for years. It started when I hit puberty. They say that about poltergeists and ghosts. They feed off the energy of the young."

I don't like the way her gaze rests once more on Matthew. There is plenty to say but I bite my tongue. I have to tread carefully with regard to Tommy. It is a big grey area, and it might just be possible that Rowena has faced the same trauma as me. *It's always a person you know.* I should have that tattooed to my brow. But I find myself unable to ask her. The diary. That's the key. Perhaps, like me, she cannot speak of it and she wants me to read her testimony instead. This is not what I was expecting. Suddenly the ghosts have taken a back seat and I feel all raw inside. Tentatively I reach across the table for her hand.

"Do you – shall I read your diary?"

She withdraws her hand, as if she cannot bear to be touched. I know that feeling.

"Perhaps that would be best, love. Now, do you want to heat up some food for the little lad?"

CHAPTER TWENTY-EIGHT

After lunch, Matthew goes for a nap in the travel cot, and I stay with him until he drifts off. It feels really good to be back in this cool, clean, soap-scented room. Until now, I hadn't realised how on edge I've been, how twitchy. Constantly listening for noises, jumping at shadows. This room harbours nothing but a timeless sort of hush. I haven't yet broached the subject of staying here for a few nights, but I don't think it will be a problem. Steve will be the problem. I haven't contacted him yet.

As Matthew slumbers peacefully, I open Rowena's diary. Her girlish handwriting is neat and disciplined, but her schoolgirl thoughts spill out all over the page, peppered with doodles and biro love hearts, entwined initials and references to obscure bands and song lyrics. It isn't too hard to figure out who RH and TB are. There's a book list in the back: Stephen King's *Carrie*, James Herbert's *The Fog* and Catherine Cookson's *The Dwelling Place*. Strange mix. Was that what she was after? Romance and horror? She certainly got that last one

It's a page-a-day format, and Rowena seems to pack a lot into each entry. I dip into it, searching for mention of the sort of chilling phenomena I'd been experiencing, malevolence, shifting shadows, dark thoughts, but most of it is centred around what she did at school, what she had for tea (mainly Crispy Pancakes and Angel Delight) what boring/mortifying/ unjustified things her parents said. All pretty cringy, if I'm honest.

Monday:

♡ Another week. Double Maths. Yawn. Met TB at break time. He's driving a van for his dad. Seen it parked up outside school, and we snuck out (Debs, Janice, me) and he gave us fags and chocolate. He's drop dead gorgeous- Janice was trying to get off with him but he was looking at ME. I go all wobbly when he smiles at me. He has hair like David Cassidy

Debs says he looks like Woody from Bay City Rollers but he's much dishier than him. And he's 21- so cool. He likes Thin Lizzy.

Presumably Lizzy, whoever she was, earned him even more cool points. I wonder what Rowena's dad, he of the heart condition, thought about a 25-year-old tempting his sixteen-year-old daughter with cigarettes and a sexy flick of his mullet. Girls back in the day were so naïve. I shiver with unease and flip through a few weeks until I find something more substantial.

Saturday. Not sleeping. The scratching in the walls was so loud last night. It's freaky. I don't know how Mam and Dad don't hear it. I felt something sitting on my bed. It woke me up and I'd only just got to sleep. I properly heard the mattress creak, and then it sank down at the corner like there was a weight on it and I felt it pull the sheet off me, dead slow. I jumped out of bed and stood on the landing screaming...

I feel my own throat constrict with fear. This is more what I was expecting. I can relate to this; that pull of fear so strong it glues you to the spot. How could her parents not hear anything? Maybe they were sound sleepers. I bet they heard her screaming though. What on earth did they make of that? An hysterical teenager wailing on the landing. That iconic 70s image of Kate Bush springs to mind, the flowing white gown, wide eyes and crazy hair. No wonder the media jumped on this; it must have put their circulation figures up. I feel an immediate flicker of pity for the troubled teenager I never knew. Rowena seems a million miles away from full Kate Bush. She is steady and together and… normal. Whatever that is. I read on.

It's gonna be ok. Met TB in the village and he can help. He knows about this stuff. Mam and Dad are going out tonight even tho they don't want to leave me. It's been mental lately, with reporters. Old Mrs Finlay had a go at me yesterday when I went to buy sweets, Said I was an attention seeker. Old cow. I told my folks Debs is coming round to do geography homework, but TB is gonna bring his Ouija board. He says it's the only way. Can't wait to see him. So excited!!!!!

Alarm bells are ringing now. I know she's an impressionable teen, but seriously? An unseen hand pulls off your covers to the point that you get hysterical with fear and by morning you're mooning over some lad. It doesn't add up. I read on:

I was a bit scared about the séance. I know Tommy does this all the time, Some of the Sixth Form hang out with him. They do dark Masses or something. I'm not sure about all that but Janice's face when I told her he was coming over to my house was ace! She was CRUSHED with jealousy.

I cannot wait to tell them all what happened. We light candles in my room- TD in my room!!! I have to nick Mam's white candles that she keeps under the sink for power cuts, but Tommy has some black ones. I didn't even know you could get black ones. Anyway, he brings out this Ouija board and it was so cool- all this archaic writing and magic symbols and he has a special velvet cloth to lay it on. Something about the energy. So we settled down and I was supposed to close my eyes but I couldn't stop looking at the way his long hair shone in the candlelight...

Oh, dial back on the Mills and Boon, Rowena. Can't you see he's taking advantage? There's more:

I show him where last night a book had flown off my shelf. I left it on the floor. It was *Alice Through The Looking Glass*, the copy I got as a Sunday School Prize. Tommy laughs at that.

"It's mocking you," he says. "Good little Christian girl like you. I've got something that might appeal to it."

And he dives into his haversack (he has Tubular Bells painted on the flap!) and pulls out a doll. He calls it Hetty and I know they use it at the Thing they do in the churchyard because Debs overheard one of the prefects. I reckon it already has bad vibes. It looks like one of those Victorian dolls with the blonde ringlets and rosebud mouth, but its petticoats are stained with earth and it only has one glass eye, which is all dull and dead. I fight the urge to take it from him and dust off its clothes.

"I'll set this up on the shelf where the book was pushed out. The Entity will draw near, maybe take possession of it. Let's see what it does."

"Have you done this before?" I whisper, even though I know he has. The fact that he knows stuff I don't excites me. There's a cold draft about my shoulders, but I'm used to that now. There are a million little ways in which my poltergeist makes his presence felt."

My? Him? Rowena is really owning this thing. That can't be good. It's getting late but I cannot tear myself away. This is the sort of page turner where you're kind of reluctant to turn the page and see what is lurking between the lines.

We both sit cross-legged on the floor. It's really lovely sitting here with Tommy in the candlelight. He's wearing new Levi flares. We place our fingers lightly on the planchette, just touching, and the heat makes my belly all fluttery. I cannot believe he is here in my room and we're gonna do…this. And maybe more…

Dot dot dot. Oh Rowena. What are you thinking? There seem to be entries missing, and two blank pages and then the writing starts up again. My heart is as fluttery as the teenage Rowena's hormones. What the hell had happened? The next few pages are in retrospect. The change in tone hits me like a sledgehammer, and suddenly I know. I know what happened in that dense, candlelit atmosphere, and it had nothing to do with ghosts...

When I return to the kitchen, Rowena is tidying the already spotless worktops.

"Your phone has been ringing, love." She jerks her head towards the table where we'd been sitting. "I didn't want to answer it, but I did have a peek. It's Steve."

"Steve?" A familiar twist of annoyance accompanies his name. Even though he's apparently so busy at work, he can still find time to check up on me. There are four missed calls. Four? I'm already rehearsing my argument in my head. *I refuse to come back unless you take this seriously. You need to bring in an expert. A priest to cleanse the house. You need to DO something or...*

Or what?

With a shiver, I imagine myself on a train home, back to Dundee. But no, that route is closed off to me. Steve was my only option, my salvation, and now that bridge is burning like the fires of Hell. As I return his call, I study Rowena's neat figure, her deft, competent movements as she scours the sink. I want to stay here, in this citrusy homemade environment, to be looked after. Rowena is the mum I longed for growing up, the safe, organised mum, who makes sure your uniform is washed, provides a decent breakfast and kisses you at the school gate. Poor Rowena, who, like me, has had a torrid home life.

Steve's phone goes to voicemail.

"Typical. All those missed calls and when I try to get him- nothing."

Rowena makes a face. "Better keep trying. It could be urgent."

"He just wants me home, but I'm not going back to that house." I hit redial.

"I wouldn't set foot in there," Rowena agrees, turning back to her tasks. "He'd be better off to sell it for redevelopment. That's what they do with houses like that. Start again."

"Oh wait- he's left a voicemail." I peer at the screen. I'd been so busy planning my speech, I hadn't checked the most basic detail. I retrieve the recording and listen intently. There's a second or two of static, and then...

"Kat...fell...I was in the loft..." Steve's voice, but mumbling and gaspy. What? I draw in a stuttery breath to reply, before realise I'm talking to a machine. "Rowena! He's hurt!"

The recording has ended. With shaky fingers, I replay it, Rowena peering over my shoulder, as if we might see some kind of vision, an explanation, on the screen. Steve's faint, wobbly words burst forth again.

"Kat...I fell...I was in the loft...I'm hurt."

CHAPTER TWENTY-NINE

My gaze slams into Rowena's. "Oh my God. He's fallen out of the loft. What the hell was he doing in the loft? He's supposed to be at work."

There's something else on the recording. Rowena hears it first.

"What's that...is that another voice?"

"A voice? I never heard anything."

"Play it again."

We listen intently, and we both hear it. A grunt that is not Steve, a dull, drawn-out dragging noise.

"It doesn't sound like he's alone," Rowena says slowly, and the way she says it makes my entire body freeze. I am rooted to the floor, gripping the phone so tightly it's a miracle the screen doesn't crack.

"What do we do?" My own voice is a whisper.

"We go there." Rowena's eyes are bleak. "Maybe this wasn't an accident."

We debate for a minute about whether to call the ambulance or the police or both, but Rowena's car is parked outside, and she persuades me that it makes sense to just *go*. I run upstairs and pluck the baby from the cot. He's already awake and gurgling at the ceiling. Despite all my anxious hustling, he remains in good form, merely frowning in puzzlement as we skid to a halt beside the waiting car.

"You don't have a car seat!" I wail.

"Get in," Rowena snaps. "We can't worry about that now."

I guess she'd right. It's started to rain, we're getting wet and my choices are limited. I strap myself into the front seat with Matthew on my lap. "This isn't right. I don't like this."

Rowena ignites the engine and flicks on the wipers and the headlights.

"We'll be there in five minutes."

"I'm going to call the police."

"Like I said, we'll be five minutes. We can decide then. We don't want the police involved."

"But we heard another voice! Didn't we?"

Her tight-lipped silence conveys everything I'm scared to admit about that house. Who says it was a human voice? I squeeze Matthew against me, in a way that is precarious and illegal, but I don't care. This is not the worst danger we are about to confront.

Rowena is an erratic driver. Maybe around town she is sedate and meticulous, but with the clock of doom ticking, she produces her A-game. We squeal around corners, splash through puddles and snare chunks of vegetation with the left-hand wing mirror. I swear we killed a sparrow who didn't manage to fly clear in time and it reminded me horribly of the cat's skeletal leavings. I still have a hundred questions for Rowena, but right now my mind is already in that house, floating up the staircase, willing Steve to be okay. What if he's unconscious, or injured and bleeding out? My stomach is churning like a washing machine at the thought of what we might find.

"I'm going to call the ambulance."

I jab 999 on my phone. Better a false alarm than to be waiting around for help. Rowena brakes outside number 11, clipping the pavement with a jolt that rocks Matthew's head back. Luckily, I've been protecting his skull for the last few miles. His wide blue gaze locks lopsidedly on mine. He looks drunk and bewildered.

"I know, I know," I croon. "It's okay. *Ssh*."

Rowena slips back her seat and pats her lap. "Give him to me."

"What?"

"You can't take him in there. I'll sit here and look after him."

I realise with a jolt that she has no intention of entering the house. She never had, and Matthew is a convenient excuse. She's correct though. It's no place for an infant. Reluctantly I hand him over like a parcel as the wipers continue to dance across the windscreen. I want to stay here where it is warm and dry and safe, but I have to face this. I have to open the door and place my feet on the ground. My body is so unwilling to move I mentally give it instructions, just as I'd instructed the ambulance controller moments before. *Number 11. Green gate. Front path.*

I open the gate, set foot on the path. The afternoon light has been sabotaged by black thunder clouds, and the windows of the house are illuminated; lamps in the sitting room, the bare bulb in the hall. The Crying Boy picture springs to mind. I should have chucked that in the skip when I had the chance. I'm untangling my keys, ready to wrestle the lock, when something catches my eye in Len's front garden.

Tamsin is standing there, in the rain, without her coat. Okay, teenager's seldom wear coats, but there's something about her stance, the way she's hugging her damp upper arms, the way she's letting the rain flatten her hair and course down her face like tears…Something is not right.

"Tamsin?"

She springs to life. "Hi, Kat. It's horrible out here, isn't it?"

She continues on her way down the path, even though I'm convinced that she isn't continuing anything. She had been there all along, a statue in the rain, watching, with intent. I have no time to work it out. My key turns and I am in.

The Crying Boy scolds me silently. That all too familiar smell is present. Stone and rot and age, as if something that should be firmly closed has been left ajar. I burst into the kitchen. The door to the staircase is hanging open. I hear a groan, and call Steve's name. There is a faint answer, and I race towards it, taking the stairs at a gallop.

Steve is sprawled on the landing, his head jammed against the banister and his phone abandoned near his elbow. Weirdly, the loft has never been on my radar, but now my gaze travels upward to the deep rectangular hatch, securely battened down. An aluminium stepladder is toppled drunkenly against the wall, the bookcase knocked out of kilter. It resembles a stage set from a slapstick farce.

"What on earth were you doing?" I sink down beside Steve. His lips are paper white and there's a lot of blood soaking into the carpet. He half-opens one eye and makes a noise, which I guess is a positive sign. I try to comfort him while hunting around for something to stem the bleeding.

"Stay still. It's okay- I called an ambulance. Oh God- hang on- I'll get towels."

I duck into the bathroom and return with the most absorbent hand towel I can find. I don't know what to do with it, but the injury appears to be skull-related. At least, when I tentatively part his hair, my fingers come away scarlet, so I press the towel against the likely spot. I'm not cut out to be a nurse, but I do my best to reassure him. He seems to be flickering in and out of consciousness.

"Don't you dare…" I swallow painfully. *Don't you dare die.* "I mean, stay with me, please. I- I love you, Steve. I know I don't always show it, but…you need to know this. You were never just part of my escape plan. I would have gone with you anyway. Anywhere. Please believe me."

I don't know if he can hear me. Both eyes have been closed for a while. At this point in the movies, the female lead would ease open an eyelid to reveal the white, and everyone would panic and start weeping, but what good would that do? All I can do is stay calm and listen for the paramedics. Only when I finally hear them coming up the stairs, do I allow the tears to escape.

The paramedics settle us in a cubical of a crowded A&E department. They'd told me which hospital, but it could have been anywhere. I don't have a clue where I am, and the Durham dialect sounds foreign to my ears. I feel totally at sea.

There had been a couple of strange moments as we'd left Derville's Lane. One of the paramedics had asked me if I wanted to go with Steve in the ambulance and of course I'd said yes, before remembering the obvious. I couldn't really take Matthew to the hospital. Rowena had been decisive.

"Do you have you Steve's keys? I can borrow his car. I was just having a look- there's a car seat in it."

"But I couldn't-"

"You can't let Steve go on his own. Matthew will be as right as rain with me. I'll strap him safely in and take him back with me- all his stuff is in my house, and I think I can manage to open a jar of baby food. Pop in and get the car keys."

She was so convincing, I ran back into the house. Steve was a creature of habit. He always hung his keys on the rack in the hall.

"Ready? In you get," said one of the paramedics. I could sense they were getting impatient, although they'd managed to stabilise the bleeding and Steve was a better colour. And then Tamsin had popped up out of nowhere.

"I saw the ambulance," she said. "I just wanted to find out if he's okay? Is he seriously injured?"

"We're going to get him checked out. He got a nasty bang on the head."

She'd bit her lip. "Wish him a speedy recovery. From all of us."

And then she turned away and disappeared.

A long time afterwards, two things hit me. How did Tamsin know he was injured and not simply ill? And why had the hatch door to the loft been firmly shut?

CHAPTER THIRTY

They decided to keep Steve in overnight. He had regained consciousness, but the very young doctor who checked him out seemed a bit wired, out of her depth, and eager not to mess up. She wasn't going to let him go anywhere in a hurry and ordered a battery of tests. Concerned about the blow to his head, she put him under observation for 24 hours. I kissed him tenderly on the undamaged side of his head. His hair smelled of attics, damp and musty.

"I'll come back tomorrow, first thing," I'd promised, already doing mental somersaults around fitting that in with the baby's routine. Something else had occurred to me. "I'd better let your kids know."

Why hadn't I made an effort to contact them before? I should have at least tried to show an interest. Goodness knows what they thought of me, a strange woman with a kid, latching onto the family home, and now the bearer of bad news about their father.

Steve's eyes strayed painfully to his phone, which the nurse had placed on the bedside locker.

"Call Uncle Jeff," he said.

So, I'd called Uncle Jeff, the patriarch of the family business. He seemed bad-tempered with the intrusion, or maybe with me, but promised to inform 'those who need to know.' A shiver ran down my spine at that odd phrasing. It felt like the sort of thing you'd say about someone recently departed.

"He's going to be alright," I'd added hastily, as much for my own benefit as Uncle Jeff's. The connection went dead, without him asking about how I was coping, or how I would be getting home, or whether I would be okay on my own in the haunted house on Derville's Lane. It was a nasty reminder that I was an interloper, not part of Steve's family circle. I wasn't part of anyone's family circle.

I'd left the hospital feeling lost and hopeless, and now I am waiting, alone, with Steve's bloodied clothes in a plastic bag, for an Uber which is taking forever. Plenty of time to churn over Things That Don't Add Up. You'd assume, if you fell out of a roof space, you wouldn't exactly have time to secure the hatch door. Perhaps Steve had done that before he fell? It looked like an old-fashioned sort of access, obviously not attached to one of those slinky, telescopic ladders, and the stepladder Steve had been using was a worn, paint-splattered one I'd last seen leaning against the garden shed. Maybe it had buckled, or he'd simply lost his balance as he'd closed the hatch. What was so pressing that he couldn't wait for me to help him? That was the first rule of home improvement- never climb a ladder without having someone there to hold it.

Inevitably, a more uncomfortable explanation presents itself. What if Steve had been pushed by some unseen force? Rowena and I both heard unexplained noises on his voicemail. The paranormal could not be ruled out. Steve might be an unbeliever, but I'm weary from trying to find rational answers for what is going on in that house.

As for Tamsin- no mystery there. She'd simply spotted the bloodied towel as they wheeled Steve to the ambulance. That was the second time I'd caught her in Len's garden. It was odd, but none of my business. I have more pressing things to think about.

My immediate alarm over the accident begins to subside in the taxi. I give the driver Rowena's address and sit back against the seat, forcing myself to take deep, steadying lungfuls of air. When I press a hand to my stomach, it feels empty and I cannot remember when I last ate. My thoughts turn to Matthew. He's not used to being looked after by strangers, and I hope Rowena has coped. If she hasn't- the alternative fills me with dread. I cannot wait to be reunited with my son, but the cab is taking forever. Every traffic light seems to be red, and despite the lateness of the hour, every road is snarled up with traffic. It's all catching up with me; the constant threat of unexplained happenings, the house's sinister back story, the creepy trolls and now Steve being blue-lighted to hospital. No wonder I cannot settle. If anyone pricked me with a pin I think I would burst like a balloon, collapse into a hundred worthless shreds.

At long last, the cab crawls to a halt outside Whitecross Villa, and I pay my fare with Steve's credit card and disembark. As I wait for Rowena to open the door, I check my phone. It's only just after 10pm, although I feel like I've been hanging around that hospital all night. The hall light is beaming yellow through the top pane of glass, but it's very quiet. No television murmur, or music, or even the baby crying, which would be the worst possible case scenario.

Impatiently, I ring the doorbell again, rub the toe of my trainer against the coconut door mat. It's plump and clean, unlike the threadbare one at home. I realise I'm still thinking of my mother's house as home, and the pull of it is overwhelming. I suddenly want my mother here more than anything, taking charge of the baby, heckling the nurses, spouting gloomy adages for all she's worth. The longing is so sharp I might bleed.

My gaze shifts to the side, to the empty driveway, separated from the neat front lawn by a rank of hybrid tea roses. Their fragrance drifts on the air in the gathering dark and I can just make out the outline of them, a crown of thorns against a navy blue sky. And then it hits me. There is no car. Rowena had borrowed Steve's car and it should be parked here, occupying the driveway. Matthew should be tucked up in his cot and Rowena waiting for me with a large glass of wine and sympathetic concern. I hadn't realised how much I'd been longing for all of that, and now the glaringly obvious slams the breath from my body.

There is no one home.

Suddenly, Matthew's crying is no longer the worst case scenario I can imagine. A whole heap of ghastly possibilities yawn in front of me like an open grave. What if Rowena has had an accident? She was driving a strange car on some seriously dodgy roads. I can visualise it- a bad bend, the baby distracting her with his fretful cries, an oncoming tractor.

Oh shit. *Shit.* My legs go weak. I sleepwalk to the driveway, staring stupidly at the gravel as if the bloody car might somehow materialise like Doc Brown's DeLorean. What do I do? *What do I do?* I haul out my phone. No missed calls, which is positive: my mother always says bad news travels fast. Rowena must have left Derville's Lane hours ago, just after the ambulance. That's assuming she did leave. Is it possible she decided to stay there? Surely not. She's shown no desire to re-enter the scene of her teenage torment, and she herself had pointed out that Matthew's things, his food and his changing bag, were all at Whitecross Villa, so of course she would have brought him here.

I pace back to the front door and peer through the letterbox, as if that might reveal some clue- toys dropped in the hall, Matthew's little blue jacket, Rowena's walking shoes -but there is only an echo and the faint tang of bleach. I draw back. My anxious fingers have left prints on the polished brass flap. I fumble with my phone, find Rowena's number and press call.

It rings out. I wait, fretfully. From the hall, there is an answering trill. At first, I don't get it, and then it dawns on me. The truth feels as sick and hollow as the drumming of my heart. I am calling Rowena's landline. I do not have her mobile number. I don't have a key. I don't have a car. I am stuck here with no way of communicating and no means of transport, while somewhere out there my precious baby is with a woman I barely know.

CHAPTER THIRTY-ONE

The only thing I can do is call a cab and return to 11 Derville's Lane. If Steve's car is absent, that's a problem. There should be absolutely no reason for Rowena to disappear with a child she's responsible for ...unless Matthew wouldn't settle, and she's taken him for a drive to soothe him? He always falls asleep in the car. My anxiety climbs down a rung. That might be the answer, or maybe she ran out of milk, or nappies and had to go to the corner shop.

Okay, there are answers which don't involve a major incident. It's just possible I'm catastrophising. That reminds me horribly of Steve's unsympathetic reaction to my distress at the spooky occurrences in the house; distress which now seems horribly irrelevant in the face of this new threat. I'd rather face a thousand spooks than have anything happen to my child.

As I wait for the cab, another scary beast raises its head.

What if Matthew's father has made good his threats and appeared on the scene? He's an opportunist, and he knows the address. Suppose he was hanging around the house, and he spotted the baby with Rowena and...A sharp chill shoots through me. Has he done something stupid like snatching the baby? He wants to scare me, I know that. I have the power to destroy his cosy little life. Unfortunately, he has the power to destroy mine. For months now, we have been balancing on a tightrope of fear. It would only take one of us to move for the other to fall.

By the time the cab arrives, I am in a state of paralysis, imagining Rowena forced to give up Matthew to his father, pleading, hysterical. Maybe even now she's in some police station. Surely she would have called me immediately?

I sit rigidly in the back of the vehicle, knees clamped together, hands clasped, as if by not moving I can keep myself from falling apart. All will be well. I tell myself. I'm sure I heard that at some church service long ago. My mother never bothered with church, so maybe it was a family funeral. I remember the minister saying it one time. *All will be well.* I liked it, because it sounded hopeful and comforting and I need that comfort right now. I say it time and again- *all will be well* -like a mantra or a little prayer, all the way to Derville's Lane.

The cab slows. The only car parked up outside number 11 is Rowena's white Fiat 500. She definitely followed through with the plan to borrow Steve's car, but where the hell is she? The absence of any other vehicle does nothing to set my mind at rest. Matthew's father does not own a car, unless he's borrowed or stolen one, but I cannot rule out the possibility that he has turned up out of the blue.

It takes a great effort to talk to the Uber driver. He's young, disengaged. He has no idea of the pain I'm going through. Even as I speak, he's starting to scroll through his phone.

"Can you wait here for me?"

He grunts. I peel myself from the back seat. My top is stuck to my back with sweat and my legs are shaking. I've often wondered what I'd feel like if Matthew ever went missing. I'd tested myself, letting my imagination run wild in idle moments, the way you re-examine bad dreams on waking. *A parent's worst nightmare.* That's what people call it, a situation like this. Now, the nightmare has arrived and I cannot predict or control when I will wake up.

The lights are still on at number 11. I hadn't thought to switch them off. It gives the illusion of someone being at home. Knowing what I know about that house, the thought does not raise my spirits. I can imagine that dank, peculiar smell wrapping its tendrils around the place, squeezing all human life out of it.

With a shudder, I turn my attention to the neighbours. Next door seems to be in darkness, but it's hard to judge, because the curtains are firmly drawn and they look thick and heavy, Bizarrely, I think I can hear a distant bass note of music, something pounding and funky. Not Len-type music. I walk on. Perhaps Tamsin, with her habit of lurking in gardens, might be able to shed some light on Rowena's plans. To the best of my knowledge, she was still around when the ambulance left. It's a disappointment to find Tamsin's house in darkness too. The family car is absent, making me wonder if the whole family have gone out for the night.

Tamsin does not look like the kind of teen to willingly accompany her parents for pub grub. Perhaps she's holed up in her bedroom, snapchatting with her mates. I make my way up the path and ring the bell, but there is only stubborn silence. I want to bang my head against the glossy exterior paintwork. A tear slides down my nose. I ring three more times until I have to accept that there is no one home.

I hurry back to the cab, hesitating as my fingers grip the door handle. The driver is oblivious, wearing ear buds now, lost in a world of sports pundits or rap music or whatever he's into. I take out my phone, bring up a number and call it.

It's answered on the third ring. There is a bubble of pub noise-chinking glasses, muffled banter, someone calling for a pint and a woman laughing. He speaks and the bubble bursts.

"Yeah?"

I don't answer immediately, buying time as I attempt to find the right question, to regulate my breathing, but the words still come out light, without substance and not in the least threatening.

"Where are you?"

I can almost feel the spread of his cat-like smile.

"Hi, honey."

"Don't call me that. Where are you?"

"In a pub. Stick me on video call and I'll show you."

"I don't want to see you."

"Bit harsh."

"Fuck right off. Matthew is gone. I just need to know it's not you."

He makes a dismissive noise which I cannot quite get a handle on. He either doesn't believe me or he doesn't want to know. The woman in the background laughs again, and the bottom falls out of my stomach. I'd know that laugh anywhere. Without warning, he hands the phone over with a curt:

"You'd better speak to your mother."

And then my mother's voice, a muttered, "Who is it? Kat? Why is she…?"

And then she takes the phone and addresses me directly.

"Kat, I haven't heard from you for ages. You're still alive then? Why are you phoning Billy?"

I stammer something about Matthew. At least I now know that Billy hasn't made good his threat, that he isn't lurking around, waiting to pounce. Billy is in his local, in Dundee, with my mother. In their world nothing has changed, nothing has been riven asunder and the sky has not fallen in. Only I have the power to do that, and if I do, I will be collateral damage.

"You gave him to a woman? What are you saying, Kat?" My mother's voice is tetchy. I can imagine her tossing back her hair and blocking her ear against the pub noise. "What woman? This would never have happened if you were still at home with us lot to babysit."

"Well I'm not at home!" My voice finds its strength at last." I'm in the middle of nowhere. Steve is in the hospital and the woman I trusted to look after the baby is gone! I don't fucking know where she is and I don't know what to do."

There is a pause. I hear Billy swearing good-naturedly about football to one of the other bar flies.

"Have you phoned her?"

"Of course I've fucking phoned her…"

"Don't fuckin' swear at me, Katherine."

"…but I only have her landline number and I came back to the house but she'd not here and-"

"Call the cops."

"You think I should?"

"That's what they're for. Finding lost kids. I'm sure he's not lost, and there's a simple explanation but call them, or go into the cop shop, that might be better. Pin them down. Those wifies on the phones just try and fob you off."

"Right, I will."

"Let me know what happens."

"I will. Mum…"

"Yeah?"

The silence fills again with pub noise, like beer trickling into a glass. My throat constricts, squeezes down the words I want to say. I want to tell her I miss her, like you do in normal families. That I love her.

"I've gotta go, Kat. Call me back later. It will be okay."

"Okay, bye." I cut the connection. Tears are leaking down my face, and I have to dash then away the sleeve of my jumper. Composing myself, I get into the cab and slam the door so hard the driver finally pays attention to me.

"Where to?"

"The nearest police station."

CHAPTER THIRTY-TWO

He takes me to Darlington. It's not the nearest, he says, but the only one that's likely to be manned.

"It's Saturday night. They'll be waiting for the fights to start."

Great. I huddle in the seat. I can sense him watching me in the rearview mirror. Now I've got his attention, I find I don't really want it. My brain is a revolving door of bleak scenarios and guilty secrets and I don't want to have to speak, to explain myself. I cannot get rid of the image of a leering Billy slumped on a bar stool. Affable, matey Billy. Manipulative, despicable Billy, wearing his sins as lightly as his fake leather jacket and forcing me to speak to my mother when he knew exactly what was on my mind. The thing that is always on my mind. The one thing I can never ever share with my mum.

"Are you looking for someone, pet?" The taxi driver asks.

There is no escape. I rouse myself.

"A woman I know- she was babysitting for me and I've no idea of her whereabouts. She has my son with her."

"Eeh, that's rough, like. Is she not answerin' her phone?"

I cannot be bothered to go through all that again. I gaze out of the window and watch the dark countryside flash past; illuminated cottage windows, yard lights.

"Is she a local woman?" He tries again. "It's just that- when we stopped at yon address, it seemed familiar, like."

"She's called Rowena…" I pause, watch the man's face in the mirror. "Rowena Howden."

His eyebrows shoot up. "The poltergeist woman? Jesus, she's a bit of a legend. That was the house, wasn't it? That's how I recognised it. I remember my folks talking about it. People were scared to go in there. Talk of Devil worship, there was. All this stuff is getting popular again. I saw something on Facebook."

"Yup." Popular. Social media has made gut-wrenching fear *popular*. Glumly, I turn my gaze back to the window. The scenery has turned suburban, farms and barn conversions giving way to terraces, semis and streetlights.

"And she's got your kid?"

"Yup."

"Jesus." He falls silent.

The atmosphere in the cab becomes thick and cloying, whirling with unsaid things. I feel nauseous. If we don't stop soon, I'm afraid I'm going to puke over the guy's perfumed upholstery.

Eventually, mercifully, we swerve to a halt in front of a long redbrick building. The outside is bland and institutional, the inside pretty much the same. A uniformed copper sits at a counter behind a Perspex screen. He's tapping away at a keyboard, but looks up when I approach, attempting to chase the boredom from his expression.

"How can I help?"

He sounds like a checkout operator. I swallow, compose my voice so that it mirrors his rational, neutral inflexion. I explain the situation. He seems to get it, but it doesn't alter his unhurried demeanour. He takes my details, and my back story and enters it onto his database. I swear he's typing with two fingers. I chew my lip and fidget, rubbing one toe of my trainer against the lino until it squeaks.

"Do you have Mrs Patterson's landline there?" He picks up a receiver. "No harm in trying again. No reports of any incidents matching the description you've given me of the car, so she probably went late-night shopping."

He makes it sound so simple. There is a pause as Rowena's phone trills in an empty hall. The police officer averts his eyes from mine. And then suddenly:

"Hello, is this Mrs Patterson?"

Adrenaline floods through me. I want to reach through the gaps in the Perspex and grab the receiver. "Is it her? Is Matthew okay?"

The cop ignores me. His routine tone doesn't flicker. "Durham Police here. Nothing to worry about. We're just checking up on a welfare concern about the child you're looking after-" he checks the computer. "Matthew Riley. Yes. Yes, that's correct- his mother. Oh, you did? Yes, that's what I thought. Here she is."

He hands me the receiver, his face carefully neutral. When I go to voice my myriad questions, Rowena interrupts before I get a word out.

"What were you thinking?" Her tone is low and fierce.

"Sorry?" I go cold. This does not sound like the motherly woman I left my son with.

"I popped out for five minutes, that's all."

"With Matthew?"

"Of course with Matthew. What do you take me for?"

"I just-"

"Are you in Darlington? How did you get there? I can't pick you up. Matthew is asleep."

I rally, and try to recover. In a heartbeat, I have transitioned from wronged parent to irresponsible schoolgirl.

"It's fine. I've got a cab waiting."

The policeman extends his hand and I surrender the receiver.

"Alright? False alarm, eh? It happens a lot. Most missing kiddies aren't actually missing at all."

Flushed with embarrassment, I stammer my thanks and make my way from the overheated building. The cab driver, now fully invested, demands an update. He seems genuinely delighted.

"All's well that ends well, eh, pet? Just as well." He guns the car into action. "I wouldn't want any bairn of mine disappearing with the Poltergeist Woman."

CHAPTER THIRTY-THREE

I stroke Matthew's soft hair. He's sleeping peacefully in the travel cot, blissfully oblivious. while Rowena looks on from the bedroom doorway.

"He was sound asleep in the car seat," she says. "So I didn't want to wake him up."

This is her explanation for why he's sleeping in the same stripey hoodie and little denim jeans that I'd dressed him in this morning. He'll get too hot and wake up in the night. The hood might catch on something and tighten around his neck. Is he still wearing his little trainers? Gritting my teeth, I straighten up and turn towards her.

"He's fine. Thanks."

We are being icily polite after a tense stand off on the doorstep. I'd paid the cab- not as much as I'd anticipated. Maybe he felt sorry for me- and there I was, back on the immaculate doormat, ringing the bell. This time, there were footsteps. I could hear the cab idling, either because the driver was concerned for my welfare or, more likely, he wanted a bit of gossip to share with his mates down the pub. *See that Poltergeist Woman? Remember, from years ago? Saw her tonight. She kidnapped a bairn in broad daylight.*

Such is the stuff of urban legend, misplaced mythologies, the sort of 'folklore' that Tamsin's mother had alluded to. What you don't know, you make up. I've got to the stage where I don't even know what I don't know. I'm confused, weary and a bit humiliated. The easy way the police officer had called up Rowena and got an answer, as if the emergency had only ever been in my head, makes me flush with embarrassment.

Rowena had answered the door and let me in. The smell of herby, wholesome cooking wafted from the kitchen. Nothing out of place here. She was warming up lasagne, perhaps, steaming some broccoli, with garlic bread in the oven and a glass of wine on the side. My stomach had rumbled with hunger and rage. How could she stand there, so bloody normal?

"What the hell do you think you're doing, giving me the runaround like this?" My voice had echoed fretfully around the uncarpeted hall.

"Ssh." She'd raised her dark eyebrows to the ceiling. "The baby's asleep."

"*My* baby is asleep! What were you thinking, taking off with him at this time of night? I've been frantic! You'd better have a good reason…"

She turned and went into the kitchen. If she did have a good reason, she was taking it with her. I hurried to catch up.

"I had an errand to run. Matthew was absolutely fine. He fell asleep in his car seat."

"You could have let me know! You have my mobile number."

I was right about the glass of wine. She took a sip, motioned to the bottle. I shook my head. I didn't want to let normal win. None of this was okay, and I just wanted her to acknowledge it, apologise and concede that I had every right to be angry. Just like I had every right to be scared, in that house. I was not hysterical, crazy or overreacting about any of this.

"I'm going up to check on him," I'd said defensively.

Rowena had shrugged and gone to adjust whatever she was cooking.

Now, she looks less confrontational and maybe even a little unsure of herself. How did I ever think that the white hair made her look vulnerable? She has it clipped back into wings, either side of her head, and her exposed features are thrown into stark relief in the dim light from the landing; her sallow skin, strong brows and the strained hollows around her eye sockets make her look old, tired and, if I'm honest, *haunted.*

"I'm going to eat. I'll plate something up for you and you can microwave it later, if you like." Her tone is appeasing, but I just want her to leave, so I can be alone with my son.

"Fine." I turn back to the cot, listen to the definite flounce as she turns away, her footsteps ebbing back downstairs.

Never wake a sleeping child, is one of my mother's maxims, but I don't care. I scoop up my baby and hug his relaxed body to mine, stroke my cheek against his rosy mouth, revel in his soft, sleepy breath.

I press my lips to his hair. He smells. Pulling away slightly, I sniff again. He smells…*peculiar.* It could be his hair, or his hoodie, there's a distinct whiff of something that should not be there: mould, damp socks, a sort of mossy, rank odour overlaid with… smoke? It's so alien, my heart does a triple jump. The thought of my baby being somewhere without me, someplace foreign, is too much to bear.

Heedless of my mother's words of doom, I lay Matthew on my bed, where he squirms and grumbles, eyelids flickering. As gently as possible, I strip off his outerwear and change him into a dry nappy, eagle-eyed for the upcoming squall as this new outrage dawns on him. I'm going for lightning fast and efficient, but it is really hard to dress a limp, drowsy baby. I stick a loose tee shirt on him, wrap him in a blanket and hold him close, rocking him back to slumber.

I cannot resist another sniff at his hair. The strange smell is masked by Matthew's usual baby conditioner fragrance. Laying him gently in the travel cot, I pick up the clothes I've dropped on the floor, press the hoodie to my nose. The whiff jostles something in my memory but I cannot place it. There's a certain similarity to the dusty, masonry reek that I've come to dread, the one that accompanies unexplained occurrences in the house on Derville's Lane. But beyond that…I sniff again. And then I have it. It smells exactly like my brother Ryan's bedroom, when Mum is out and he lights up a spliff. He's not supposed to smoke in the house, but he's always chancing it. He opens the window and exhales next to it, but still, his room reeks of that rank, mossy smell, with an undercurrent of raw hormones, sweaty trainers and cheap body spray.

If you distilled all that and sprinkled it on a child's sweatshirt that would be the smell. *Oh my God.* The hoodie drops to the floor.

What the hell has Rowena been doing, with my baby, in a teenage boy's bedroom?

Rowena is sitting at the table with a newspaper, her empty plate pushed aside and a glass of wine at her elbow. Even though I'm starving, and I know I need to eat something, the lingering taint of leftover cooking is unappetising. Rowena glances up from her crossword, biting the tip of her biro.

"Twelve across," she says. " 'Go forward on tiptoe.' Three words."

The newspaper is so covered in her workings-out it resembles an alchemist's journal; characters and dashes, half-formed words, random circles of letters, like mind maps, where she's been trying to decipher an anagram.

"How fucking dare you?"

This time she looks up and locks her gaze with mine. Her eyes are cold.

"What is your problem, Kat? Come on, Spit it out." She nudges the chair beside her.

I don't want to sit, or be placated or made to feel this is not a big deal. I remain standing.

"You took Matthew some place, and you're not telling me where and I want to know."

She shrugs. "I thought you'd be ages at the hospital. I thought Matthew might fall asleep in the car, so I popped in on an old friend."

"Which old friend?"

"Oh, really. Is that even relevant?"

"Yes, it is." I think of the time Steve took Matthew to see his father and I went ballistic. "I have a right to know where people are taking my child! Is that so hard to understand?"

Rowena sighs deeply. Her attention drops dismissively to the crossword once more, as if she has disclosed all she is willing to disclose. Should I mention the smell, or will she think I'm overreacting? That word again. What am I so scared of? An inner voice chides me. *You're scared to trust your own judgement.*

"I know you took that child somewhere unsavoury. Somewhere I would never have taken him. Call it a mother's intuition, but I know you did, and I *will* get to the bottom of this."

I'm glaring at her profile now. The slight flicker of a nerve near her mouth gives me a little pang of joy. I'm onto her. What the hell is she mixed up in? I want to press the blade deeper.

"Tomorrow, I'm going to visit Steve's father."

"Oh, yes?" She doodles on the newspaper, a hard, scratchy black line.

"I feel he should know about Steve, for starters. And maybe he could shed a little more light on your poltergeist story." The vague inflection on the word *your* makes her spin around.

"You know he's a bit…" She spins her fingers near her head. "I'd take whatever he says with a pinch of salt."

I smile tightly. "Really."

She turns back to the crossword. "Ah- twelve across. Got it. 'Proceed with caution'."

From the outside, Thomas Burns' care home resembles a country house hotel- imposing stone, Georgian windows, wraparound ivy. A tree-lined drive ends in a wide sweep of gravel and stone steps lead to the front door, which has been left enticingly open. As I climb the steps, I can see that the invitation is a bit of an illusion. Only the vestibule, with an antique table bearing an open visitor book, and a vase of roses, is accessible to Joe Public. The inner sanctum lies behind a second (locked) door, with 'Farthing Hall' etched in elaborate curlicues on the glass panel. In contrast to the Victorian ambience, there's an ultra-modern security set-up, with a buzzer and doorbell camera. I cannot decide whether the residents are extremely blessed to be inhabiting such elegance, or doomed to end their days in rural isolation. It could just as easily be the setting for a Hammer Horror movie and I, for one, have had enough of uncanny settings to last me a lifetime.

When I woke up at Rowena's this morning, I knew I could not stay there. I was convinced she was being deliberately evasive about where she'd been with Matthew. Perhaps she'd merely dropped in on a boyfriend, or stopped by to have a nightcap with a mate, but she shouldn't have done that with my child, the child she'd offered to look after. *That* made it my business. Rowena had broken my trust, and I had a niggling feeling that her late-night visiting was somehow linked with that house on Derville's Lane, and since I didn't want to go back *there* either, I was quickly running out of options.

To avoid having to confront Rowena again, I'd stayed in bed as long as I could, messaging Steve and trying to read between the lines of his answers:

Nothing broken, just bad bruising. They say I can get out today.

That's brilliant. When?

Not sure. It's only 7.30

Get them to give you a time

You must have missed me! Xx

He's carefully made that last one *not* a question. He must be scared of the answer. Before, I might have skirted around it, like a pothole in the road, but my bridges are burning. Even though I was quick to accuse Steve of withholding information from me, what if he is the only person I can trust? We need to talk. There are things he needs to know. But first, there is something I must do, something else I will probably keep from him. I bite my lower lip and message back:

I've really missed you. I can't wait to have you home xxx

The 'home' bit makes me uneasy.

Taking my leave of Rowena had been strained.

"I could drive you?" She'd offered. "I have to return Steve's car and pick up my own. I could drop you off at the care home and wait for you."

"No, it's fine, thank you. I don't know how long I'll be."

There'd been a distinct pause at that, as we both weigh up the implications of this visit, and she'd looked a bit squeamish, the way you do at the thought of a customs man trawling through your post-holiday suitcase.

I'd packed up Matthew's things and walked out. She hadn't come to the door, and I was glad. I wanted to make a swift, pain-free exit, but travelling with a baby is not conducive to a speedy getaway. It is undignified at best: my backpack is bulging with nappies and toiletries. There's a white rabbit and a spare soother hanging off one strap and the pockets are stuffed with emergency rusks and juice cups. Matthew himself, lording it in the sling, is an even greater encumbrance. I feel like a squaddie about to yomp over the Brecon Beacons.

Taking a deep breath, I press my finger to the buzzer.

CHAPTER THIRTY-FOUR

"Yes?" A starched voice crackles over the intercom.

"Um, I'm here to see...Thomas- Tommy Burns." There's a pause, which I swiftly fill. "I'm his daughter-in-law. Katherine."

Matthew looks into my face and giggles, whether at the downright lie or the use of my Sunday name. I stroke his head as we await the verdict.

"Just sign your name in the visitor book, date and time. Have you been here before? No? We'll send someone down."

Down from where? It all seems much more formal than I'd anticipated. I'd imagined diving in, extracting information and scuttling out again. Now I'm faced with the reality of vulnerable adults and safeguarding issues. If the poor soul has dementia, as Rowena had said, raking up the past might do more harm than good. Something else occurs to me. My biro stutters mid-date. How does she know the state of Tommy Burns' health? She'd never given any indication that she knew Steve, or had kept up with his dad over the decades. *What other secrets is she keeping?*

A young girl in pink scrubs arrives at the door. Unlocking it, she admits me with an airy,

"For Tommy? In you come."

Her blonde hair is gathered up into a showy ponytail on the crown of her head, and her make-up is flawless; gleaming base, heavy eyeliner, black brows which remind me unsettlingly of Rowena's. Even her manicure, when she re-locks the door behind us, is an unchipped candyfloss pink. Feeling lost and inadequate I follow her through a maze of narrow passageways. It doesn't smell the way care homes normally do- the ones I've been in anyway- but more like a motel. Not homely, but clean with a whiff of chemicals, as if the carpets have just been steamed. I wonder who is paying for all this. Not Steve, that's for sure. Maybe the grumpy Uncle, Tommy's brother, is more generous than he sounds.

We stop at a nondescript brown door. The Victoriana doesn't extend beyond the front lobby. There's a laminated sign on the outside which reads TOMMY in primary school script. Perhaps he is indeed a bit confused. This is depressing. I should never have come here. The girl taps on the door and pokes her head around it.

"You've got a visitor, Tommy." Singular. She hasn't even glanced at the baby. "Your daughter-in -law."

I wince with guilt. She steps aside to usher me in.

"Would you like a cup of tea? I'll be doing elevenses shortly."

"No, no. It's fine, thanks. I won't be staying long." I indicate Matthew ruefully. "Some people have a short attention span."

The girl smiles without understanding or humour. Maybe she thinks I'm referring to her patient. The man in question is sitting near the window, watching the exchange with some amusement. The carer clip clops away down the corridor as the door closes and I am left alone with a man I have never met, but whose house is now my home.

"My daughter-in-law, eh?" he says. "Did I miss something?"

It soon becomes obvious that Tommy Burns misses nothing. I can tell in ten seconds that Rowena is either misinformed or is lying. This man is as sharp as a tack.

"I just said that to get in the door. They're a bit fierce, aren't they?"

"Oh aye. Some of 'em'd give Nurse Ratched a run for her money." He gives a wheezy laugh. I can tell from the way his mouth moves that the stroke has had consequences. One side of his face has dropped, and he manhandles his right arm onto his lap. "I cannot shake your hand, lass, but sit yourself down. And there's the bonny lad? Matthew, isn't it? He cam' to see me a while back, didn't ye, son?"

Matthew kicks his legs as if he's excited. I wrestle him from the sling and place him on the carpet, where he sits and claps his hands. He's only just learned to do this and he knows it gets him attention. Tommy continues to make encouraging noises. I can feel my shoulders relax. This feels perfectly right, and normal. A woman taking her child to see his...grandad. A unexpected flicker of warmth springs into life. This is not how I expected the meeting to be.

Suddenly, Tommy switches his focus to me. He appears old, weary and stooped, a forlorn figure in an institutional armchair, but there is something magnetising about his blue eyes, as if they belong to another man entirely, a younger, fitter man, who might once have possessed black candles and led weird rituals in the woods and seances in young girls' bedrooms. I am not altogether comfortable with that other man, but I let him size me up.

"I wondered when I'd get to see ye. Steve was yappin' aboot ye non-stop the last time. I says to him, lad- I've never seen ye so happy. That's what I said. He deserves it, after all that went on before he took off for Scotland, and then *afterwards*...but hang on, ye probably knaw all that."

I shrug awkwardly. It's all a shady grey area, both Steve's past, and the history of the man in front of me, who left his imprint on my cushions, and the kitchen piled with junk because he simply could not cope. A big strong man reduced to ashes and probably tears, as he was forced to leave his home. I should have done more research, developed more of an understanding for the people whose lives I carelessly gatecrashed. And then I remind myself that Tommy Burns was not always a frail old man. He manipulated a teenage girl and subsequently inveigled the house from her mother, and a generation later, his son had not disclosed the history of the house to me. That's why I'm here.

"Steve not with ye, love?"

"Steve took a bit of a tumble, actually, and ended up in the hospital. Don't worry though. He's alright."

"Away. Is that right, lass?" He looks concerned. "Daft lad. What's he bin getting' up to?"

"He was coming down from the loft and the ladder toppled out from under him. He got a concussion and bruising but he's getting home today."

"Imagine that." He fixes me with those eyes again, as if he can see through me.

"That's the thing," I say carefully. "There's no telling what's going to happen next in that house."

His gaze darts from mine, and he claps his hands for the baby again. Classic avoidance strategy. Matthew joins in the pretence, dropping his teething ring in favour of a much more exciting game. For a moment, I think Tommy simply hasn't heard me, but maybe he's just figuring out an answer. Sighing, he turns back to me.

"You don't like it there?"

"I'm terrified. There's a ginger cat which freaks me out and a hamster corpse and a door with a life of its own and shadows in the bedroom…"

He puts up a veiny hand. "There's nothing in that house."

"You didn't see anything, when you were living there?"

"I did not, because there was nothing to see."

"Not according to Rowena."

"Rowena? Have you spoken to Rowena? Is she still running that B&B out Fordham way?"

I nod miserably. Matthew, bereft of attention produces a pet lip and starts to winge. I pick him up, and let him play with the tassely tie-backs on the very high quality Farthing Hall curtains.

"Well, well." He shakes his head. "She must be about sixty now. She was younger than me."

"You never kept in touch?"

He shakes his head and inhales gingerly with a backwards whistling sound. "Ee, no. I never stayed in touch with any of them. Got a bit embarrassing-like, once I hooked up with my missus. That's the curse of small places. You reputation lingers like a bad smell. I got called Psychic Tommy well into my forties. Embarrassing that, when your bairn gets teased about their dad in school. My old neighbour, Len, comes to visit, now and then."

"Rowena says you were a fake."

He gives a soundless chuckle. "Rowena always saw right through me! It was all hocus pocus for the ladies. I was a wrong' un and no mistake. Played up to the newspapers and all that. I was in my element. But what's past is past."

His blue eyes seem to cloud as he gazes unseeing out of the window.

"What about Rowena? She thought you could help her. That family were going through hell."

"*She* was putting her family through hell, more like!"

"What does that mean?"

"I mean she made it all up! Poltergeists my arse. Pardon my French, bonny lass."

"You mean neither of you …believed in any of it?"

"She wanted to get my attention. I wanted to get into her bedroom. Sorry, but that's the God's honest truth. The papers can say what they like but there were never any ghosts, no conspiracy, no mystery."

"No supernatural phenomenon?"

"None."

"But the haunted doll. There was a doll- it ended up in Matthew's cot."

He shrugs his bony shoulders. "I don't know what to tell you. The doll came from a flea market and Rowena is delusional. Always has been. I expect she told you she was possessed?"

"Something like that. She's been on some guy's podcast just recently."

"Still milking it."

The remainder of my regard for Rowena is upended like spilt milk. I'm having trouble breathing. Her journal had led me down a certain path, shown me a young girl struggling with real or imaginary demons. I know those demons. Even now, they are squatting at their keyboards, discussing me, tearing apart the fabric of my home with lurid fantasies. I have fallen into the same deep well as Rowena. We were flattered by our reflections in the water, the attention, the notoriety perhaps, but we have been the architects of our own undoing.

I need some space to get my thoughts in order. Tension is pinching my temples and I suddenly want to get out of here. I start to gather up my things.

"Tommy, it was good to meet you. I'm sure Steve will pop in as soon as he can."

"By, that was a short visit." Tommy raises one snowy eyebrow.

"I know, I'm sorry, but I have to get back." I cannot bring myself to use the word 'home'. "The baby will be needing his lunch and

I expect they'll discharge Steve soon and I want to be there."

"O' course you do. Don't let me keep you, lass. One thing…" His keen eyes pin me to the chair. He knows how to manipulate an audience. "Did Rowena ever hook up with someone- marry, like?"

"Yes, she did. I don't remember his name, but he died a few years ago."

"So it wasn't Len, then."

"Len? Next-door-Len?"

"Aye. I always wondered." He's gazing mistily out of the window again, back into the past. "Len and me we were rivals, you see. We both had our eyes on the same prize."

"The same…you mean Rowena?"

"Aye. But when her father chucked me out, she dumped me. Couldn't go against her father's wishes, and I had an inkling that Len stepped into the breach, so to speak."

"If he did, she didn't marry him." I was no longer certain of anything. Len and Rowena? This back story gets more bizarre by the minute.

"Ah well." His face cleared. "It was just a thought."

There's a sharp rap at the door, which opens immediately. The same blonde head appears.

"You have another visitor."

CHAPTER THIRTY-FIVE

"Hi, Grandpops."

A young woman wearing a too-warm rust sweater, stone combats and pink flip flops enters the room. I have style-envy. Her fists are stuffed in her pockets, like one of those edgy models on a catalogue shoot. She's wearing the same expression too; neutral with a hint of reluctance. Quite what she is reluctant about I have yet to discover. The resemblance to Steve is unmistakeable; solid frame, messy cropped hair of midnight black, even darker eyes and straight, uncompromising brows. I feel slightly intimidated.

She plants a kiss on her grandfather's cheek before turning to me with her hand extended. I clasp it without getting to my feet. It would have been mannerly to rise and introduce myself, but awkward with the baby, and it's too late and now she is staring at me as if I owe her some kind of explanation.

"I'm Kat. I just came to introduce myself to Tommy, and tell him about Steve…about your dad."

"Oh, that's nice," she says, although the 'nice' is difficult to interpret. Her gaze slides to Matthew and away again. "That's why I'm here too. I'm Laura. I guess we're family."

I cannot make my mind up on the 'family' either, but the last thing I want is to alienate Steve's kids before I even get to know them. A persistent little voice warns that it may be too late, that Laura is already making assumptions about me.

"I've been really looking forward to meeting you." My bright smile falls on her averted head as she turns away, searching for a seat.

She glances up. "Long overdue. What have you been doing with yourself?"

What have I been doing? Let's see, battling with unseen forces, clearing up rodent skeletons and rogue dolls… "Oh, you know- I just haven't had a minute."

"We should have a barbecue," she announces, brightly. "Once Dad is feeling better, and the builder is off the scene."

"That sounds lovely." I'm already quailing at the thought of our chipped glasses, mismatched tea sets and non-existent garden furniture, even though, ironically, the Burns family sell garden furniture nationwide. There's an assumption there too, which I don't like, but it's easier to go along with it. "Something to look forward to. We can get disposable plates and sit on blankets on the lawn…"

"I don't do meat or plastic cutlery, but yeah, it will be a blast!"

I can picture Laura blasting into our lives. She has a bullish look about her, from her blunt nose, to the slight puffiness around the eyes that suggests lack of sleep. For some reason I can see her burning the candle at both ends, pursuing her interests with dogged determination. I'm sure Steve must have told me what she did for a living, but I've forgotten.

"What do you do, Laura?"

She eyes me up for a second, as if I should know, and it's a massive black mark that I don't.

"Works in the family firm," Tommy supplies, with a raspy cough. "We couldn't manage without her. She stepped into the breach when I got ill and her father took off up north…" The cough loosens in his lungs. He cradles his chest. Laura proffers a glass of water with a speed which suggests she's done this before, that she has, for some time, been his staunch support and has no intention of letting the side down now. I decipher all this in a matter of seconds.

They are a unit, tight-knit, with no need for another two members. It feels like the right time to leave.

A different pink-clad girl tells me where I can get a bus, and the next two hours are spent negotiating timetables, bus stops and connections until eventually, we locate a Shopper Hopper that will drop us off near the end of Derville's Lane. Matthew loved the bus, staring unblinkingly through the mud-splattered window as the countryside rolled past. I'd crooned 'The Wheels on the Bus' beneath my breath as we barrelled along and he'd insisted on standing on my lap, paddling his feet against my thighs as he danced in excitement.

It felt like my visit to Tommy had achieved something- clarity. There must be a rational, everyday explanation for the things I've been experiencing. The old man had flatly rejected any notion that the house was haunted. Rowena had made it all up for a number of reasons, and Tommy had encouraged it in pursuit of his own murky objectives. There'd obviously been a lot of murkiness, a lot of deception surrounding number 11, but I remind myself that none of that has anything to do with me.

Armed with this new knowledge, I feel unburdened as I step off the bus; happier than I've been in weeks. It has started to rain, a soft, fine spray, blowing across the fields to soak the back of my jeans. I pull up Matthew's hood, and he peers out at me, flame-cheeked and curious. I hug him to me, eager to protect him from the rain, from ghosts, from this new life that I've dragged him into.

"It's going to be okay," I whisper. "Steve will be home soon and we'll start afresh. The builder will come back to finish the sun room, and we'll do the garden like we planned and silly mummy will delete her blog. All those nasty trolls will vanish like that- poof!" I blow air against his cheek and he giggles. He throws back his head and lets the rain coat his eyelashes.

The hedgerows look fresher, greener, as if they've been washed and spruced up in my absence and the scent of garden flowers hangs heavy and exotic on the air. As the end of our lane comes into view, wild hawthorn merges with cultivated privet where the pavement begins. The privet has been artfully clipped around a red post box, and under the white street sign, one of the neighbours has planted marigolds.

But today, the sign does not read 'Derville's Lane'. The sign has been vandalised. Shock swoops through me and all my sunny feelings seep away. Someone has taken white paint and blocked out some of the letter's, the 'r', the 'l' the 'e'.

It now reads 'Devil's Lane.'

I groan aloud, causing Matthew to trace my mouth with his fingers. He frowns, like a little old man with too many cares.

My fingers are so unnerved and clumsy, I nearly drop the front door key. Despite what I've learned about the deception played out a generation ago, part of me refuses to accept it. A unwelcome thought surfaces. *The house does not want me here.*

"Oh, stop it!" I scold myself. Matthew's face begins to crumple. "It's okay, baby. I wasn't speaking to you. I just need to get over myself."

The door swings open and I am faced with the Crying Boy. That's why I hate it so much, that association with upset children. His unshed tears seem luminous. I take a deep breath. There is nothing to see here. You need to get a grip on your imagination.

But there is a definite presence, as if someone unfamiliar has just left. It's like when Leanne borrows my clothes. I can always tell when they've been moulded to a slightly different form. I know. This house feels subtly altered in a way I'm at a loss to explain.

I venture into the kitchen, dropping my keys onto the table with a substantial clatter to re-establish my presence and mark my territory. The sink is just as I left it with dishes piled in the drainer, table still set with salt and pepper, and a couple of table mats with a scuffed Autumn leaf pattern. I ease Matthew's heavy weight from the sling and plonk him gratefully into his highchair. I stand for a moment, flexing my shoulders. Steve has left the butter out. Crossly, I return it to the fridge. Something still feels a bit off.

I stroke Matthew's hair absently. "Stay here for two seconds, baby. I'll just check the sitting room."

The sitting room door is closed, which is unusual. I know, even before I open it, someone has trespassed. Violated this space. Slowly, I walk across the threshold, bracing myself for what I might see.

CHAPTER THIRTY-SIX

The sitting room walls have been daubed with graffiti. Mostly symbols of the Occult: five-pointed stars, hexagrams, all-seeing eyes, horned circles and an upside down cross. In case I cannot interpret them, the artist has helpfully added SATAN ROCKS in foot-high red letters, just so there can be no mistake. Above the fireplace, the mirror has been smashed. Lethal shards litter the carpet. In the space vacated by the mirror is another bold scrawl. The message is stark.

GET OUT OR DIE

In true horror movie fashion, the paint has dripped in places, staining the wall with long melting rivulets of red.

A braver person might have done a bit of detective work, checked whether the paint was still tacky in order to estimate the likely whereabouts of the perpetrator, but I am not that person. I do not want to remain in this house for a second longer. Even though I know this is not paranormal, this is the work of a ned with a spray can, I slam the door and run into the kitchen to scoop Matthew from his chair. It definitely feels safer outside.

I walk around the exterior, checking for open windows, entry points, but nothing seems out of place. If nothing has been forced, that means only one thing. Whoever did this had a key.

My mind flips into overdrive. Who would Steve trust with a key? A neighbour, a family member, the builder. Me. Had someone had access to my keys? I wrack my brain and come up with nothing. My keys have been in my bag all the time. What about Steve's ex-wife? I've never met her, and despite Tommy's dark hints, I have no idea what went on between her and Steve before I came on the scene. Satanic graffiti isn't typical ex-wife territory though, is it? It's hardly in the same league as cutting up your husband's suits.

My thoughts turn to Gary the Builder who has been MIA for weeks now. He might have a key. One of my online comments comes back to haunt me:

I wouldn't let my baby anywhere near that builder.

But unless the genial Gary is completely deranged, why would he do this?

I need to call the police. Memories of my recent bruising encounter make me hesitate. They've probably already got me logged on the database as a complete fruitcake. The mother who thought she'd lost her baby when it was with the babysitter all along. But I am not imagining the desecration of the sitting room. Someone means to scare us, and I need to find out who.

When I eventually get through to the central police call centre on the non-emergency number, the call goes something like this.

Operator: You think someone broke into your house and vandalised it?

Me: They didn't break in, exactly.

Operator: So, you left the door unlocked?

Me: Oh no. The door was locked. I distinctly remember locking the door.

Operator: And the windows were closed? All of them?

Me: Yes, all of them. There's no way anyone could have got in. I'm thinking someone had a key.

Operator: Okay. And do you know how many keyholders there

are for the property?

Me: I don't know. You see, it's not really my house.

Operator: It's not really your house?

Me: I'm just living here. Steve – that's the homeowner- he could have given a key to anyone.

Operator: And where is the homeowner?

Me: He's in hospital.

Pause. Sigh.

Operator: Is the homeowner a vulnerable adult?

Me: Oh no, He's not like an old man living alone or anything.

Operator: Look, I'll see if I can get someone to swing by. Do you feel unsafe in the house? Is there somewhere you can go for now? If you're saying there's no evidence of breaking and entering, and you think it may have been a keyholder, I can only log it as criminal damage, and that's not a priority.

Me: Okay, so I guess it's not a priority.

I'm left with the distinct feeling that I'm on my own with this. Miss Marple without a clue.

Because I don't know what else to do, I go next door. You always leave a key with the next-door neighbour, right? My doorbell action goes unnoticed and I try to resist the urge to peer in Len's front window. The heavy, lined curtain remind me uncomfortably of a Victorian séance parlour. I content myself to peering through the letter box. The hall is a mirror image of next door, but the smell of trapped air makes me step back. I ring the bell another couple of times for good measure and wait. I'm about to turn away when the door opens with the sort of creak that jars my nerves even more.

Len's face is surly, suspicious. I expect it to alter when he recognises me, but it doesn't.

"Len, I need to know- do you have a key for next door?"

He looks surprised. "No, I don't. Are you locked out?"

I shake my head. "No, but someone got in and...vandalised the place."

"What? Last night?"

"I was away. You know Steve is in the hospital."

"I heard." He didn't elaborate. I expect he saw the ambulance, or maybe Tamsin told him. She seems to get everywhere. He added as an afterthought. "He's alright though?"

"Yes, but it could have been a lot worse."

His attitude is making me a bit defensive.

"Do you have any idea who it might be? There's no sign of any forced entry. And you definitely don't have a key?"

"Are you saying I done it?"

"No! Of course not. But someone might have stolen the key, or something."

"They might have." He looks like he might close the door. "But seeing as I do not have a key…"

Behind him, instead of a Crying Boy print, there is one of those teak hat racks that resemble a horizontal garden trellis. My mother had one, until it came apart under the weight of all our coats, and even superglue couldn't fix it. This one is in much the same condition; it's peeling off the wall. Surreptitiously, I make an inventory: one of those old- fashioned black umbrellas with a tortoiseshell handle, a woolly tartan scarf, a beige overcoat, a smart trilby and a lime-green sweatshirt suspended by its hood.

"Is that it?"

Guiltily, I refocus on the old man's face, where his suspicious expression has set like concrete. I'd handled this all wrong.

"Yes, it's fine. I'll-" I slip my phone from my back pocket. "I've reported it to the police."

"Huh, They'll do nothing. Waste of time. Got my wheelbarrow

stolen last summer and they didn't even come out."

"Still. I thought I should..."

But he is already withdrawing. The door closes in my face, displacing a draft of musty air. There is something about the smell, like a reek of perfume that casts you back to another place, another time. I am back in my brother's bedroom. Unwashed clothes, rank trainers, a hint of weed...

A car crawls past. I can feel eyes on me. It's Steve's car, with Rowena at the wheel, and someone in the passenger seat...Steve himself. But how...? Just as I'm trying to figure out this equation, the riddle of the smell hits me like a truck. It is the same odour that had been clinging to Matthew when Rowena brought him back from their mystery destination.

The car parks up and she gets out. Steve emerges from the passenger side with some difficulty. From here, he looks uninjured but I can see he's trying to keep his head still and he has a deep furrow in his brow which wasn't there before. As I retreat down Len's front path, I hear him thanking Rowena profusely.

"Don't." I say.

They both look at me like I've sprouted horns. I continue. "Don't go in. The place has been trashed. I'm waiting for the police."

"What?" Steve grips the front gate. He has an unaccustomed indoor look about him.

"Satanic symbols. *Get out* written in blood. That sort of thing." I say it very deliberately, as if I'm reciting a shopping list. I cannot get a handle on Rowena's expression. I can tell she's put on fresh make-up, rosy lipstick and a summery frock. This morning she'd been in black leggings. I feel a crazy spurt of hatred. I'm standing here, terrified, in crumpled jeans and a sweaty teeshirt, while she looks like the calmest of oceans. And what is she doing, interfering in our lives?

Steve is already hurrying up the path. I call on him to wait, but I can hear his exclamations before I enter. I cover Matthew's ears. I do not want his first words to be *fucking twats*.

"Steve, I think we should stay out. It's a crime scene. Maybe the police will need to do forensics on it."

It's just another excuse not to enter the building, not to have to lay eyes on all those vile words and symbols again. I look around for Rowena, but she is already getting into her own car. I watch as she calmly buckles up and pulls away without a glance.

Steve comes up behind me, wraps an arm about my waist and rests his chin on my shoulder. It should be a romantic pose, but given what he's just seen, I feel like I'm holding him up.

"Who the hell would do that?"

"They didn't break in, Steve. There's no evidence of a forced entry. The police were asking about your keyholders."

He withdraws contact, goes to rub his hair in typical Steve fashion, before remembering the crack to his skull, and thinking better of it.

"Are you sure you didn't leave the door unlocked?" he says

"Of course I'm sure." My temper flares. "I'm not an idiot. You're the one who's always telling me you can leave your door open around here and be perfectly safe!"

"Alright. No need to bite my head off. Look, I have to sit down." He presses his fingers into his pouchy eyes, pinches the bridge of his nose. He has three-day stubble and uncombed hair. His lips are pale. I don't have the heart to argue with him.

"Len says the police won't bother coming out. They did say it isn't a priority."

Steve sighs heavily. "If they don't come out tonight, I'll give it a lick of paint tomorrow. We can't leave it like that. All those symbols- the words- it's enough to give you the creeps."

I muster a tentative smile. "Gives *you* the creeps? I thought nothing gave you the creeps. You don't believe in all that stuff."

His answering grin is weary. "At least we know this isn't ghosts. I never heard of a poltergeist painting walls."

"Come on in." I hitch up Matthew and guide Steve by the arm. "Go and lie on the bed. I'll bring you up a cup of tea."

At least, for now, we are on the same page. We can put up a united front. This is not supernatural, this is the work of a human hand. A human who wants us out.

CHAPTER THIRTY-SEVEN

With Steve settled upstairs, I call Rowena.

"Do you know anything about this? If you do, tell me."

She swallows. I get the impression she's drinking something. Wine, no doubt.

"Why on earth would I know anything about Satanic graffiti on your walls?"

"You disappeared pretty quickly."

"Not surprisingly, given the face you had on you."

"Excuse me?"

"Well, I brought Steve home to do you a favour, and what thanks did I get? I was about to bring his car back, and I thought, why not call the hospital, see if he's ready to be discharged. Thought I'd save you the hassle of getting a taxi with the little one. I even gave him one of James' old shirts to wear. I presume his other clothes were blood-stained?"

I hadn't even noticed what Steve was wearing. That, and the fact that what she's saying makes perfect sense incites unreasonable fury in me.

"Stop pretending to be the good guy, Rowena. I went to see Tommy and he told me everything. You let me feel sorry for you, encouraged me to imagine that this house to be in the grip of demons, when all the while it wasn't true. You'd made up the poltergeist to get attention."

"Is that what he told you? Tommy has memory problems, I explained that. Oh-" she cuts off my protests. "- he may seem lucid, but we all remember things differently, don't we? Like I said, Tommy was all talk back in the day. The seventh son of a seventh son, my eyeball. He didn't have a clue what I was going through, and in many ways, he made it worse."

"And you are a liar."

"Fake or liar. Who are you going to believe, Kat? Who do you *want* to believe? If you are certain you live in a house that isn't haunted, then you have your answer." She gives a light laugh. "As you know, I love a puzzle, a riddle. Something with no clear answer. Usually, the answer is there all along. You just don't see it until the last minute."

I take a deep breath. I have no time for riddles right now.

"You've never even been to see Tommy. He says you never stayed in touch, so how do you know about his medical condition? Maybe Len told you. Let's talk about Len, Rowena. Is he the old friend you were visiting yesterday evening?"

There's a slight pause, another gulp of wine. "Whatever I say, you're not going to believe me."

"Just answer the question!"

"You seem to know it all, Kat. Answer your own questions."

And with that, she disconnects. I am fuming. How could I ever have thought Rowena was a kind, motherly person? Probably because I was looking for a kind, motherly figure in my life. She is shady and manipulative, but is she a liar? I'm no longer sure. I so want to believe Tommy, that there is nothing here, but an insidious voice keeps reminding me of all the things I cannot explain. I feel pulled in all directions until I'm no longer sure of my own mind, and that's the scariest thing of all.

Steve smells of hospital, disinfectant and all things sterile. I fuss over him, make him scrambled eggs, with grated cheddar and a pinch of paprika on the top, and hot tea with extra sugar for shock. He looks genuinely chuffed that I've gone to so much trouble. I give him some smart answer about him being no good to me dead, but inside I feel so happy to have him home.

He'd been lying on top of the duvet, and now he raises himself up on the pillows, wincing a lot. I balance the tray on top of his knees, and perch carefully on the end of the bed.

"How are you feeling now?"

"A bit like I've been trampled by wildebeest, and my head's aching."

I nod towards the tray. "I brought up your painkillers."

"I checked the rest of the place," he mumbles, through a mouthful of scrambled egg. "Nothing else has been disturbed, apart from the ladder and the bookcase, but that's all down to me. The carpet will need a bit of a scrub. Who knew your head could bleed so much?"

I make a face. "I'll do that later and I'll take the ladder back outside. What the hell were you doing up there, anyway?"

"I was just…nothing, really."

"Nothing really? You could have killed yourself."

I watch him sharply. It doesn't seem like the right time to tell him about my visit to his father, or my suspicions that Rowena is somehow involved with Len. That last bit is none of my business, but why the hell would she think it okay to take Matthew in there? Steve breaks into my thoughts.

"Don't look so worried! I'm still here. If you must know, I was putting that scraggy doll in the attic, so you wouldn't have to see it again."

"Aw, Steve." I'm genuinely touched. "I should have been there to hold the ladder. That thing belongs in a museum."

"I'm not sure we can blame the ladder. I – I kinda felt something pushing down on the loft hatch. It knocked me off balance."

I go cold. "You're kidding?"

He shakes his head carefully. "I probably imagined it. Anyway, it was really nice of Rowena to run me home. She's quite worried about you."

"Why should she be worried about me?"

He chews on a piece of toast. "Well, I told her you were having a hard time adjusting to being out in the country."

"I'm not. I like the country."

"Oh, come on. It freaks you out."

"It's this house that freaks me out!"

"Exactly." He shifts uncomfortably. "I was telling her about…all the things you thought you'd seen, and how upset you've been."

"Oh, great!" I throw up my hands. "Why not tell the whole neighbourhood I'm imagining things."

"It's not like that. She's genuinely concerned about you. She says this house has a bad history, and that it's maybe not the best place for a family home. She says you might be happier away from here."

I jump to my feet. "What business is it of hers? Honestly, Steve, I don't trust her."

"Don't be like that, Kat. She understands the pressure you've been under, being away from your family, and she was asking questions about- Well, she was suggesting that perhaps we left Scotland too soon. You know, like a knee jerk reaction on my part."

"She- she knows nothing about my decision to leave Scotland, and neither do you."

"What does that mean?"

"Steve, there are things you don't know about me."

CHAPTER THIRTY-EIGHT

Earlier...

"On your own tonight, hen?"

"You know I am."

I'm ironing my freshly-laundered jeans. My mother is at the Bingo, and Leanne is out with her latest boyfriend. My brothers, no doubt, are somewhere they shouldn't be, with people they shouldn't be with.

"You're like fuckin' Cinderella." Billy watches me from the kitchen doorway, beer can in hand. This is his perpetual stance. I've lost count of the times I've glanced up to find his eyes on me, or parts of me. Today it's my legs. The jeans are straight out of the airing cupboard, so I'm standing at the ironing board in just a strappy black top and knickers. I used to do this all the time around Mum and Leanne, and even my brothers, who would just make vomiting sounds as they passed by. But not Billy. I'd miscalculated with Billy.

He'd been in the bedroom watching the football, and I'd thought I'd be undisturbed. The ballsy part of me says this is my home, and I'm entitled to walk around stark naked if I like, and what I wear, or don't wear, is entirely my own concern. But there is another part, the realistic, savvy, female part, that understands that this is not the way the world works, that I need to protect myself.

Hurriedly, I park the steam iron and shake out my denims. They are new, a rich clingy indigo. Even as I thread one foot into them, I know what's coming.

"Don't put them on." Billy's voice is a tone or two heavier than usual.

I don't look up. It's imperative I put the jeans on, but somehow, pulling them over my thighs and zipping up the fly feels even more exposing.

"Come and watch the football. Here, I'll get you a can. Name your poison." He crosses to the fridge without even looking at me, making me wonder if I've mistaken his interest. He opens the fridge door. "Beer? Lager? Cider? Nice fruits cider for the ladeees."

His cheesy banter makes me grimace, but I need to get him off my back. I zip up the jeans while his back is turned, and when he offers me a fruit cider, I am fully dressed. There is a flicker of disappointment, but that doesn't stop his gaze lingering on the tops of my breasts.

"Come on," he says. "Keep me company watching the footie."

"Not in the bedroom."

"Of course not, ya numpty."

He laughs uproariously. "Imagine your ma coming home to that. She's cut aff ma balls with nail scissors."

I wince, but he's probably right.

Billy finds Sky Sports and we sit on the couch. Immediately, I realise we're too close for comfort, but if I move now, he'll know what I'm up to and laugh at me. I despise his mockery as much as his leering. My strategy is to have one can of cider and make my excuses. I wish the bedroom I share with Leanne had a lock, but it doesn't, and twice lately, he's walked in on me when I've been getting dressed. He's done it to Leanne too, but she doesn't seem to find his creepiness a problem.

"He's a bloke of a certain age," she shrugs. "They get like that. Look at him with his leather jacket and his cowboy hat- and that moustache! He looks like the bastard child of Johnny Cash and the Grim Reaper."

We'd giggled until we'd had to wipe our eyes, and it had taken the sting out of his behaviour for a short while, but I was beginning to dread being alone with him. I lacked Leanne's sassiness and quick put-downs and my only tool was appeasement. I'd seen the way he got when he was drunk and argumentative. He'd slapped Mum once so hard she'd had to double-down on her foundation for a week. I didn't want to make him angry.

He tips his can towards mine in a matey gesture that gives him an excuse to encroach on my space. His aftershave is so flowery I can taste it. Leanne insists he sprays himself with Neutrodol, which he gets in a 2-for-1 deal in the Pound Shop and she could be right. He strokes his thin moustache and displays his teeth, which are in surprisingly good shape, given the amount he drinks and smokes. There is such a wolfishness about the grin that I distract myself by speculating about whether or not they are dentures.

I raise my can of cider to my chest like armour.

"You're missing the footie."

"I'd rather look at you."

My blood runs a little colder. Best to try and make light of it. "Remember the nail scissors."

I feel his breath on my collarbone,

"It might just be worth it," he murmurs.

The last of the blood red letters disappear beneath my roller, and I stand back to assess my handiwork. We'd decided that there was zero chance the police were going to get involved and go full CSI on this, so I'd found Steve's stash of emulsion and painting supplies in the garden shed and got to work. With Matthew down for his nap and Steve snoozing too, I'd swept up the mirror shards and vacuumed the carpet. Obliterating the tobacco- brown wallpaper has been equally as difficult as covering up the scrawl, and it could do with a second coat, but for now, the threats are veiled. The idea that they are still there, beneath the paintwork, makes me feel queasy. Crude symbols, pulsating beneath the thin skin of emulsion, gaining power, still able to harm.

As I tidy up and double-check that I've managed to suck up every last fragment of glass, I reflect on the old saying that if you break a mirror, you can expect seven years bad luck. I hope fervently that it applies to whoever did this. I've trawled through the suspects repeatedly. Len is a taciturn but innocuous old man. I cannot imagine him being in league with Satan, and Billy, who might well be a disciple, is still in Dundee. The builder has zero motive that I'm aware of, but is there something I'm not seeing?

Tamsin might possibly be in the frame, but it's hard to imagine her being so destructive with a spray can. Bright and confident, with a middle -class upbringing – could it be an act of rebellion? It seems unlikely.

Steve appears in the doorway. He still looks tired, pale and under the influence of something pharmaceutucal but manages to raise a smile at my efforts.

"Whoever did this, they're not going to win." I state with a bravado I don't feel.

He steps into the room, head lowered, and captures my gaze in such a way there is nowhere to hide. Some kind of honesty blooms between us, as if we've been hiding from each other all of this time. It seems natural for me to go into his arms, and easy to lean my head against his navy fleece to be lulled by his heartbeat.

"I'm glad you realise it's a 'they' and not an 'it'."

"I don't know what to believe." With a heavy sigh, I let myself settle into the sturdiness of his embrace. "I've told you what I've experienced in this house, and you don't believe me. You keep trying to talk me out of it."

"I'm not. I just don't want you to…I just don't want you to leave."

I lean back, place a finger on his lips. "I'm not going anywhere. Steve. I've only ever wanted the truth."

"I keep telling you the truth. There is nothing here."

"Maybe. I went to visit your dad. He says Rowena lied all along; that there was never a poltergeist. Did you know about your dad and Rowena?"

Steve frowns. He's reeling from that fact that I've taken matters into my own hands. "My dad and Rowena? *Our* Rowena?"

"She's not *our* anything. She gave me her diary to read, and it all pans out. She was besotted by him, a real schoolgirl crush. At first, I felt sorry for her. She was supposedly traumatised by all this ghost hysteria and along comes Psychic Tommy to save the day. I thought she'd been…" I try to choose my words with care. You never want to hear sleazy things about your own family. "…groomed. She was very young, and your dad was a good bit older. I suspected that she might have been coerced into doing things she perhaps didn't want to do. Back in the day, women didn't want to call it out."

Steve looks stricken, and I chide myself for bringing it up now, when he's still feeling frail and vulnerable. Like I say, you never want to hear the unpalatable truth about your own family. It's a taboo that leads to untold secrets and misery.

"I know my dad was a bit of a lad, but-"

"Being a 'bit of a lad' is no excuse for forcing a woman. For rape."

Steve looks aghast. "You're talking about my *father*! I swear he'd never…"

"As it happens, I'm not talking about your dad." My voice sounds oddly calm, even to me. "I'm satisfied that it was a mutual thing, your father and Rowena, although with the age gap, it's very questionable. But I'm actually thinking of someone else." My gaze fixes on the carpet. I feel like I am very far away, watching myself from the doorway, a defenceless young woman ironing her jeans.

I raise my eyes, and hold Steve's gaze. "I have something to tell you."

CHAPTER THIRTY-NINE

I hear myself tell Steve things I have never told anyone before. How, afterwards, I threw those jeans in the bin. Straight after I'd shredded them with a kitchen knife. It was Billy I wanted to shred. I wanted to take the same kitchen knife and hunt him down. I had nightmares about going into his room and stabbing him as he slept, only to fling back the sheet and discover that I'd killed my mother instead, and she was lying, open-eyed, in a pool of her own blood. I'd wake up gasping, and once I'd cried out in horror and woken Leanne. I told her I'd been having a hard time at work, that I was partly true, because I couldn't focus.

"Sometimes, I get flashbacks," I whisper to Steve. "I taste his aftershave in my mouth. Fruit cider still makes me nauseous. The hideous thing was that it was nothing to him. It was like he was entitled. As soon as it was over, he zipped his fly, took a swig or beer and started watching the sport, as if somehow I was part of the fixture. I remember rolling onto my side, curling up. I was so cold and shivery. The light was too bright. My clothes were on the floor and all I'm thinking is why? Why didn't I put up a fight?"

Steve has been listening in silence. He's slumped against the cushions on the couch, one arm spread across the back of it, while I'm perched on the edge, staring at the carpet, my attention running around each square of pattern like a mouse in a labyrinth. It's odd how you focus on the miniscule when you're in distress, as if your whole existence shrinks to a spot on the landscape. Billy has made me feel so small for too long and it is a relief to finally tell someone.

Steve touches my back. Not a caress, but a simple laying down of his hand. It is the right kind of touch, and for once, I do not flinch. My spine feels like the shell of a crab, brittle and scraped clean. If he applies any pressure I will surely shatter.

"You're not to blame," he says. "*He* is the criminal. You need to make him pay, Kat. You deserve justice."

I swivel to face him. His expression is so grim I feel like he is about to break too. He doesn't try to touch me again, but when I lean in close, he wraps his arms around me and strokes my hair.

"I wish you'd told me. Our relationship makes so much sense now."

I inch back. "I wasn't using you as a means of escape, I swear it."

His eyes hold sadness and regret. "Not that. I mean *sex*. You should have said. I might have gone about things …*differently*… if I'd known what you've been through. No wonder you didn't want me to touch you."

"I've been keeping everyone at arm's length, not just you. Everyone except Matthew."

He makes a face, as if he'd forgotten about Matthew's role in all this. I hadn't. I can never forget that something so beautiful and fresh and innocent could come out of such an ordeal.

"So your family don't know who Matthew's father is?"

I shake my head. "I never told them. Couldn't tell them."

"But you have to. Your mother needs to know what sort of a man she's hooked up with and your sister needs to be protected. He could be a danger to any woman."

Fear grips me. All those anxieties come back to crush me. I raise my eyes to the newly painted wall and it occurs to me that I will never smell fresh paint again without remembering that relief of unburdening myself to Steve. Billy still looms large in my consciousness, but the truth has whitewashed his presence and like the graffiti, he has lost a bit of his power. Steve is correct. If I love my family, I have to protect them, whatever that takes.

"There's a chance that my mother might take his side. If she chose his word against mine, it would break my heart."

"I know, it's hard. I'll be here to pick up the pieces. It's a chance you have to take."

Despite the dormant graffiti, or maybe because of it, the house feels calmer tonight, safer. It's as if things have come to a head and I'm working hard to make my peace with them. Steve has volunteered to approach all his keyholders (Uncle Jeff, his father, and his kids) and find out what they know. He maintains that his son's mates may have taken the key as a prank. It isn't the first time that number 11 has been on the wrong end of a can of spray paint. They were probably winding each other up about that time back in the day when the place was a derelict squat and thought they'd create a bit of mischief. Mischief. Steve's word. A victimless word, which didn't come close to describing the panic they'd created, that horrible plunging fear I'd experienced on reading those words, dripping with menace:

GET OUT OR DIE.

"You know what lads are like, when they've had a skinful." Steve had seemed determined to make excuses, and I'd listened and nodded, as if I had no opinions of my own. That's exactly the sort of mindless lunacy my own brothers, out of their skulls on special lager and skunk, might have got involved with. As much as my brain longs to accept this explanation, my body refuses to compute. It suspects a trick. How else can I explain the tightness in my throat, the constant weight on my chest?

I cannot leave this place. I need to make this life work and now that I've confided in Steve, I can see a way forward at last. We are a team, and…and I do love him. Despite my primitive brain's attempts to hold my system in some kind of lockdown, a little spurt of pure joy escapes. I crave happiness, normality. Could it be within my power to find that here, at number 11, Derville's Lane, if I can only lay the ghosts to rest?

As Steve deals with his pasta bake, I decide to take Matthew for a walk. We go through the gate in the back garden and set off through the trees. The sun is setting somewhere just out of sight, and the sky above the canopy resembles poached salmon, with clouds like silver-grey skin. The place looks just as it did on my last visit, but now I give a wide berth to the tree where Bobo was found hanging. Taking deep breaths, I force myself to relax and recalibrate.

"Someone probably found Bobo and hung him on a branch," I tell the baby. "Old people do that all the time. Gate posts and walls are full of baby hats and odd gloves and kicked-off shoes. It's a thing."

In response, Matthew catches the ends of my hair in his fist and piles it into his mouth. I extricate it carefully.

"The shadow in the bedroom- just a trick of the light, exactly as Steve said. And all that babble on the baby monitor- it was probably picking up some other wavelength. Police, or a cab company. The doll…"

How could I explain the doll? I was tired, the room was dark. I picked up the doll from one of Tommy's old boxes, thinking it was Bobo, or Mr Fox or one of Matthew's other toys…That rationale seems flimsy, even to me.

At the top of the hill, I sit on a stone, remembering my first days here. The birdsong soothes me. I jiggle Matthew on my knee and try to identify all the separate calls. I'm no child of nature but I manage to spot a blackbird wobbling on a sprig of conifer, its fluid notes more piercing than the rest. I point it out to Matthew, try and copy its whistle for his entertainment, making him giggle. Even though its creeping towards his bedtime, he looks very wide awake. His joy in everything, from trees to birds to pebbles, is infectious. I feel totally alive and in the moment. *Fresh start, fresh start, fresh start.* This new mantra kicks off in my brain, as persistent as a song thrush.

In my back pocket, my phone trills. I thought I'd put it on mute. I really don't want to look at it, not now, but the pull of the screen is irresistible.

It's a message from Leanne.

Don't want to worry you, but they're at it again on that Facebook group...

MountainAsh: The word is that there's been new phenomena at the house on Devil's Lane

Melody Hughes: You're kidding!

Jane Merriman: OMG IT'S STARTING AGAIN!!

Bill Bunter: Details? How do you know this?

Mountain Ash: I have a source. Photos to follow.

Posted to the comment line is an image of the street sign with the whited-out letters. Devil's Lane. And then, another. The interior of the sitting room with the hypnotic pentagrams, the dripping, red-blood scrawl. The words GET OUT OR DIE.

Jane Merriman: OH NO! What's going to happen to that baby?

Melody Hughes: She's doing it, the mother. You can see from the blog she just wants to monetise the poor child. She's looking for attention.

Mountain Ash: No, she isn't. This is for real. Graffiti in a locked house? It's the Entity. It's returned. That place is a portal between dimensions.

This is followed by a link to a website, which, when I click on it, prompts a security warning. Immediately my imagination travels to the murky edges of the web; dark entities murmuring about even darker entities, picking over the bones of my mind like carrion crows. What have I done? Mountain Ash is not finished.

Mountain Ash: This is concerning too...

Another image. The hallway. Our Crying Boy print.

Bill Bunter: What idiots! That's asking for trouble, right there.

Jane Merriman: WHY? WHAT DOES IT MEAN?

Elan Del Silva: They'll never find luck in that house. It's a disaster waiting to happen. Check this out..

Another link, leading to yet another paranormal blog:

'The phenomenon of the Crying Boy painting was born one morning in 1985. The Sun, at that time the most popular tabloid newspaper in the British Isles, published under the headline: 'Blazing Curse of the Crying Boy,' the story of a Rotherham couple who blamed a devastating fire at their home on the painting, which they believed to be cursed. They were not alone. Before long, the story gathered momentum, and a rash of fires all over the United Kingdom were blamed on the cursed child. The pattern in each one was the same. Nothing was left intact but for the painting itself, which remained unblemished.'

I cannot read any more.

This person- this troll- has been in my house, or they have

obtained images from the bastard who carried out the crime. I need to report this to the social media platform, to the police, but I feel so powerless. Weakness floods through my body, real, physical weakness. When I stand up, I can almost feel my energy seeping into the earth. I am a drained battery.

It crosses my mind that whatever it is that inhabits this place wants me like this.

CHAPTER FORTY

"I need to find out who these people are!"

"You don't. You just need to delete your accounts and stop sharing your life with them," Steve says flatly.

"But they've been in the house!"

"Old images. There are probably loads of pictures from back in the day when this place was sitting empty."

"What about The Crying Boy?"

"Bullshit. That could be a print on anybody's hall wall."

That makes me pause. Could he be correct?

I glower at him doubtfully. "But even if that's true, the Eighties graffiti isn't going to match the recent stuff. The photos are identical. Unless it's some kind of copycat stunt?"

Steve sighs heavily. I can smell his tuna pasta bake crisping in the oven. He would rather be anywhere but in this conversation, and to be honest, so would I. I keep thinking about that fresh start I had promised myself, with my secrets revealed and all the supernatural shite explained away. It had seemed so easy, but I should have known better. This house has a stranglehold over us.

"I need to find out the identity of these people," I repeat stubbornly.

"Keyboard warriors. They have no limits, no filter. All you're doing is adding to the feeding frenzy. They'll do anything for a bit of attention."

I think of the teenage Rowena. Was that what she was doing? Stoking that media storm with crumbs of invention? Posing for photos in her school uniform, and getting her teenage kicks from appearing on page 13 of The Sun? And here am I, inventing, titillating, performing for 'likes' while the same strangers dissect me and share out the pieces.

I sink onto one of the kitchen chairs.

"What have I got myself into?"

"It stops here." Steve appears in my line of vision, his hands sunk into claw-like oven mitts. I feel an overwhelming affection for him. I rise slowly from my seat, tears already dripping onto the floor. The crab claws encompass me, and there is something so homely, so right about it, it makes me weep all the harder.

Steve eases me away from him, wipes a stiff, padded thumb beneath my eye, which, in other circumstances would have made me giggle.

"This is what you do," he says, in a voice designed to cut through my arguments. "Report the Ghost group to whoever moderates these things. Deactivate your blog and block all these so-called followers. And that *thing-*" he jerks his head towards my phone, lying innocently on the table. "Get rid of all these bloody apps. Would you carry around a bottle of poison in your back pocket?"

I sniff. "No."

"Why?"

"It could fall into the wrong hands, or leak or...cause havoc."

"Hmm." Steve leaves me standing, picks up the phone and waggles it, the way you'd shake a box of Smarties at a naughty child. "These things should have a health warning."

I wipe my own cheek, follow the tender track Steve had touched. "You're right. I've been carrying around all that toxic stuff."

Steve smiles, not in a smug way, but with a tender sadness.

"There is an off switch."

He hands over the phone and watches as my screen fades to black. I imagine all those weird figures, hiding behind fake identities- Melody and Mountain Ash, Bill Bunter and Elan Del Silva and even vacuous Jane Merriman with her pathetic shouty capitals- crying out in frustration as they vanish down a drain, a whirling vortex to oblivion.

The next morning, I feel better. Usually, the first thing I do is check my phone, but when I pick it up, the screen is still resolutely black, and then I remember what had transpired the night before. I'd amazed myself by taking Steve's advice. After our meal, he'd brought down the laptop, and I'd deactivated by blog and closed my account. It was weird, giving over control to someone else, but it felt like a turning point. This is what trust feels like, I thought.

Afterwards, with Matthew tucked up in bed, we'd fallen asleep in front of a movie and then staggered up to bed. For the first time since I'd been assaulted, I could actually imagine myself making love with a man. We didn't. Steve's analgesics saw to that, but it was perhaps this very lack of pressure that allowed me to snuggle up to him without fear. I'd let my hands wash over the steadfast plane of his back, and he'd stroked my face and kissed my eyelids. I'd fallen asleep with my face pressed into the curve of his throat, and his hand cradling my bottom. I learned a new word, intimacy. This is what I want, I congratulated myself as I drifted off to sleep. Full disclosure, trust and intimacy. Secrets are hard to keep, destructive, but *this...This* is something to hold fast.

Ironically, it's the closeness that wakes me in the night; I am sweating, and have to peel myself away from Steve and kick off the duvet.

She's doing it, the mother. Looking for attention. Graffiti in a locked house?

Even though I've done the right thing by pressing the 'off' switch, the comments are still living rent free in my mind. They are inescapable. They accompany me to the bathroom, and into Matthew's room as I hover over his cot. He is fast asleep, spreadeagled like a starfish. *She just wants to monetise the poor child.*

Sick to my stomach, I creep back to the bedroom to collapse onto my pillow, but sleep eludes me. Melody Hughes, Mountain Ash, Elan del Silva- they wail like ghosts in the haunted attic of my brain.

Graffiti in a locked house?

I sit up abruptly. Who knew the house was locked? Someone who'd been present, that's who. A person who had tried the handles and the windows and discovered another way in. Someone who had turned the key in the lock...

Melody Hughes, Mountain Ash, Elan del Silva.

Mountain Ash...

That's it! Mountain Ash. Rowena...rowan, another name for Mountain Ash.

"Steve!" I descend on the mound beside me. "I think I know who it was! And who's been trolling me!"

Steve's head appears, slow and dishevelled, eyes screwed into slits.

 "It's not even light. What are you on about?"

I round on him. "It's Rowena, I'm sure of it. There's something about her- she's been dishonest from the start, lying about the ghosts, letting me think she was a victim, when all the time..."

Steve sits up, scrubbing his face with one hand. "She looked after you when I had the accident and brought me home from the hospital."

"She was trying to inveigle her way in."

"I'm not sure about that…"

"She has a motive. I just have to find out what it is."

Steve groans and collapses onto his back. "You're seeing things that aren't there."

"What if the answers are all there in front of us?" I demand. "The writing on the wall."

I am alone in the house with the smell of new paint. It sits uneasily at the back of my throat. Steve has gone back to work, although I'd pleaded with him not to, tried to badger him into another day of rest. He was showered, dressed and making up his sandwiches by 8 am, and short of holding onto his leg like a toddler, there was nothing I could do. When I first met Steve, I hadn't thought of him as someone with this sort of work ethic. When I thought of him at all, I imagined him cruising in his taxi, having a bit of banter with the late night punters, sharing his patter with the ladies. Affable, relaxed, a one-arm-resting-on-the-window sort of guy. I'm sure cab driving is right up there on the list of stressful occupations, but Steve made it look easy.

He's changed since we came here. There are new lines around his mouth and every night his stubble grows in grey. I'd watched him shave this morning, examining his reflection in the mirror with the sort of scrutiny I couldn't muster face-to-face. He'd scraped away at his whiskers the old-fashioned way, a Gillette razor slicing through meringues of foam. It was easy to imagine a younger version of him with his father, in this very bathroom, learning the finer points of exfoliation, the place reeking of the peculiar scent of men's toiletries. Butch floral, I've always thought. My mind strays to Ryan and his Africa body spray, and I feel a pang of homesickness.

Had Steve lost weight? There was a slackness around his clavicle as if he's losing muscle. Steve has always been about muscle and strength and dependability. I'd felt suddenly scared, an urgent, deep-seated stab in the bowels. While I've been scanning my surroundings for ghosts and ghouls and nefarious things, Steve has been wasting away before my eyes.

"Tell me what's wrong." My voice was so small it got lost beneath the thunder of the running tap. But he heard me. Like the Phantom of the Opera, one portion of his face still covered in white, he turned towards me for a second and then back to the task in hand. his eyes crinkling in a sad smile.

"Nothing. I'm fine."

"That's exactly what men say when they're not fine."

He'd scythed through the remaining foam. "Just a bit of family stuff. Nothing to worry about."

"Is it Laura? Is there anything I can do? Why don't you invite the kids round? Laura suggested having a barbecue…"

"No."

I'd taken a step back. "It was just a suggestion. Although when she said it, I was a bit worried about how we're fixed for entertaining. When is the builder coming back? By the time we get a sun room, the sun will have retired for the winter."

"Just leave it, will you?" He'd rubbed his face with a white towel, hiding his expression from view. He never normally snapped at me. It was new and strange.

"Okay. I still don't think you should be rushing back to work. That uncle of yours must be a shit boss."

The towel dropped. There was such a bleakness in his eyes, I was reminded instantly of Laura. It's a mistake to think that brown eyes don't have chilly depths.

"It's just I have a lot of ground to make up with a lot of people."

"What's that supposed to mean?"

"*Leave it.* Have you seen my denim shirt?"

I'd watched him from the hall, zapping his car lock with the impatience of a younger, cut-price Jeremy Clarkson and climbing aboard without a backward glance. I may be none the wiser about his problematic family dynamic, but he has left me with a mission, should I choose to accept it.

CHAPTER FORTY-ONE

He'd suggested it the night before as we cuddled in bed.

"Why don't you write to your mother?"

"Write to her?"

"Sometimes it's easier to write things down. You need to tell her what you told me."

I'd physically shifted away from such an idea and he'd tightened his embrace, as if that alone would force me to see the benefit of his suggestion. I thought about it, lying quietly with the comfort of his warm breath against my scalp. I know I have unlocked a box and Steve will see to it that it remains open.

"Okay." I take a deep breath. "I can do that."

"Write a letter, stick it in the post box. That's all you have to do. The simple truth. The ball is in her court then."

"I know what'll happen. I'll get a phone call and she'll be yelling and shouting abuse and threatening violence. She *knows* people, that's what she always says. She *knows* people."

"She's not going to hurt her own daughter."

"She already did." I didn't want to burst into tears again but my throat was tight from holding back the dam. "She should have known. She should have spotted what Billy was up to, with all his slyness and his watching, and headed it off. She should have *known*."

"Life is full of *should haves*," Steve had said gently. "People make mistakes. You've got to let them make amends."

What *should haves* does Steve have in his past? Sighing, I lug Matthew into the sitting room and set him up in a corral of toys and safe household plastics. He is very fond of measuring jugs and sieves and I promise him, that once Mummy has completed her mission, we will go outside and play with the sieve in the builder's sand pile.

I find proper, lined notepad in one of the sideboard drawers. It smells faintly of lavender, or perhaps mothballs. I wonder if it's a relic of Steve's anonymous mother. His father's presence so overshadows this place, how can the ghosts get a look in? The thought of ghosts prickles the back of my neck, as if I have let down my guard and they are reminding me that they are assembling, just a mere breath away. I gather up the notepad, an envelope and a selection of biros and plonk myself down on the couch. I rest the pad expectantly on my knee. The first three pens are dry, so I chuck them in the direction of the fireplace. The fourth one I chew, as I try to marshal my thoughts.

Matthew loses his rattle and starts to whine. I watch him as he grunts his way onto his stomach and crab crawls towards mischief, propelled by one determined little knee. He's so independent and stubborn, taking after me, in that respect. My mother taught me how to be resilient and ballsy and not to ask for help, or to expect it. Maybe that's why I don't know what to write. I know she loves me, but I don't expect help, or empathy or understanding. All I can do is write down the truth. I don't even know where to start.

Dear Mum,

I don't even know where to start with this letter. It was Steve's idea to write it all down. I've been keeping something to myself for too long, and when you do that it's really hard to let go of it.

You know I love you Mum, but something happened that you

should know about…

Over by the sideboard, Matthew starts to cry, an angry little bleat. He's managed to get himself stuck under there. He's realised he's in the dark, heading down a one-way track.

"I know the feeling," I mutter as I go to rescue him. Not for the first time, I wish I had a mum like me.

With the baby down for his nap, I nip out to the post box, bearing the scrapings of my soul in a blue envelope with a second-class Christmas stamp I found in my purse. I'm not happy about leaving Matthew, but I can literally see the post box from the front gate, and as I approach, I realise that Charlie, Tamsin's dad, is engaged in a spot of neighbourly DIY. He's couching on the pavement beside the street sign, dabbing black paint on the missing letters, obliterating the 'Devil' and restoring 'Derville' once more.

He twists round to smile at me.

"Bloody kids!" he says. "This happens quite a lot."

"Does it?"

I pop the envelope into the post box. His presence somehow lessens the agony of hearing it plop to the bottom, knowing that it will soon be winging its way north to destroy my family.

Charlie has a calming presence. He rises to his full height, a good eight inches taller than me, and looks like he wants to shake hands, but that would mean putting down his painting stuff,

I hold up my palms.

"Carry on. You're doing a great job."

He shakes his head at the sign.

"The power of words. Rearrange a few letters and boom, you have a whole new, sinister meaning."

I think of Rowena messing around with her crosswords and anagrams.

"Some people like a bit of wordplay."

"And some people like to cause mischief."

Mischief. The same word Steve had used, the get-out-of-jail free card.

"We had the same kind of mischief yesterday. Someone spray painted our lounge."

"No!" Charlie tosses the paint brush into the pot and sets it on the wall, as if he expects to have to catch me if I faint or something. His concern is quite gratifying, so I elaborate, telling him about the Satanic symbols and the hateful words. He looks a bit sick.

"Oh, my days. That's awful. Do you want a hand?" He glances doubtfully at the small pot of paint. "I have some white emulsion?"

I smile at him. "It's sorted, thanks. The police didn't seem inclined to come out and - well, I think they thought it was an inside job. Nobody broke in. They must have had a key."

"Oh!" Charlie raises his hands as if that explains something I can't yet see. "Joel. Bloody Joel."

"Who?" I wrinkle my brow.

"Tamsin's boyfriend. He's Len's grandson. He lives there."

"He …oh, that's why Tamsin was going to visit Len!"

Charlie grimaces. "Try keeping her away. Kat- you don't mind if I call you that?- I try to see the best in everyone, but Joel Langton is bad news. He has a lot of issues, which in my opinion stem from pot, but nobody listens to me and Len lets him do whatever he likes. It's not altogether Joel's fault, I have to say. His parents died in a car crash about five years ago." He acknowledges my sharp intake of breath and carries on. "The parents been to visit relatives, leaving Joel with his grandad. They had car trouble on the way home, so they pulled onto the hard shoulder to call for help. The first that Len knew about what happened was when the police showed up at his door. A lorry driver on his mobile had ploughed straight into them. Both killed outright."

"Oh no! That's awful."

"It was, and in one way, I feel sorry for the lad. He's obviously traumatised, but there's a limit, you know? At the start, we invited him over for tea, that sort of thing, but he became more and more withdrawn, he dropped out of college and now…" He gives an elaborate shrug. "I bet that's your culprit. Does Len have a key?"

"He says he doesn't."

Charlie gives me a look that suggests he doesn't believe that for a minute. "Devil's Lane…" he indicates the sign. "Pentagrams on your walls. Joel is your man."

Thanks to my vivid imagination, I can almost hear a bleak wind whistling down the quiet lane and the sky seems to darken. I back away, remembering with a twist of guilt that I've left my baby asleep in an empty house.

"I- I have to go." I indicate the direction of home. Charlie's expression slips from pensive to concern. Like all helpful people, he has a burning desire to rescue me.

"Do you want me to speak to Len, about Joel?"

"No, no, it's okay. I'll tell Steve. Maybe we can get the police to have a word, frighten him off."

"Yes, I expect that's best. He could do with a short, sharp shock. He needs to get out of that house, get a job…"

"I have to go." Head down, I hurry away. I can imagine Charlie's narrowed gaze fixed on my back. What is he seeing? A harassed, hesitant woman, scared of her own shadow? Maybe he feels sorry for me. The Bakers don't seem like the sort of neighbours who would willingly get mixed up in the sort of things which happen at my end of the terrace.

I hope that Matthew is still asleep. I'd planned to be two minutes tops, stick the letter in the post box and sprint back, but Charlie and his weird DIY task had completely derailed me. The front door opens without incident. The Crying Boy seems oddly luminous, his tears multi-faceted globules, set to quiver and fall at any moment. With more roughness than necessary, I grab the frame and turn the image to the wall, slamming it with unnecessary force against the wallpaper. It gives me a measure of satisfaction as I march into the kitchen.

The staircase door is closed, even though I left it open. I always leave it open when Matthew is upstairs, so I can hear him. But now it is closed. I approach with caution. There is no indication that Matthew is awake. If he wakes after a restful sleep, you can hear him chirping away to himself, practising the words that are still unformed in his head. If something wakes him up, he emerges from rest as a snotty-nosed disgruntled mess, with a red face and real tears, which, recently, has made me think uncomfortably of the Painting That Shall Not Be Named.

Suddenly, I hear a sound, a sort of dragging, banging noise; the heavy duty sound of furniture being moved upstairs. My heart misses more than one beat. Poltergeists move things. I've seen the evidence. My inner voice tells me not to be so stupid, that it's all a big hoax. There is *nothing here.*

But there is.

Another voice enters the fray, stronger than any logic.

You've always known there was something wrong with this place.

I feel frozen with fear, my feet welded to the spot, but my baby is upstairs and I *have* to move. Whatever is making that noise…An involuntary moan of stark terror leaves my throat.

I have to get to him.

Whatever that thing is…I have to get to my baby first!

CHAPTER FORTY-TWO

I fling open the door. The gloomy staircase lies in wait, yawning upwards. The landing light is swaying. I can see the yellow glow making patterns on the walls like a magic lantern. It is the middle of the day – had I even turned the light on? I am suddenly a cartoon mouse, moving so fast it feels like I'm windmilling in reverse. The steps take on mammoth proportions, a moving carpet of bumps and obstacles out to trip me up. By the time I reach the landing I am gasping for breath.

The bookcase has been moved. That's the first thing I notice. It's slanted away from the wall as if the unseen furniture movers have been interrupted. I stare at this inanimate object until my eyeballs threaten to burst, as if I am willing it to move, to betray its secrets, to do *something*. And then, the faintest sound of closure draws my attention ceilingwards. I did not actually *see* anything move, but a thin veil of dust has been displaced in the fretful glow of the landing light. Unless I'm very much mistaken, that sound was the loft hatch being firmly closed.

Matthew is just waking up. I grab him unceremoniously from the cot and run with him, protesting loudly, down the stairs. My foot slips near the bottom, jolting us both into the kitchen, and land heavily on one knee, nearly dropping the baby. Sensing his almost-fate, Matthew starts to cry in earnest, ear-splitting shrieks which, for once, I ignore. I run outside, and down the path, leaving the door standing open. With luck, Charlie will still be painting. *Please be there, Charlie. Please…*I stand at the gate and yell.

"Charlie! Come quick! There's someone in the house!"

He is at my side in seconds, as if he had a hunch about me and has been loitering with his paint brush ready to dive into action. He comes over all FBI, and I wonder if in a past life he was in the military.

"What location?"

"Upstairs landing. I think there might be someone in the loft..."

He is already gone, sprinting into the hallway, turning right at the backwards-facing Crying Boy and I follow, a little slower, with Matthew, bemused and sullen, in my arms. Charlie takes the stairs two at a time. When I catch up with him, he's examining the top of the bookcase.

"Have you seen this?" He's still holding the paintbrush, and uses it to point out evidence as if he's been dusting for prints. At first I see nothing but dust, and then it reveals itself- a footprint.

"Looks to me like the intruder has been using this bookcase to boost themselves up into the attic. That's why its shifted."

I stare at it doubtfully. "That might be Steve's footprint though, from when he fell? Maybe he kicked it, trying to save himself, or something."

"Does he wear trainers?"

"Yes,"

"Converse?"

"Um...I doubt it. Just generic trainers, I think. He probably buys them in Primark."

Charlie narrows his eyes and stoops closer to the furniture. He's doing a good impression of Hercule Poirot.

"Look at that diamond pattern. Definitely Converse."

"Are you an Agatha Christie fan?"

"Nope. Tamsin walked in some newly laid concrete last summer. Her footprint is immortalised like on Sunset Boulevard, and she wears Converse with tread like that."

His face takes on a gloomy aspect, and I can guess what he's thinking. The stepladder is still languishing against the wall in the bathroom – I never did get around to taking it outside. With Matthew on one hip, I manhandle it towards Charlie, reflecting on how babies definitely slow you down in a crisis. All those Attenborough documentaries where the impala or the zebra fall foul of a lion because the youngsters hold them back- it all makes sense. If I put Matthew down, he'll crawl towards the stairs; if I return him to his cot, he'll scream blue murder. Thwarted, I can only observe from the foot of the ladder as Charlie clumps his way to the top and lifts up the hatch. A rush of cold air reaches my nostrils, and that damp stone stink from before. Ash, soot, brick dust; the bouquet of chimneys, roofs and crawl spaces.

Charlie vaults into the roof space with measured grace, heedless of his neat slacks and polo shirt. His voice takes on a new disembodied form, as he recounts his findings with the tone and speed of a buildings inspector.

"Evidence of some kind of visitation. Mice, most definitely. Mummified rodent corpse here, and…pigeon feathers. They must be getting in somewhere. Place could do with a good clean…" He makes a spluttering sound that suggests a mouthful of cobwebs.

"Any *human* evidence?" I call up to him.

"Well…" There's a pause. "Several empty beer cans, a half-full bottle of lemonade, some crisp packets and …looks like a plastic box of…muffins?"

My mouth gapes. "I made those muffins ages ago. I thought Steve had taken them to work!"

"Nope. Here they are. So, yes. Plenty evidence of human occupation. No sleeping bag, or anything so, as I suspected…"

I hear his shoes clump over the rafters. A shower of dust coats my hair. Automatically, I move Matthew away from the hole, and although Charlie is speaking, I cannot make out his words. It's like he's gone into a tunnel and I am on the other end of a vital call. I cannot stand it any longer.

"Charlie, come down, I want to go up there. I want to see what's been happening. It's been driving me crazy for months and I need to get to the bottom of it…"

I'm ranting. Charlie's head appears, his hair and goatee shrouded in grey powder.

"I'm coming down," he calls helpfully. I watch his steady tread on the ladder.

"When was the last time you held a baby?" I ask sweetly.

Each rattly rung of the ladder feels like a step nearer to some awful disaster. This is like entering a mine in reverse. I don't like heights. I hate small spaces. In particular, I hate what might be up here, but I have to go. I can hear Matthew, safe in Charlie's arms, practicing a word which might, at a pinch, be *mama*.

"Be back soon," I croon without conviction. The black rectangle swallows my head and I am lost, suddenly part of this alien world of mildew and creepy things. It reminds me of the game show where they put a Perspex square of creepy crawlies on a celebrity's head. Even watching that on the TV made me want to scream. There's a huge gap between the top of the ladder and the loft hatch, and I'm forced to channel the young athletic me, the pre- pregnancy version, who could run for the night bus and bound up the stairs to the top deck as the vehicle swayed precariously around the city centre. I manage to heave my backside onto the edge of the opening and teeter there for several minutes.

"It's not floored," Charlie calls up. "Keep to the joists or you'll fall through."

"Great." I clench my teeth and rise cautiously to my feet.

Charlie has switched on a bare bulb which is doing its best to illuminate the space, helped by daylight struggling through a square skylight. It also illuminates silver skeins of cobwebs, looping between the rafters like Christmas garlands. Below the skylight, a peculiar organism that looks like some kind of fungus, clings to the beams. I wrinkle my nose. Who in their right mind would want to linger here?

Stepping away from the safe rectangle of the access, I search for the evidence Charlie had noted: beer cans, plastic lemonade bottles, crisp packets. Whoever has been here has a fondness for Monster Munch. The mundanity of it all infuriates me, and then I come face-to-face with Hetty the Haunted Doll and all complacency deserts me. It's lying on top of a box, and looks pretty much as it did the last time I saw it, and the effect it has on me is pretty similar too. My insides shrink with a primal dread. The doll stares with its one eye towards the skylight. I have a visceral urge to smash the glass and hurl it into oblivion,

"Calm down," I mutter to myself. "This is *not helping*."

I pick up the stub of a black candle. My mind wanders to The Crying Boy painting. That's a fire risk, right there. If someone has been lighting candles up here, we could have been burned in our beds. I shudder. The icy cold has seeped into my bones.

"Can you see a bricked- up area in the adjoining wall?" Charlie calls. "I suspect the roof spaces were once interconnected…"

I'm no longer listening. My gaze has already fastened on the wall in question. The adjoining wall between number 11 and number 10, between the Burns household and that of the Langtons. It's still some way distance, but I can see a definite outline of red brick against grey stone. It's almost in the shape of a person, I muse, as if someone or something has broken through. The dread escalates, making me heavy and slow. My feet adhere to the joists. Even from some way off, I can see that a section of the brickwork has been knocked inward, creating a recent, jagged scar. I sense a heartbeat that is not my own, a steady thumping bass, origin unknown.

"*Oh shit.*"

I approach with caution. There is a hole just big enough for a skinny person to wriggle through. It is covered on the far side by some kind of blanket or throw. When I press my ear closer, I can hear music.

I call down to Charlie.

"Charlie, take Matthew and go next door. I'll meet you round there."

This skinny person is going to wriggle through that hole, no question. There is no going back now. The dread has drained away in favour of pumping adrenaline. I'm going to lay the ghosts of this house to rest if it's the last thing I do.

CHAPTER FORTY-THREE

I look around me. An attic bedroom, a revamped version of the squalid space I've just left. I have certainly made an entrance. The crude covering on the inside of the skinny hole has turned out to be a sort of New Age wall hanging, deep mauve with black symbols that looked like runes, and by the time I've battled my way from one dimension to another, I seem to be wearing it.

On this side of the divide, the walls have been painted matt black and sprayed with graffiti. Not unnerving threats or occult symbols but really cool stuff - JOEL surrounded by red and black guitars and the silhouette of a skateboarder hovering above the skirting. The occupant of this space is an artist. There are fairy lights and lamps draped with black muslin and a Gothic mirror straight out of a Hammer horror. The rumpled quilt is patterned with skulls.

It's hard to make a judgement on Len's grandson, given that, up until an hour ago, I didn't even know of his existence. Quite what he thinks of me, as I blunder so unexpectedly into his bedroom, is impossible to guess.

Joel and Tamsin are sprawled on a bed, listening to a thumping riff. She has her head on his chest, he's smoking a spliff. I can smell the sweet reek of incense masking all the more unpleasant odours of a teenage boy's room; sweaty socks, cheap spray, hormones and, of course, weed. All the odours that had been clinging to my baby's clothes now make perfect sense, and the knowledge hits me like a sledgehammer. Rowena brought my son here, but I'm still not sure why.

The pair on the bed leap up as if I'd thrown scalding water on them. By now, I'm enjoying a bit of a power trip. They've tormented me long enough, and the victim is about to turn the tables.

"I know you've been visiting our attic. Don't try and deny it. You could at least have taken home all your rubbish."

That last bit makes me sound like a disgruntled mother, and in a way I am. The boy now facing me looks like he's in need of a mother. I think of all the little things I do for Matthew on a daily basis, making sure he's happy and cared-for and safe, and I cannot imagine a day when this will not be so. I cannot imagine not being there for him, but Joel's mother didn't have a choice. Her role was snatched from her, and I can see something in this young man's eyes that tell me he is neither happy, nor cared-for, nor even safe.

That is my first impression, but he has mastered the art of concealment, and it is only a fleeting one. He is hiding beneath a uniform of black hoodie and jeans, and his tee is emblazoned with some kind of Marvel character. One that haunts attics and lonely places, perhaps. Long dark hair spills from under his hood, obscuring part of his face and most of his emotions. Brow and lower lip piercings glint in the fairy lights. Tamsin is wearing a tartan skirt with ripped black tights and a cropped top. They are both barefoot, but I can see two pairs of trainers thrown randomly about the carpet. One is lying on its side, allowing a glimpse of the specific motif Charlie had referred to.

So far, Joel has not uttered a word. It's Tamsin who speaks up.

"It's not Joel's fault. He wanted somewhere to get away from things. I helped him knock out the bricks."

"Get away from things? It's like the Seventh Circle of Hell in there. Is that what you were looking for?"

"Whatever. Anyway, what gives you the right to bust your way in here?"

We are facing up to each other, rather ridiculously, on either side on the single bed. Tamsin's aggressive stance is something to behold; hip jutting out, blazing eyes. In a fight situation, I would definitely rather take on her boyfriend, who is hanging behind, scrubbing his spliff into an overflowing ashtray. On this side of the veil too, there is evidence of teenage occupation: takeaway cartons, crusty plates, sticky tumblers.

"You have some nerve!" I countered. "You two have been breaking into my loft, into my *life*! Do you realise how scared I've been? Do you even care?"

That last bit sounded a bit desperate, but doubt flickers in Tamsin's brown eyes, and even Joel seems a tad shamefaced.

"It was just a place to hang out," he says lamely.

"We haven't been introduced," I say icily. "I'm Kat, your next-door-neighbour and the woman you've reduced to a nervous wreck."

Unexpectedly, and probably because he doesn't know what else to do, he offers a polite handshake. I am completely disarmed. I'm not sure what I'd expected to find in the roof space but it really wasn't a bored Monster Munch fan. My anger deflates like a birthday balloon. I take his hand. which is cold and rough. In the weird light I can see flaky skin on his face too, pimples and fine soft bristles on his chin. A boy-man stuck here in this bat cave. This isn't healthy, or right, but I cannot let myself be swayed. Desperately I try to recall all the spooky outrages of recent months, to connect all the dots.

"So, let me get this straight- you didn't just stick to the attic, did you? You've been *in* our house! All the times I've been hearing noises, and seeing things in the house, it's been you?"

I've not quite sure who I'm addressing that remark to, but it seems like they're in cahoots.

"Depends what things you're talking about," says Joel.

"Let me give you a list. The skeleton of the rodent with the red lace around its neck? The ginger cat?"

They glance at each other. Joel shrugs.

"Dunno about the cat. When you got locked outside that time, we'd crept down and turned the key."

Tamsin sniggers. "Yeah, we stole some biscuits and ran back upstairs. We unlocked the door at the last minute, so you could get back in, but Joel broke a mug."

She gives him an evil side-eye. I'm not sure who the mastermind is, but frankly this is an anticlimax. Sometimes the logical explanation is too mundane for words. I'm looking at a couple of daft kids with too much time on their hands.

"What about the shadow I saw at the window? I was in the garden and I saw the outline of someone in the baby's room. I nearly *died*. Did you put that filthy doll in Matthew's cot?"

Joel nods slowly. "Yeah. I'm sorry. We found it in the attic. We posted a picture of it on Reddit and all these randoms started talking about what happened here years ago. They said it was the doll Psychic Tommy used to lure the demon. It was just a prank."

"Lure the de- *what*? Reddit? Jesus, does everyone know about this house but me? And it isn't ever *just a prank* when you're hurting someone. I was terrified. Wait until you have kids and you'll understand. What about the graffiti?"

This time, they don't say a word. They're smart enough not to admit to criminal damage.

"We're kinda sorry about Steve though." Tamsin says quietly.

I'm stunned. "Steve?"

"Yeah. He was just climbing down from the attic and closing the hatch behind him. We crept up and pushed down on it. We only meant to scare him. We were gutted that he fell off the ladder."

"You could have bloody killed him! You've gone too far. Look, we have to go downstairs. Your grandad needs to hear about this. This is serious shit. And you-" directed at Tamsin. "Your dad is here. No doubt he will have something to say to you."

Her face falls a fraction, and I see her swallow nervously. Not as bold as she makes out, then.

"Did you tell him?" she asks in a small voice.

"He worked it out for himself." I spare a glance at the trainers. "You're not exactly masters of disguise, once we figured out you weren't ghosts. Downstairs, now. Come on. Scoot."

I flap my hands, suddenly all teacher-like, and they move with the same reluctance as a bunch of Year 10s heading for double maths.

Len is predictably baffled by my appearance in his kitchen. He's standing with a tea towel in one hand and a spatula in another. Behind him, fat is spitting in a skillet and, more distant, a persistent rapping on the door.

I stalk past him.

"I'll answer it."

"What the- ?" He glares at Joel, as if the boy is sure to have a hand in whatever weirdness is about to unfold. I swing open the front door. Charlie is gripping a red-faced Matthew like a rugby ball. He hands him over with relief.

"He's very feisty. I've been ringing the doorbell and knocking- what's going on?"

"Come in. That hole in the wall leads right into Joel's bedroom. He's in there-" I indicate the kitchen. "With Tamsin."

"Right." He pushes past me, the embodiment of a father about to do battle. I take a minute to soothe Matthew, He's hot and tetchy, in need of a clean nappy and a drink.

"It's okay. Two minutes and we'll be home." I cannot wait to get out of here. I feel weary, as if I've spent the day trekking up a mountain in poor visibility, and not merely climbing up one flight of stairs to come down another. I feel like a lot has happened in the space between, and I can hear Charlie scolding Tamsin. By the time I join them, her heavy eye make up is suspiciously smudged, and she looks years younger. She's being inventive with the truth, though. None of it was Joel's fault. None of it was *her* fault, Well, maybe some of it, but…it just felt like a *blast*, at the time.

"All that graffiti…" I wave angrily in the direction of the adjoining wall. "It was disgusting! I had to paint over it. You'll need to at least pay for the paint, or …or…Oh, I don't know. It's not even my fucking house."

All eyes swivel to me, as if I've just screamed in a library. I take out my phone.

"I'm calling Steve. It's up to him. You can sort it all out with him. That graffiti- it was just awful. Can you imagine what it was like to come home to that? *Get out or die*. I mean, really- what the hell were you thinking? That goes way beyond teenage shenanigans."

I jam the handset to my ear. The repetitive trill at the other end is like nails on a blackboard. Is it my imagination, or did Len just catch Joel's eye? Did he hold his gaze for a second too long? I cannot make sense of it but right now, I just want to get home, to speak to Steve, but Steve is not answering.

Meanwhile, Charlie is reading the riot act to his daughter.

"You are grounded, young lady."

She tosses her hair. "Whatever. That is such a cliché."

"Home. Now. And you are not to contact *him*-" A evil glance at Joel, who is staring at his socks. "- for the foreseeable. You're going to have to apologise to Steve and-"

"Wait." I hold up a finger, as if I'm testing for wind direction.

Indeed, a tiny detail has just blown in and settled. "Have you been commenting on my blog?"

Joel glances up. "No, not me. I don't agree with social media, the way it can influence and ultimately persecute people."

"Ha! That's rich coming from someone who almost made me want to move out."

"It was me." Tamsin seems, on the surface, unrepentant. I bet she was the sort of child who would sit on the naughty step for a week rather than apologise.

"I knew it. Which one of my many trolls were you?"

"@MountainAsh."

"What?" For the moment, I cannot remember all the subversive comments that originated from the keyboard of Mountain Ash, but I'm taken aback. I had convinced myself it was Rowena.

"It was both of us," Joel admits reluctantly, no longer able to hide completely behind his girlfriend. "We used the same account."

"Yeah, I guess we were egging each other on." Tamsin bit her lip, risking a glance at her father.

"You just lost computer privileges for a month, girl. Come on." He pushes her towards the door and she resists him with a flex of her shoulders. She has wide, proud shoulders, like a swimmer, lots of potential locked in her athletic frame. She is vital, intelligent and I can only imagine the disappointment her father must feel, witnessing this. The sub-optimal boyfriend, the mediocre setting, the twilight troublemaking and now the trolling. I hug Matthew closer, already wanting to protect him - and me -from the pitfalls ahead.

"I'm going home too. But one more thing…" My gaze sweeps them all. "Can someone please tell me why Rowena was here? I know she was here, the evening Steve was taken to hospital. She came around here with my son and I want an explanation."

CHAPTER FORTY-FOUR

"So what did they tell you?" Steve looks exhausted, slumped in the chair just as his dad must once have done before they took him away. He has that look about him, feeble, as if he doesn't have the strength to hold himself upright, while I am still full of adrenaline and outrage.

"They told me a bit about the Rowena connection..." I assess him carefully. He never believes me. Why would he believe this? I change tack. "We need to get the builder in to seal up the hole in the wall. The thought of those kids wreaking havoc in our home-" I shudder. "Maybe he could do it when he eventually comes back to finish the bloody sun room."

"About that..." Steve begins, but Matthew bites hard on a sharp play brick and starts to squall. I lift him from the floor.

"How was work? Did you feel okay?"

"I wasn't at work."

I sense a story that isn't being told. "You weren't?"

"No." Steve sighs and rubs his face with both hands, letting his finger wander into his hair, He looks like he wants to tear it out by the roots, but makes do with a good scrub of the scalp, carefully avoiding the injured side. "I went to see Laura."

"Oh. Is she still having problems?"

"In a manner of speaking. Look- I don't want to discuss all this now. I'm sorry I wasn't here when all this was going on." He waves a hand towards the wall. I think we are now both hyper-aware of our boundaries and who dwells beyond. "At least you got to the bottom of it."

"Hmm. There are still loose ends." I stare off into space, or rather, towards the chimney wall where, despite my best efforts, the lurid red of the GET OUT OR DIE legend still glows like a light anomaly.

"Talking of which- did you write to your mother?"

I'd forgotten all about the letter. Events had somewhat taken over. Now the pit of my stomach drops a notch. The letter, even now winging its way to Dundee, on cheap lined notepaper which smells of old musty cupboards, is a ticking bomb. Very soon I will be caught up in the blast.

"Shall we order pizza?"

With an effort, I switch my attention back to Steve.

"We'll drive to the pizza place, via Rowena's." I go to fetch my coat, as if the act of putting it on can fortify my defences. These loose ends will not tie themselves.

"Kat, are you sure this is a good idea? Does it matter whether she was visiting Len or.."

"It does, actually. It wasn't just a social visit. It just got personal."

Rowena had recently got out of the bath or shower. She opens the door smelling of soap and wrapped in a snowy towelling robe several sizes too big. Her white hair is loose and damp, curling slightly on her shoulders. She stares past me, out to the road beyond the privet hedge where Steve is waiting with Matthew in the car.

"Just you?"

"Just me."

She steps aside to let me in and closes the door. It's almost as if she'd been expecting me. My gaze wonders round the still, serene hall. Even after all that's happened, it's still fragrant with wholesomeness and safety. Rowena had provided me with a port in a storm, a listening ear. I feel disappointed, dejected.

I fix my eyes on the plaster cornice, clean as icing. How on earth does she dust up there? With a sigh, I begin.

"I sent a letter to my mother earlier, detailing how...telling her all about how her fiancé raped me and fathered my baby. I've burned most of my bridges, so I may as well set fire to the final one." I muster up all the anger that has been building over the last few hours, but Rowena refuses to meet my gaze. "You were a bit sketchy about your whereabouts the other night, when you took off with Matthew, but I know exactly where you went."

Her face is carefully neutral. I notice she's stuck her hands wrist-deep into the pockets of the robe, giving her an air of nonchalance that pisses me off even more.

"I know that you're an old friend of Len's." I push.

"We go back, yes."

"And yet when I first met you, you made out you had no knowledge of Steve, or even number 11."

"I never said I didn't. I just- held some things back."

"There's been a hell of a lot of holding things back. I know what secrets can do. Instead of telling me what you knew about the place, you let me find out the hard way." To my embarrassment, my voice breaks. I clear my throat and hurry on. "You and Steve, letting me piece the story together and coming up with conclusions I wouldn't wish on anyone."

"It wasn't personal." She says it in such a blasé way, like a boss announcing redundancies. Armed with the knowledge I've just learned, I have to fight the urge to grab her by the towelling lapels and dunk her in her own dirty bathwater.

"I was stuck in that house, a single mother with a baby and nowhere else to go. Except here. Oh, yes, you were so understanding, so welcoming, when all the while you were plotting to drive me out. Scare me so much I had no choice but to pack up and go home, back to Dundee." My throat constricts. "Don't try and deny it. I know everything."

Rowena's mask finally slips. I can see real venom in her eyes, poison that's been building in her system since she lost her father in horrible circumstances, since she was forced to relocate to Durham with her widowed mother, since she experienced her home lying derelict and unsellable, haunted by late-night Occultists and fornicating couples. When she speaks, her voice is brittle and unguarded.

"I was cheated out of that house! I was a young girl and Tommy Burns took advantage of me. Nowadays it would be called grooming. He encouraged me in this- this Poltergeist charade and I'm still dealing with the legacy. Things which happen to you...they shape you in strange ways."

"You don't need to tell me," I say, equally as harsh. "That is the worst betrayal, that you could do this to *me*. I was vulnerable, hurting, when I came here. I liked you, and I thought you understood. Instead, I find that you have been *paying* young Joel Langton to trick us into believing the house is haunted. You knew about the roof space. He says it was you who told him about it! You've been taking advantage of him to get your revenge. They've been playing games with my mind, and all because of you!"

Rowena has the grace to look away, although I still don't think she's grasped the severity of this, the sheer audacity.

"I didn't think you'd stay in the house if you thought it was haunted. It was a gamble which might not have worked, but-" She shrugged her shoulders. "I thought it was worth a shot. If you'd gone back up north, Steve would have gone with you - he has a very rocky relationship with his family, so he wouldn't have needed much persuasion. If the property was empty, I might have been able to persuade Tommy to sell me the place for a song. Reparation, you might say."

"You have *this* place!" I spread my arms. The woman is clearly bonkers. "What the hell are you doing scrabbling away in the past and talking revenge and-"

"This place belonged to my husband's family. It was their legacy, not mine. I never had a legacy. My family home was desecrated- not by poltergeists but the media scrum, the attention, the stigma. I completely lost my teenage years. Nobody helped me through it and when the attention got diverted elsewhere, I was left to figure it all out myself. I lost my father, my family life, my home and even Tommy Burns, although that was probably a blessing. Kat, this is no place for you, but I didn't ever mean to harm you-"

"*Get out or die?* Oh, that's not scary at all!" I'm yelling now. She is so implacable, so unheeding of what she has done.

She brushes this away like a mere cobweb. "That was over-the-top, granted. I think Joel and Tamsin got a *little* carried away with their mission."

"Carried away?" I cannot believe what I'm hearing. "And not only did they- you- invade my physical world, but my online world too. I was so excited, setting up my blog and everything and it became a living nightmare. All these comments, every hour of the day and night, discussing my house, my baby, the alleged hauntings and their own worst imaginings. *Ugh*." I shudder. "I was trapped in the middle of it."

"That wasn't anything to do with me."

"For a while I thought you were @MountainAsh."

"Not me. I don't do all that social media. Cannot abide it."

"That's exactly what Joel said. Why should I trust you?"

"Not my M.O., Kat."

"I know you're not 'Mountain Ash'. Tamsin has confessed to that. You're Elan Del Silva, aren't you?"

"Who?" She scrunches up he nose in a way that may have been cute, years ago.

"Elan Del Silva. It's an anagram of Devil's Lane. I know how you like an anagram."

"Oh, yes, I see. That's clever." She nods, eyebrows raised as if she's impressed with a particularly good puzzle solution. She neither confirms or denies. I suddenly feel very, very tired.

"If Elan Del Silva it isn't you, who the hell is it?"

CHAPTER FORTY-FIVE

I slip into the car, slamming the door hard behind me and tugging my seat belt so hard, it jerks to a full stop.

"You'll never fasten it like that," says Steve mildly.

"I KNOW." Eventually, I manage to shove home the clip, and sit there, fuming.

"Did she admit to it all?"

"Oh yes. Everything the kids told me was true. It started out as a bit of a joke, and I guess that's the way she sees it. Something and nothing. She hasn't a shred of remorse. I just couldn't seem to get through to her about what she's done."

"What she *tried* to do."

I turn on him. "You don't get it either! I thought your house was a safe place and it turns out that you're living next to a bunch of deadbeats who basically tried to scare the crap out of me FOR MONEY! Rowena seems to think she's- *entitled*. That she had a shitty time in her youth so somehow, in her warped logic, your family owes her big time."

"My family has a lot to answer for."

Something in his voice makes me turn. He's staring straight ahead. Without returning my gaze, he starts the ignition, checks his mirrors, moves off. The streets are early evening quiet, that time when people are thinking about tea, settling down in front of the telly.

"What does that mean?"

"Nothing." He slows at a pedestrian crossing. A woman with a buggy crosses, and I automatically check Matthew who is dozing in his car seat, which means he'll not be sleepy tonight, right when I need some me-time to sort out my head.

"What are we going to do about her?"

Steve shrugs. "She hasn't really done anything, has she?"

"Steve- she paid the kids to do this! Like the leader of some shitty Scooby gang. I still cannot believe it."

"Nobody is going to take this seriously, especially not the police. Look how interested they were in the graffiti."

I heave out a sigh. Steve pats my knee.

"Let's get some food. Things always seem better on a full belly. We can talk about it later."

I turn my head to watch the streetscape pass by. I don't have it in me to think about anything else, and pizza is the last thing on my mind.

Predictably, Matthew is still bright and breezy at nine. Steve is reading him The Three Little Pigs for the fourth time, while the baby tries to flatten each pig picture with a clap of his hand. Who needs wolves? I skulk around the kitchen, tidying up, rinsing out cloths. I want to call Leanne, but I'm scared I'll blurt out the contents of the letter and she'll go off on one. I can just picture my mother and Billy being called to the phone and some big, boisterous family meltdown taking place. I cannot face that right now. My imagination is seething.

I storm back into the sitting room.

"Elan Del Silva isn't Rowena."

Steve looks up from the story book. There's a guarded expression in his face that says he really, really does not want to have to deal with this right now.

"You mean- is that one of these people that were commenting? The trolls?"

"It's an anagram of Devil's Lane."

I can see him working it out, doing one of those funny character-maps in his head, the sort that Rowena scribbles on her newspapers.

"Coincidence?"

"Hardly. And if it isn't Rowena, who the hell is it? It's someone who knows about Devil's Lane."

"Tamsin or Joel? They might have two accounts, or Rowena could be lying. It doesn't matter. You've deactivated your accounts- they can't spew out any more nonsense."

I sit heavily on the edge of the couch. "But they can, can't they? Just because I can't read it, doesn't mean it doesn't exist. It's like that thing about the tree in the forest- you know, if it falls down when nobody is there to hear, does it still make a sound?"

"What are you getting at?"

"I'm saying the trolls are free to write about me, or the baby, or the poltergeists- whatever they want. They can make up stories and lies, they can be as preposterous as they like and influence a whole pile of people who have never even heard of this house on Devil's Lane. Just because I'm not engaging with it doesn't make it go away. I've opened a door, Steve, and I don't think we can ever close it. Rowena is right. This house is poison."

Matthew will not consent to sleep until after ten, by which time I am exhausted. I've tried everything, warm bath, low lights, soft music, but even when I leave him tucked up in his cot with Bobo, he is still stubbornly wide-eyed and fidgety. I pick up the baby monitor and watch a while from the doorway, appreciating the cosiness I've created for him. Thankfully, Steve's paint choice has mellowed, or maybe I've become accustomed to it. For a few precious moments I enjoy the golden glow, and hum along to the whimsical chime of the mobile above the cot. Matthew is having a conversation with the ceiling which makes me smile, all the words which are not quite words, the inflexion and the bubble-blowing. At least now I know that he is just talking to himself. There are no bogeymen left, no darkness creeping across the light, no misinterpreted shadows. However difficult today's revelations have been, I feel relaxed, as if a weight has been lifted. I whisper goodnight and pull the door until its open a crack, just enough to let in the landing light.

When I go back downstairs, Steve has turned off the television. This is unusual. His habitual position post ten p.m. is slumped in front of some cop show with an open can of something alcoholic, but the sitting room is strangely silent. Steve is standing over by the window. He looks like he might have been pacing, or just moving around aimlessly, picking things up and putting them down. But he is not aimless. I can see that in the set of his jaw and the tense bunching of his shoulders. When I enter, he looks startled, but collects himself and goes to stand behind his father's easy chair (I cannot think of it any other way), rubbing the back of it with nervous fingers. My gut reacts. I can tell he has something on his mind

"Is he asleep?" He speaks softly, as if the baby might hear him.

"Heading that way."

He pats the chair. "Sit. I have something to tell you."

I don't sit. I try to look him squarely in the eye, but he moves away, turns his back to contemplate the curtains. A host of things rage through my mind.

"You've met someone else. You cannot stand me anymore. You're emigrating to Australia."

He ignores me. I wonder if he's been rehearsing what he's about to say all day. That's what I do if I have to confront someone. Is he about to confront me? My insides squirm.

"It's kind of ironic, all this." He turns to face me, arms folded, shoulder hunched. His face is partly in shadow, and it makes him look older, more unsettling. "Rowena trying to get her hands on this house, by fair means or foul."

"Foul, mainly."

"The irony is- it's not even mine. We are not the people she needs to see off. Even if I wanted to sell it, I couldn't."

"You mean it still belongs to your dad? But she knew that. She had plans to approach him once we- the sitting tenants- had fled to pastures new."

Steve shakes his head, stares at something of interest on the carpet. "It's not even his. When I left here, I was having money troubles, with the divorce and all that. My uncle Jeff paid my solicitor and lent me a sum of money- a big sum- to start afresh. I was to pay it back, so much a month, but I couldn't stand the thought of being stuck here, in the family firm, where everyone knew my business. Christ, my ex-wife does the accounts! It's – claustrophobic. So, I left. I didn't tell them where I was going and they didn't ask, until…I fell behind with the payments."

"Oh. Could you not come up with a new agreement?"

"I just stopped paying." He spreads his hands and looks up, pleading for understanding. "It was stupid, and dishonest, but I thought, if I don't go back, and they don't know where I am, that it would all go away."

"But it didn't?"

"You always have to face the music, don't you? Life has a way of forcing you to face the music. My dad got ill and then I met you, and…well." He shrugs.

He looks so sad I want to touch him, but my hands bunch into fists and I cannot seem to move. What I thought of as my home has been given a new twist that I didn't see coming.

"So what happened when you came back?"

"I came back to find that my father had changed his Will and signed this place over to my daughter, Laura. Partly it was to do with getting rid of his assets, but that didn't work out so well. If you sign your house over to a family member to avoid being liable for social care fees, you have to basically survive in good health for seven years. Now he's in permanent care, they're both in the shit, financially. It was also a way of making the point that when I'd defaulted on the loan, I'd defaulted on my place in the family. Honestly, it's worse that The Sopranos."

The joke falls flat. I repeat the lesson cautiously.

"He signed the house over to Laura, so Laura can chuck us out, basically."

"Oh, she wouldn't do that, but she did have one or two objections. The sun room, for instance."

"She called off the builder." Things are starting to become clear.

"Yup, and she was a bit pissed that she only found out about it through your blog. Furious, in fact. You were doing videos about her house. That's the way she saw it, anyway."

I suddenly cannot think of any suitable words.

"So where does that leave us?" My voice sounds high and tight.

"I'm working at the firm to pay off the debt and Laura doesn't have any plans for the house as yet, so nothing has changed, really. I just thought you should know. Rowena was on a hiding to nothing all along. The main loser is me, right? The humiliation of facing up to my mistakes, having to work in a job I tried to escape, with a family who despise me. I don't have a pot to piss in and no prospects, so maybe it's time you thought about the future and whether you want to spend it with me."

His last words come out in a mad rush and then there's a pause which I cannot think how to fill. When I don't speak, he lifts his hands and drops them to his thighs,

"So there you go. All the secrets are out. Maybe you want to sleep on it. I'm for bed, anyway."

With that he shambles from the room, leaving me alone to wonder what the hell I've got myself mixed up in.

CHAPTER FORTY-SIX

It's after midnight before I go to bed. I end up watching episodes of Gavin and Stacey until my brain settles and I start to feel sleepy. When I slip into bed beside Steve, his eyes flicker. I position my head level with his. We are inches apart, our breath mingling. I reach under the quilt for his hand.

"It's okay," I whisper. "Whatever happens, wherever we go, I want to be with you, And so does Matthew."

"You've asked him, have you?" The white of his teeth glint in the semi-darkness.

"We have had that conversation, yes. He says he cannot live without your story reading skills."

I am rewarded with a chuckle. I haven't heard Steve laugh for a very long time, and I hadn't realised how much I'd missed it. Life has been so overshadowed by things which weren't even real.

Steve scoops me into his arms. It is so good to lie in a tangle of warm limbs, his chin on top of my head, my arms about his waist. We probably should talk this thing through, but we drift off to sleep still holding each other as if our lives depend on it.

I wake up in the very early morning with the smell of smoke in my nostrils. I'd been dreaming of hot buttered toast, and as I open my eyes I have a sinking feeling that I may have left the grill on. But we had pizza. I remember the boxes stacked on the kitchen counter ready for the bin. I come fully awake with jolt.

"Steve! Wake up." I shake the bundle next to me, already throwing my legs out of bed and reaching for my robe. There's nothing to see on the landing; the low energy bulb is still operating normally. I can definitely smell smoke. Suddenly the shrill beep of a smoke alarm pierces my doubts.

"Oh God. It's a fire. Steve! Steve!"

"Get the baby." Steve is behind me in tee shirt and boxers. He takes the stairs at a jog. As I haul the sleeping Matthew from his cot I can already hear Steve cursing. I run into the bedroom and grab my phone. When I get downstairs, Steve's face is ashen. He's struggling to open the back door.

"Call the fire brigade. I can see flames in the hall. Come on, out this way."

He ushers us out onto the path. Matthew, at first baffled by the interruption, is now bawling, the sound more nerve-grating than the smoke alarm. We hurry around the front, to be greeted by acrid smoke and crackling flames. The porch is alight. As we watch, stunned, there's a pop and sparks fly into the dim sky. It is barely light. I don't even know what time it is.

I hand the phone to Steve, and he gives directions as the baby squirms in my arms. Someone flies through the gate. It's Joel.

"Jesus, I saw the fire. Are you alright?"

I round on him. "Was this you?"

He looks aghast. "No, I swear it! I couldn't sleep, but I wasn't hanging around, I just…"

"Did you see anybody?"

He looks puzzled. "I was down the road. At a mate's house. I heard a car, I think, just driving off, but I didn't pay much attention. Could have been Charlie. He often leaves in the early hours if he has a flight."

"So you didn't see where it was parked?"

He shakes his head. Steve hands back my phone.

"They're on their way. Joel. help me get some buckets. I cannot just stand here and watch it burn."

"Yeah, no worries. Grandad has a hose connected round the side. It might reach. I swear it wasn't anything to do with me."

He's looking to me, the person he's hurt the most, for some kind of approval. I nod and wave him away.

"Just go. Do something good."

The professionals put out the blaze in a matter of minutes. Little structural damage, the fire officer says.

"You were very lucky we were in the vicinity. Barn fire over at Skelmerside. Have you accommodation for tonight? We'll have to let it cool and assess the damage later. I've just done a preliminary and…" He scratches his head. "I'm going to have to radio the police. I

can smell petrol."

"Can you think of anyone who would want to frighten you in some way?" The detective has introduced himself as DC Webster. He is young, friendly, but with the world-weary expression of a much older man. His sidekick, a young Asian woman in a sharp suit is currently in Joss Baker's kitchen helping make tea, although I suspect it's her way of obtaining the sort of background information that only neighbours can provide. I've seen the way this goes on TV. It strikes me that we might all be under suspicion. They don't know that the house doesn't belong to us. They might suspect Steve, or even me.

He'd explained that arson is the likely cause of the fire. In his report, the fire investigator had noted that he had detected an accelerant and the remains of fabric.

"Classic petrol-doused rag," the detective had mused. "Not very sophisticated."

I wanted to ask how sophisticated arsonists do it, but any flippancy might just count against me.

"What kind of fabric," I ask instead.

He checks his notes. "I do not have that information."

"It's just- Rowena Patterson. She sews. When I went to her house she had piles of fabric there."

"And this Rowena Patterson- does she hold a grudge against you?"

"She has a huge grudge against the family in general," I say without hesitation. "I can give you her address. She's been waging some kind of…vendetta against us. You should question the family at number 10. They're in on it."

I stop short, realising I am implicating Tamsin, when the Bakers have been kind enough to take us in. Even as we speak, Tamsin is taking Matthew for a walk around their garden.

"And anyone else you think might have been tempted to do this? For any reason?"

"Yes." My voice comes out all squeaky. "There is someone. It's probably a long shot, but…"

"Take your time." The detectives young/old eyes are watchful, waiting.

"I recently told my mother something that she wouldn't have wanted to hear. I told her that her partner raped me. This guy, Billy, is my son's father."

"I see. And can you give me details for your mother and her partner?"

"Yes, but they live in Scotland. It's unlikely…"

"We cannot rule anything out."

"Sure." I subside. Could it possibly be that Billy might want to kill me? Or the 'people' that my mother knows? I'm getting really tired of people wanting to do me harm.

"Can I ask a question?" I've been building up to this for a while, perhaps from the moment I woke up with the smell of smoke in my nose.

"Of course." The officer gives me his full attention. Even if they didn't follow up on the graffiti, the police have certainly come up trumps.

"There was a picture hanging in the hall. I just wondered if it had survived." I can feel Steve's gaze burning into my profile, but I don't look.

DC Webster checks his paperwork.

"No structural issues in the hallway, but lots of smoke damage as you can imagine, and water incursion. I have an additional note here- a print was found on the floor, which appeared to have escaped harm. The Crying Boy..." The man looks up and catches my eye.

"Do you believe in ghosts, detective?"

He does not look unduly surprised by the question. I suppose he hears all kinds of things in his job. "What are you getting at, Ms Riley?"

"I'm saying- suggesting- that there might be a paranormal option. The house has history."

He glances back down at his clipboard. "I am aware, yes. but I think we can rule that out." His lips twitch. "People love a mystery, but I like to stick to the evidence of my own eyes."

"Exactly," Steve agrees.

"One more thing, Mr Burns." DC Webster is making notes. Probably about me. He looks at Steve.

"Are you the home owner, sir? Or a tenant?"

Steve looks at me before answering.

"It's complicated. You should probably speak to my daughter, Laura. Laura Hughes. I can give you her number."

SIX MONTHS LATER

We never spent another night at 11 Devil's Lane. A contact of Steve's heard the news and offered to let us housesit his bungalow while he took up a work contract abroad. It's a new-build, with no history and a clean slate. No baggage of any kind, a bit like Steve and myself. We have made our confessions. That's not to say the past doesn't have long fingers.

I ache to speak to my mother, but Leanne says she isn't ready yet. Billy is still on the scene. I'm not sure whether she believes his story or mine, or whether she's simply too afraid to speak her truth. Sometimes it's easier to say nothing.

The house on Devil's Lane remains empty, although sometimes I walk past it when I'm taking Matthew out in his stroller. Maybe I do it just because I can, to prove that it no longer holds any power over me. I recall the day I first saw it, and how charming I'd thought it was. Now, the damaged porch still stands there like a blackened tooth, a reminder of that awful night, and the smoke damage remains smeared across the stone frontage, as if someone has tried to rub the entire place out with a giant eraser. I suspect it won't go quietly.

Once, I saw the ginger cat sitting on the bench at the front. It looked bored and a bit smug, and when it saw me, it opened its mouth in a silent pink scream. I felt physically sick. There was something else on the bench beside it, a tiny scrap of something, but I didn't stop to look. I knew what I'd see. A grisly skeleton with a red lace about its neck. Steve might be a non-believer, but the house doesn't fool me. Not *everything* has a rational explanation.

The Durham Echo

Insurance scam goes wrong: Local woman named.

A local woman has been charged with setting fire to a property at Derville's Lane, Blackwater. The woman, named as Laura Melody Hughes, who owns the property, works for local firm J.D.Burns Ltd.

No-one was injured in the incident, but relatives of Hughes, including a nine-month-old baby, were in residence at the time. Police say that a greater tragedy was avoided by sheer luck. Fire Officer Bob McDermott reported that the family had been alerted by a smoke alarm and were able to evacuate the building safely. A local resident, Joel Langton, helped keep the fire under control until the fire service arrived.

The house in question has experienced its fair share of notoriety, being the location of the infamous Poltergeist Hauntings of 1976. Local resident Rowena Patterson lived in the property at the time of the phenomenon. She commented:

"This house has something of a history. I don't think anyone locally was surprised to hear about the fire. I'm just so glad the family got out safely. It is definitely not a home for the faint-hearted. I just hope that when it comes on the market later this year, it attracts the right owner."

THE END

ACKNOWLEDGEMENT

Much love and grateful thanks to my family and friends, my 'chief cheerleaders' who have encouraged me to keep writing and to never lose sight of the dream.

Special thanks to the legendary Dawn Geddes, of Book Smart PR, for her generosity, encouragement and expertise in helping me get this story into the world; to Elizabeth Frattaroli and Gillian Duff for their friendship, endless coffees and wise advice; to all the members of Angus Writers' Circle- you are the best and it's a privilege to be one of your number.

I'm also so grateful for the support of all the lovely people I work with at Art Angel, Tay Online, Open Book, Lifelong Learning Dundee, Writing Just For You- you are my inspiration! Your wonderfully creative spin on life keeps me going.

Thank you to my lovely agent Jenny Brown, who supports me every step of the way, and to all the writers I know, near and far, who have offered me great insight and encouragement. Also to the wider writing community- the book bloggers, reviewers and all those who have our backs!

Lots of love to my boys, Jamie and Calum, who have had to wade through all my niggles and abandoned book covers on the group chat! Thanks to Linda, Jack and families for their ongoing support, and to Cameron for his publishing advice- okay, I may not have taken up your deadline challenge, but I got there in the end!

The post-pandemic years have been tough for writers, with many tempted to give up in the face of overwhelming odds, but if, like me, telling stories is your passion and you cannot imagine doing anything else - keep going!

PRAISE FOR AUTHOR

'Sandra Ireland writes about difficult subjects with sensitivity and realism, which gives the book a deeply human perspective.'

— THE SUNDAY POST

'Twists, turns and well-written pace. Ireland is good at weaving Celtic mythology into a novel which otherwise deals with very modern themes.'

— SCOTLAND ON SUNDAY

'The Unmaking of Ellie Rook cements Sandra Ireland's place as the queen of Scottish folklore-inspired domestic noir'

— THE WEE REVIEW

'Bone Deep is an exciting second novel from this Carnoustie-based author, a psychological thriller drenched in gothic suspense.'

— THE SUNDAY HERALD

'Ireland writes about powerful and troubling subjects and shows how the past can have devastating consequences'

- DAILY MAIL

BOOKS BY THIS AUTHOR

Beneath The Skin

A taxidermist with a secret. A soldier with nothing left to fight for. A mother determined to protect her young son. Together, can they fight a past that doesn't want to let them go?

Bone Deep

What happens when you fall in love with the wrong person?

The consequences threaten to be far-reaching and potentially deadly. Bone Deep is a contemporary novel of sibling rivalry, love, betrayal and murder. Set in Scotland and inspired by an ancient Border Ballad

The Unmaking Of Ellie Rook

A single phone call from halfway across the world is all it takes to bring her home . . . 'Ellie, something bad has happened.'

Desperate to escape her 'kid from the scrapyard' reputation, Ellie Rook has forged a new life for herself abroad, but tragedy strikes when her mother, Imelda, falls from a notorious waterfall.

Here, according to local legend, the warrior queen Finella jumped to her death after killing a king. In the wake of her mother's disappearance, Ellie is forced to confront some disturbing truths about the family she left behind and the woman she has become.

Can a long-dead queen hold the key to Ellie's survival? And how far will she go to right a wrong?

Sight Unseen

Sarah Sutherland wanted to be an archaeologist but now she is struggling to cope with the demands of work and caring for her elderly father, who has his own secret troubles.

Her fascination with the past still remains, and she feels a special affinity with Alie Gowdie, the Kilgour Witch, who lived in Sarah's cottage until her unjust execution for sorcery during the Civil War.

As Alie and Sarah's stories collide, can Sarah uncover the truth in order to right a centuries old wrong? And what else might modern-day Kilgour be hiding, just out of sight?